A Novel About Relationships, Loss, and Finding Your Way Home

Patricia Hamilton Shook

outskirts press

Seeking Glory
A Novel About Relationships, Loss, and Finding Your Way Home

v6.0

Outskirts Press, Inc.
http://www.outskirtspress.com

ISBN: 978-1-4787-9204-8

PRINTED IN THE UNITED STATES OF AMERICA

In Memory of

Jeanne Marie Fitzgerald

with whom I shared
many wonderful summer vacations on Cape Cod

I would like to thank my family and friends for their support and advice over the long process of creating *Seeking Glory.* My thanks in particular to those who read the drafts of *Seeking Glory* and offered many valuable suggestions that made the book better as well as to my husband and son who traveled around the Cape with me researching and photographing the sites where the story of Kate and her granddaughter Glory took place.

I would like to add that in writing *Seeking Glory* I have attempted to portray its many themes and settings as accurately as possible. Any mistakes/misrepresentations are mine and unintentional.

PROLOGUE

The sun had long since set behind the mountains and the full moon had risen, a creamy white orb resting high among the stars. A light wind stirred the grasses, blowing sandy soil across the valley. The long, low ranch buildings were dark shadows spread over the landscape, still in the moonlit darkness. A lone shadow detached itself from the others, moving quickly into and out of the cool white light such that anyone watching might have wondered if it wasn't a trick of the early autumn night. The minutes stretched by in the soft darkness until a tiny flicker of light suddenly appeared, etched into the shadows of the buildings. It remained a single, bright yellow flame for few more minutes, almost as though someone had lit a candle in one of the unseen windows, before blossoming rapidly, orange and yellow petals spreading upward and outward. Within seconds, bright columns of light were rising into the night toward the starry sky, throwing the scene into a stark contrast of light and dark. As they did so, the first scream broke the silence, followed by shouts and calls of "Fire! Fire!" People poured from the shadowed ranch buildings, spilling out into the fields, lit by fire and moonlight. A voice calling for the fire brigade rose above the others and several of the shadowy figures ran toward a nearby water tower. Some people clustered around a single dark figure commanding the shouting, weeping crowd. "We're not going to save it! Make sure everyone's out! Get over to the nursery and get the children out!"

The fire illuminated the sky, bright shafts of spreading light, now yellow and orange against the outline of mountains, engulfing the wooden structures of the ranch as another group of shadowy forms ran toward a small adjoining building. Moments later, they were racing back out, pulling crying shadow-children behind them, others, bundled in blankets, in their arms. As they headed in the direction of the dark outline of the person calling commands, another small group of shadows detached itself from the building the children and their rescuers had just left, slipping into a darkness unlit by fire, moving silently and swiftly toward the mountains until they blended once more into the blackness.

CHAPTER 1

Kate pulled the door shut to the Sea Witch Art and Gifts and sighed. Another hot summer day was winding to a close, the setting sun sending shafts of soft yellow light through the scrub pine that fringed the parking area. Business was slower than she would have liked in what should be the busiest season of the year, and Kate was worried. The Sea Witch was her baby, her dream that she had nurtured over the last twenty years of her life; she had made it a success, but the possibility of losing everything despite all her hard work always loomed for her. Kate sighed again and tried to shrug off fears of a shrinking economy, of a drop in tourism on Cape Cod. She walked slowly across the deserted parking area, climbed into her battered Toyota, and prepared to head home.

Before pulling out onto Route 6A, the "King's Highway," she looked back at the Sea Witch. Her beloved store sat there in the soft light of evening, a single-story structure built of cedar shingles weathered gray by time and salt air. In the windows, set in white frames bordered with black shutters, could be seen collections of cranberry glass, pottery, and sculptures, along with handmade dolls and wreaths, a collection of wind chimes hanging above them. Kate was proud of her stock, most the work of local artisans. When the store was open, the art and crafts spilled out onto the beach grass growing in the sandy soil in front of the store—fishermen's floats in blue, yellow, orange, and red, windsocks blowing in the breeze alongside brightly colored whirligigs, propellers spinning. The deep red geraniums in their white wooden boxes looked lonely without them. Kate smiled to herself and pulled out into the traffic on 6A. *Now I'm getting a little maudlin about this, I suppose*, she thought.

Kate drove, following the road as it wound through the village of Yarmouth Port, one of several quintessinal Cape Cod villages along the King's Highway. Shops, art galleries, antique stores, and bed-and-breakfast inns lined the route, all representing the charm of Old Cape Cod at its best. Kate rolled down her window, feeling the soft breeze caress her face and ruffle her short, dark hair. Signaling a left turn as she waited for a break in the stream of traffic, she pulled down the visor and glanced at herself in the attached mirror. The face that gazed back at her looked tired, the large, dark eyes shadowed, the lines around her mouth emphasized. She pushed her hair back from her face, running her hand through it in exasperation. Fine and straight, now laced with gray, "It always looks like it needs brushing," she mused. A car on the other side of the road honked its horn, and Kate, startled out of her brief reflection, made the turn with a wave of her hand to an elderly man driving a handsome Lincoln Continental.

As she headed south across the Cape toward Nantucket Sound, she left behind the quaint charm of the King's Highway and entered the emptier stretch of land between Cape Cod Bay and the Sound, through the middle of the Cape's upper arm. Here, charm gave way to more practical business-oriented structures. Side roads led off into groups of suburban tract homes much like those found further north around Boston. In the gaps between the tracts of ranch houses and the industrial parks and strip malls, small groves of scrub pines and oak trees stood, definition fading in the gathering twilight.

Kate continued on until she reached the intersection with Route 28, slowing to a stop as the signal turned from yellow to red. Gazing at the convenience store to her right, she tried to recall whether she needed any milk, or whether she wanted to take a quick detour down 28 to pick up a cold drink, maybe an iced coffee with a shot of espresso. Distractedly, her eye took in the commercial scrawl of this stretch of 28. The town of Yarmouth, like other Cape Cod towns, was composed of villages, in this case, three in all. But of all the fifteen towns on the Cape, the Yarmouth villages probably provided some of the greatest contrasts in terms of ambiance and attitude within one town. The portion of Yarmouth along Rte 28, where Kate was now, was a commercial strip that featured a seemingly endless stream of motels, restaurants, and stores of every description, along with miniature golf courses, bowling alleys, and video game arcades, and, in the summer especially, bumper-to-bumper traffic.

The traffic light changed, causing the current sea of cars in front of Kate to part, and with a firm decision not to consume espresso at this late hour, she crossed onto a side street leading to a small development of homes clustered on the strip of land between Route 28 and the Sound. Many of them were summer homes while others, like her own, had been converted into year-round dwellings. Kate pulled into her driveway, her eyes sweeping over the lines of her familiar house, a simple one-story, gray-shingled ranch, with a screened-in porch at one end. Kate rolled into the covered carport located at the end opposite the porch and parked. Sliding out from behind the steering wheel, she stood and stretched wearily before walking along the flagstone pathway toward the front door, her glance taking in her border flower garden, rows of pansies and golden marigolds wilting in the heat of summer flanked by clumps of dejected-looking orange day lilies, the browning grass in the front yard. Sometime soon, she was going to have to find some time to deal with the yard, Kate told herself, but it won't be tonight.

As she climbed the short flight of brick steps, she considered the state of her refrigerator and wondered what she might fix herself for dinner. *Cooking is one of the hardest parts about living alone,* she thought to herself.

It seemed such an effort to prepare a decent meal for just one person. Kate unlocked the door, letting it swing open as she stepped into the living room, immediately kicking off her shoes and tossing her purse on one of the big wing-backed chairs as she walked in and made her way into her roomy eat-in kitchen. The cool tiles felt soothing to her tired feet as she stood in front of the refrigerator and took a quick glance at the contents. A hamburger patty and some hot dogs. Cheese. A few eggs. Kate chewed her lower lip, contemplating her options. Maybe she'd just have a sandwich. Toasted cheese sounded good.

As Kate was pulling out the cheese and slipping a couple of slices of bread into the toaster, the telephone began to ring. Distracted, she picked up the kitchen phone without glancing at the caller ID screen. "Hello?" she said as she returned to a perusal of the refrigerator contents.

"I'm looking for Ms. Kate LaRue," came a clipped, businesslike woman's voice.

"This is she." Kate straightened up a little.

"I'm Shirley Randall, a social worker here at San Francisco General Hospital in San Francisco. We believe we have your daughter here as a patient. Allison LaRue."

"Ally?" Kate queried softly.

"Is Allison LaRue your daughter?"

"I have a daughter named Allison, but I haven't seen or spoken to her in ten years." Kate could feel the edge coming into her voice. "I don't know where she is or even if she's alive.

"Ms. LaRue, we have a young woman named Allison LaRue here. She gave us this number to call as next of kin."

CHAPTER 2

It had been a number of years since Kate had been on an airplane. She'd made the long drive north to Boston's Logan Airport rather than take the short hop from Hyannis, feeling uncomfortable in a small airplane and preferring not to risk long-term parking. *My car isn't worth the effort it would take to steal it,* she thought. Besides, the drive dealing with all the traffic pouring off the Cape and into Boston and its environs had kept her mind off this unforeseen and startling turn of events. But now she was strapped into her narrow tourist class seat with nothing really to do but stare out the window as Boston receded below her. *Ally,* she thought and, unbidden, images of the little girl she once knew and loved filled her sight. Ally playing with her dolls, carefully feeding, burping, changing them; riding her bike for the first time without training wheels, her face wreathed in smiles, jumping the waves on the beach, the summer sunlight gleaming off her bare, wet arms and legs, eagerly jumping off the last step of the school bus as she returned home, brightly colored leaves swirling around her. Then too there were the memories of Ally as a sullen and angry teenager, skipping school, no longer proud of getting As, staying out too late, wearing what Kate considered to be punk clothes, the multiple body piercings. And then there was the day Ally had walked out the door, vowing never to return after one last screaming match over her attitude, her lack of any ambition or direction, her punk friends, and Kate's fear of her drug use. What had happened to that sweet little girl she had read bedtime stories to and with whom she had played endless games of Candyland and checkers?

She was eighteen and an adult, the police told her when she

went to them a few days later. Kate had called everyone she knew, anyone she thought Ally might have taken shelter with to no avail. She waited days, then weeks, then months. A friend of a friend did manage to get some limited help from the police, but the less-than-mysterious disappearance of an angry eighteen-year-old months earlier didn't generate much interest. And then there was David, Kate's ex-husband, Ally's father. He had been furious when she called him several days after Ally walked out, frantic to know whether Ally was with him. Kate hadn't called right away, because she didn't think David was a likely destination and because she dreaded telling him of her latest failure with Ally. Ally was never fond of her stepmother and was resentful, Kate had thought, of her half-siblings. Her relationship with her father had soured, much as it had with Kate, as she moved through her teen years. David had blamed Kate for that too. But Ally wasn't there, and he hadn't heard from her. And it was all Kate's fault, a failure as a wife and a mother, something he would never let her forget. Thank God, he had eventually stopped calling. Of course, Kate thought uneasily, she should call him now. Tell him Ally was in California and very sick. The hospital staff were not specific on the phone, preferring, they said, to discuss the situation with her in person when she arrived. Nevertheless, she knew this was very bad.

Kate was pulled back from her musings by a nudge from her seatmate, an elderly man with thin white hair and thick glasses who, thankfully, was more interested in reading his novel than talking to her. Distractedly, she purchased a glass of white wine from the waiting flight attendant, hoping it would relax her enough so that she might sleep. Kate had slept little the night before, and she anticipated a long day ahead of her. Did they still show movies in flight? Not on this one, anyway, she thought, a no-frills flight she had booked in an effort to save money. Kate sipped her wine and went back to looking out the window at the patchwork quilt of earth far below. She pushed thoughts of Ally's condition resolutely out of her mind and thought about the Sea Witch instead. She hated leaving it, even for a short time, at this, the busiest time of year.

The time of year that could make or break her. It had only been with great reluctance that she had left her co-owner and business partner, Jerry Stafford, in charge. Jerry had been very understanding and was, she knew, very capable. He was also, of course, very familiar with the Sea Witch and with their customers as well as the local artists who supplied so much of the stock. For Kate, though, this was like leaving her child with an acquaintance, a caring, competent acquaintance perhaps, but an acquaintance, nonetheless. No one could love and care for that child like she could, a feeling she couldn't shake even though the store was really as much Jerry's child as hers.

With that, an image of Ally at about ten or so surfaced, her dark hair still in little-girl braids, walking around the Sea Witch, picking up and examining this or that breakable item, a crystal shell, a stained glass painting, and Kate hovering, fearfully whispering, "Be careful!" "Put that down!" until an exasperated Ally finally pronounced that childhood mantra, "But there's nothing else to *do!*" Kate smiled ruefully at the memory. The Sea Witch was newly hers then, purchased with the financial assistance of her mother as well as through the business investment of Jerry, her longtime friend. She and Ally had just moved into the house in South Yarmouth at the time, the divorce from David having been finalized at last.

The end of her parents' marriage had been tough for Ally, she knew that. Kate had hoped that a fresh start in a place they had all loved so much as a summer refuge would make it better, better certainly than the continual fighting and arguing that had characterized so much of her marriage. How often had Ally cried and begged them to stop when they screamed at each other? Even when they tried to hold it together until after she went to bed, she clearly knew. She either woke up or she just lay in bed listening. Kate knew because when she would go in to check on her, she would be lying there, her eyes open and tearful, or she would squeeze them shut and pretend to be asleep. Kate sighed at the memory. But in the end, the divorce, the fresh start, really hadn't helped Ally even if it had been best for her.

It suddenly occurred to Kate that despite her efforts to focus her attention elsewhere, she was once again thinking about her daughter. She may as well give in, she thought. She had managed for so long to keep Ally out of her thoughts. At least, most of the time. It had been necessary for her own survival she told herself, but that didn't mean she hadn't longed to know where she was, what she was doing, if she was okay. Now, maybe she would finally find out. Maybe Ally could come home again, get some treatment for whatever was wrong with her. Boston was a leading center of medical care and research, after all. Maybe Kate could finally figure out exactly what turned her lovely and sometimes sad little girl into an angry, resentful, and often unlikable teenager. Maybe they could figure it out together, especially now that Ally wasn't a teenager anymore but a young woman of twenty-eight.

Kate closed her eyes and tried to picture Ally as a woman approaching thirty. Did she still have all those tattoos she had given herself on her eighteenth birthday? I suppose she must, Kate thought as she played with the image in her mind, and then tried to see Ally as an old woman with the astrological signs on her arms. Kate smiled to herself as her thoughts continue to wander around images of how Ally might look and sound now. Eventually, the pictures began to blur into a mosaic of Ally-the-little-girl, Ally-the-teenager, imaginary Ally as a tattooed, middle-aged woman...

"We are approaching San Francisco International Airport..." Kate was jolted awake, unaware she had even been asleep. People were adjusting seat backs and tray tables, and refastening seat belts. When had the attendant come and taken her wineglass? "I must have really been out," Kate muttered to herself, trying to straighten her clothing and running her hands through her hair. Looking again out her window, Kate could see the outline of San Francisco Bay with the San Mateo Bridge spanning its width and the houses and freeways of the cities lining its shores. The sun was low in the sky across the Pacific, and Kate looked away from its dazzling brilliance as the plane continued to descend.

CHAPTER 3

Kate sat on a small hard chair next to Ally's bed. The rooms in the Intensive Care Unit surrounded the nursing station, glass doors allowing for an undeniably necessary full view of the patients. Nevertheless, Kate had pulled the curtains around herself and Ally, feeling a need for some semblance of privacy while trying to make sense of what was happening. She reflected on the fact that San Francisco General Hospital was a public hospital and, as such, open to all, even those without means to pay, as no doubt, Ally was. Still, Kate had noted with some relief, the hospital seemed to provide good quality care and had up-to-date facilities. She shifted in her chair, the hard plastic feeling as if it were biting into her arms and back. *They certainly don't put that much money onto the comfort of the visitors,* Kate thought with some frustration as she wriggled her behind, trying to find a comfortable position. *Well, what difference does it make?* she reminded herself. All that mattered was that Ally would be in good hands, whatever happened. Pushing thoughts of the implications of this aside, Kate looked over at her daughter. Instead of looking older and mature, she looked far more like the little girl with whom Kate had baked cookies and built sand castles. Or more likely, the little girl Kate had nursed through childhood illnesses like the chicken pox. She looked so small and thin, and her otherwise pale face was splotched with fever and framed by short dark hair, a "pixie cut" it had been called when she herself was a child, thought Kate. Ally lay unmoving, eyes closed, oxygen tubes in her nose, an IV in her arm. An arm on which the astrological signs were clearly visible Kate noted.

Kate thought back to her arrival at the hospital only a few hours earlier. As soon as she had asked for Ally's room at the front desk, she had been whisked aside by a young volunteer and taken to see a Dr. Martinez in a cramped little office nearby. There, the young, weary-looking doctor, probably a resident or even an intern, Kate thought, had told her how Ally had arrived in the emergency room three days earlier with intense abdominal pain and a raging fever. Once the diagnosis of a ruptured appendix and peritonitis was made, she was rushed into surgery and the appendix removed. At that point, Dr. Martinez had seemed uncomfortable and looked away. The resulting peritonitis was not under control, he told her, and sepsis appeared to have set in. Ally was clearly malnourished and in poor health to begin with, he had continued, a little defensively, once again meeting her gaze. His voice softened a little, no doubt because he saw the shock in her eyes. "We're doing all that we can" she remembered him saying, that standard platitude of doctors everywhere when they were out of options.

Kate's thoughts were interrupted by the arrival of a nurse who, with businesslike efficiency, checked Ally's monitors and adjusted the IV drip. She glanced at Kate and, turning back to Ally, said "You've had a long trip and you look like you could use something to eat. She's stable at the moment, but we'll know where to find you if something changes."

Kate hesitated a few seconds before replying, "I guess you're right. I could use a little something." She stood up and looked longingly at her daughter. "I didn't even know how much I'd missed her. Now I've found her, and I can't even talk to her."

"Often, people can hear even when they're in a coma, Mrs. LaRue. Have you tried talking to her?"

Unaware she had spoken out loud, Kate was startled. "Um, yes, a little. It's kind of hard, you see..." but the nurse was already gone before Kate could finish.

Kate looked back at Ally, so still and silent. She could barely see the movement of her chest as she took in quick, shallow breaths. Gingerly, Kate reached down and picked up her hand. It felt hot and dry in her grasp, and the touch of Ally's skin brought tears to her eyes. Maybe, she thought, it's better to talk to her when she can't argue with me. That brought a little smile to her lips. "Ally," she said and cleared her throat. "It's me again. Mom." Kate paused. "I'm here for you, honey. I love you, I always have. You've got to hang in there, baby." Kate paused again, searching for something else to say. "If you get better you could come home again. Get a new start. Only if you want to, of course," Kate added hastily. *And only if we could stand living with each other*, she said silently. "I'm going to get something to eat now, Ally, and then I'll come back." She gently laid her hand back down on the white hospital blanket and, with a last look at the still form in the bed, turned and slipped out from behind the curtains.

The hospital cafeteria was empty except for Kate and one young man, uniformed in white, huddled over his coffee at a table by the window, his attention focused on the book open in his hand. Probably an orderly Kate surmised, letting her gaze settle on him for a moment. Then she shrugged wearily, looking down at the remains of a tuna sandwich and coffee in front of her. Next to them was the discarded *San Francisco Chronicle* she had managed to acquire and read thoroughly without, she now realized, retaining much. It was really getting late, she thought, glancing at her watch. Visiting hours must surely be over. She was glad she had the forethought to get checked in to her motel before coming to the hospital. She was more than ready for a hot, relaxing shower and a good night's sleep. But first, Kate thought, she would check back in on Ally and tell her good night. That is, if the nurses would even let her in. Kate rose and, retracing her steps, soon found herself back in the ICU. A harried-looking nurse's aide with a nameplate identifying her only as Rosa greeted her as soon as she was buzzed through the large double doors.

"Oh, Mrs. LaRue, good, you're back. Your daughter is awake and asking for you." Rosa called the last few words over her shoulder as she headed for one of the other beds in the crowded unit. Kate, startled, stared after her for a few seconds, then turned and walked quickly in the direction of Ally's bed, her heart starting to race in anticipation. As she approached the glass doors, she could see that Ally's eyes were closed and her body as still as before, but, standing next to her bed watching her for a few seconds, Kate thought her breathing seemed a little faster.

"Ally, sweetheart, it's Mom. I'm here." This time when Kate picked up her hand, she felt Ally try to grip it. Impulsively, Kate reached down and stroked Ally's short, dark hair. Ally's eyes opened, feverish and dull, and she seemed to struggle to focus. "It's okay, it's okay," Kate murmured as Ally's breathing seemed to ratchet up a few notches. Suddenly, a series of quick bleeps began to issue from the monitors surrounding Ally's bed. Kate could hear rapid footsteps behind her, sense a stirring of activity from the direction of the nurses' station. Ally's eyes found her mother's and seemed to latch onto them. Her breath was coming in short little gasps. "Please, Ally," Kate pleaded, feeling alarm rising in her breast as Ally, having put forth a tremendous effort to focus, now seemed to be struggling to speak but all she could manage was a faint, unintelligible whisper. As she gathered herself for another try, nurses converged on the bed.

"Mrs. LaRue ..." one began.

Ally clung to her hand, now with surprising strength.

"Glory" her voice was soft, thready with fever, but it was Ally's voice, nonetheless. Even as Kate's heart beat faster just at the sound of that voice she hadn't heard in so long, she felt confused and oddly disoriented and let down.

"Glory?" she repeated tentatively, looking up at the nurses.

"Mrs. LaRue, we need to you to wait outside the unit." One of the nurses took her firmly by the elbow, pulling Ally's hand free. Ally seemed to have slipped back into unconsciousness again, her breathing labored.

As Kate was propelled away from the bed, she turned and looked back toward Ally, but the medical staff had quickly closed in on her, blocking her from view. As they moved toward the doors, Kate turned to her escort.

"What did she mean by that? Glory? Do you know? She struggled so to say it. It must have meant something to her but I..."

Her companion shrugged a little as she guided Kate to another plastic chair outside the doors. "It's the name of her little girl, that's all I can tell you."

"Her little...what?"

"Her daughter." A pause. "Your granddaughter."

As Kate collapsed uncomprehendingly into the chair, the world spinning around her, she heard the announcement over the hospital's intercom system, calling for a code blue in the intensive care unit.

CHAPTER 4

Kate stood in the bathtub of her motel room letting the hot water from the shower run down over her body, the steam enveloping her in a cocoon of warmth. She closed her eyes against the tears that mingled with the shower water on her face and let them be washed away down the drain along with this long, sad, ultimately horrible day. *My poor baby*, Kate thought, leaning her head against the wall. In that last moment with Ally it seemed as if the past ten years did not matter, nor did the difficult years leading up to her departure that sunny summer day, only weeks after she graduated from high school. Now she was gone forever and knowing there was no future as far as Ally was concerned was more devastating than the uncertainty Kate had lived with for so long.

Even as she thought this, the image of the ICU nurse standing next to her telling her she had a granddaughter came to mind. A granddaughter named Glory. In the emergency generated by Ally's dying, this incredible pronouncement had been pushed aside. Later, as Kate again sat next to Ally's bed, her now lifeless hand in hers, shock drying her eyes, she had asked again about Glory, but the nurses seemed to know nothing beyond that it was the name of her child. Ally apparently had asked for her constantly whenever she was conscious over the last couple of days. Kate would need to talk to Mrs. Randall, the hospital social worker, in the morning. She should know more, they told her.

Eventually, I'm going to have to get out of here, Kate thought, *or dry up like a prune*. She shut off the stream of hot water and stepped out of the bathtub, reaching for a towel as she did so. She stood shivering despite the steam, and slowly dried off. Getting older was no picnic, Kate mused, looking at her naked body in the harsh fluorescent light. She wasn't as slim as she once was and she sagged in places. Flabby. Maybe she should start thinking about getting to the gym once in a while. She didn't take care of herself like she should, she knew that. But she was alive. Alive and fifty-three years old, and Ally, her only child, was dead at twenty-eight. The sheer magnitude of what had happened that night, the unfairness of it all, overwhelmed her, and she stumbled into the small motel room and fell sobbing on the bed, clutching one of the hard little pillows to her face and soaking it with her tears. After she had cried herself out for what seemed like the hundredth time, she pulled herself together, tugged on a nightgown, and burrowed under the covers.

Lying in the semidarkness, light filtering through the flimsy curtains that covered the sliding doors, Kate tried to focus on happier things. The Sea Witch filled with charming, one-of-a-kind gifts and works of art, lit by the sun on a fragrant summer day. Admiring people walking through the store buying whatever took their fancy. Days spent as a buyer herself searching all over the Cape for just the right piece of art for her store. Or other long days spent lying on the beach, walking in the surf as she gathered seashells and pretty stones, and swimming in the gentle waves of Nantucket Sound. Kate could see herself younger, happier, running on the beach with her sister Maggie long before marriages and children and careers had pulled them in different directions. Suddenly, she was older, walking along that same beach hand in hand with David at night, the moon lighting a path across the water. The two of them stopping to kiss by the water's edge and feeling again the warmth of his lips, the taste of his mouth, the pressure of his body against hers. And, of course, there was Ally, skipping along the beach, a happy, carefree little girl again, a pail and shovel in her hands. Kate called to her and she ran away, laughing, down the beach. "Ally! Come back!" Kate called, running now herself. But Ally climbed out onto one of the jetties that stretched out into the Sound, clambering over the sharp rocks, heedless of the waves now crashing against them, sending sprays of water into the air. Kate screamed Ally's name, struggling in the surf, the world now dark with an impending storm. Kate could see Ally perched on the very last rock, looking out toward the horizon. Kate continued to struggle toward her, pulling herself up onto the rocks next to Ally. And as she did so, Ally turned to look at Kate, whispered, "Glory," and then was gone. Vanished into the spray and the mist, leaving Kate alone and clinging to the last rock of the jetty as the storm broke around her.

Morning sunlight filtered through the shaded windows as Kate waited for Mrs. Randall in another cramped office at San Francisco General Hospital, feeling depressed and hungover despite the fact she hadn't been doing any drinking. This chair was at least reasonably comfortable, she thought, clutching a cup of hot coffee and taking occasional small sips while ruing the fact that her favorite iced lattes could not be obtained in San Francisco. Kate's thoughts wandered back to last night's dream. She had dreamed that dream so many times over the years, although much more frequently in the early days and months after Ally left. In the dream, Ally was always a little girl running away from her, laughing, down the beach, climbing out on the jetty as a storm approached, not listening, not responding to her mother's frantic calls. Kate struggling to reach her and, just as she did, Ally turning to look at her as if to speak and vanishing. Only this time, she did say something. Glory. It was as if Ally had made one last effort to communicate with her. Glory. Kate shook her head, still unable to believe it. Ally had a child. And given that there was no one here for Ally except herself, she had to conclude that Ally was a single mother as well. Who and where was Glory's father?

A tall, neatly dressed woman in late middle age, black hair carefully styled, makeup perfectly applied to skin the color of creamy coffee, appeared, apologized for being late, and, after introducing herself as Shirley Randall, said, "You must be Mrs. LaRue." She took Kate's proffered hand between both of her own and with warm brown eyes focused on Kate's, she added, "I want to say right out front how sorry I am for your loss." Mrs. Randall turned and took off her coat and hung it on a nearby coatrack. As she settled herself behind her desk, she took a good look at the worn, slightly disheveled woman with the dark circles under her eyes seated before her, the tracks of tears clearly visible.

Kate nodded. "Yes. Thank you. I don't think I've really taken it all in yet, to be honest."

"I can't imagine you have."

Kate nodded again, her eyes filling once more with tears.

A tissue box was offered, and Kate wiped her eyes while Mrs. Randall murmured "Go ahead and cry; it's all right, I understand."

Kate straightened her back, biting her lip to hold back any further tears. "You know, Mrs. Randall, what I'd like most right now is to find out about my daughter's child. I'm sorry to admit it, but I don't know anything about her. You see—"

"Mrs. LaRue, you don't need to explain. I'm aware of the situation."

"Do you know where she is? Is she with her father, whoever he is?"

"To the best of my knowledge there's no father involved. My information is limited, I must confess. Let me tell you what I know about your daughter. As it turns out, I happened to be there when she came in to the hospital."

When Kate nodded, Mrs. Randall launched into her story. Three days earlier, she had been talking to staff in the Emergency Room when, during an early afternoon lull, Ally had come in to the ER under her own power complaining of severe abdominal pain and fever. She was accompanied by another young woman, who was introduced as a neighbor named Maria Carlos, and three young children, one of whom had clung ferociously to Ally. This little girl, Mrs. Randall explained, was about three, four at the most, and had to be all but pried from Ally's arms so that her mother might be examined. When it became obvious that she would need to be admitted, Ally was almost as devastated as her child had been. She had cried and insisted that she couldn't leave her, that there was no family to take her. Maria Carlos had been brought in to see her and had reassured her that she would take care of the girl, whose name was said to be Glory, until Ally was released from the hospital. This seemed to appease her a little, and she was able to let the child leave with Ms. Carlos. Apparently there was no next of kin in the area but just before she was rushed into surgery, Ally had provided Mrs. Randall with Kate's name and phone number. Following the surgery, Ally had drifted in and out of consciousness, but during those periods when she was at least somewhat lucid, she would call Glory's name repeatedly and could not be calmed or reassured.

"And this Maria Carlos, she still has Glory?" Kate asked when Mrs. Randall paused.

"As far as I know, yes, she does. I spoke with her once, the day after the surgery, to tell her your daughter was not doing well but that you had been notified and would be arriving from the East Coast soon. She seemed relieved and also, perhaps, a little surprised." Mrs. Randall shrugged slightly. "Apparently, she knew that you and your daughter had been estranged."

"Does she know..." Kate trailed off uncertainly.

"I haven't called to inform her yet, but I will do so. This matter is a little complicated, as perhaps you realize. Will you be seeking to obtain custody of Glory?"

Kate sighed, and the tears welled up in her eyes again. "I can't imagine abandoning my grandchild, the only grandchild I'll ever have. But raising a child again. I don't know. I'm a little afraid."

"Well, I'd be more concerned if you weren't," Mrs. Randall replied brusquely but not unkindly. "Did your daughter have other immediate family besides yourself?"

Kate hesitated. "Only my ex-husband David. He's her father, of course. I haven't spoken to him in years, so I don't have a current phone number for him." *Or I don't know whether I do or not*, thought Kate guiltily. "And I don't think Ally would have spoken with him either."

Mrs. Randall looked at Kate appraisingly for a few seconds, and then sighed. "Well, Mrs. LaRue, I'm afraid I must ask if you have discussed mortuary services with the hospital."

Kate cried again as she told Mrs. Randall of her first appointment that morning, during which she had made arrangements for a funeral home to pick up Ally's body. She could not bear to simply leave her here, where no one knew her or cared about her. She had decided to have her cremated and the ashes returned to Massachusetts for burial. She just wanted all of this to be over so she could she go home. Home with Ally's ashes and a granddaughter named Glory. No matter what she did now, she realized, there was no going back to the home she had left two days ago.

CHAPTER 5

Kate stood on the street corner and looked up at the densely packed row of buildings that provided housing in this part of the city. Wind blew old newspapers, empty fast-food bags, and other debris along the street. Here and there people were out, some walking slowly down the street, others sitting on front steps. One young man, dressed in old jeans and a work shirt, leaned against the grimy window of a corner convenience store smoking a cigarette and watching her with idle curiosity. San Francisco was a charming and delightful city, but this was not one of its more attractive neighborhoods Kate thought to herself with a sigh. All things considered, it didn't really surprise her that this is where Ally had ended up living, but on some level, Kate had still hoped that poverty had not been her lot.

Before she had left the hospital, Kate had convinced Mrs. Randall to give her Maria Carlos's address so that she might see if there was anything of value or importance in Ally's apartment—and, too, so that she might see Glory. Kate felt a twinge of nervous anticipation as she thought about this, her stomach starting to flip-flop with anxiety. Who would Glory look like? How would she feel about a grandmother suddenly appearing from out of the blue? *She must be terribly frightened and sad,* Kate told herself. *After all, how does such a young child deal with the death of her mother the only family she has? Well, actually I'm the only family she has now and she probably won't want anything to do with me,* Kate reminded herself. Kate pictured a little girl who was rebellious and defiant, a torrent of inappropriate language no child that age should know pouring from her mouth. With a quick shudder, she then tried to imagine a different scenario: Glory running into her arms crying, "Grandma! Grandma!" Not very likely, she grimaced.

"Come on, let's just do this," Kate muttered with renewed determination. She located the correct street number and made her way up a short flight of stone steps to a door consisting of black rusty grillwork. Peering through, she could see a small bare entryway or courtyard with wooden doors along two sides and another flight of stairs twisting upward. A lone battered tricycle sat in the shadows. Off to one side Kate noted a row of metal mailboxes with buzzers above them; next to the one marked "LaRue" was one that read "M. Carlos." Kate pushed the button, waited until she got an unintelligible squawk, gave her name, and then waited hopefully for the buzzer to sound. Once it did and she had stepped inside the grill, she could hear a Spanish-accented voice call from above her head, "Up here, Mrs. LaRue." Kate looked up to see a young, round-faced woman looking down at her, reddish brown curls forming a halo around her head.

Kate climbed the steps to an upper landing where Maria Carlos waited for her in front of an open door, a boy who was a toddler of about two or so in diapers in her arms and a slightly older child wearing a bright blue sundress clinging to the skirt of her loose-fitting denim dress. As Kate looked hesitantly at the little girl gazing up at her with wide brown eyes, the woman in front of her shook her head. "Glory isn't here; she's at school."

"At school?" Kate echoed.

"Yes, at school." This time an emphatic head nod. "I'm Maria."

"Of course. Nice to meet you." Kate held out her hand in greeting as Maria juggled the child on her hip to extend her own. Maria smiled and gestured toward the door. "Come in," she added as she turned and walked across the threshold, closely followed by her daughter who looked back and smiled shyly up at Kate.

Kate followed as Maria led the way into a relatively large open room that contained a few pieces of well used living-room furniture as well as a large, wooden dining-room table with mismatched chairs stacked with laundry, a television tuned to a Spanish language station, and a large number of toys scattered across the furniture and the bare wood floor. Maria set the toddler down in a playpen located in the middle of the floor and quickly cleared a spot on a frayed and lumpy sofa. The older child retreated to a corner of the room where she climbed onto an old easy chair and observed Kate from a safe distance, her thumb in her mouth.

"Oh no, I don't want to bother you," Kate said quickly. "I just wanted to see Ally's apartment, and I hoped I could meet Glory." Kate's voice hesitated over the last part of that statement.

"You will be taking Glory, yes?" Maria asked quizzically.

"Uh...well, no, I can't...not today, anyway," Kate added hastily seeing the disappointment in Maria's eyes. "You see, I can't just take her. The social services agency..."

Maria nodded slowly, and then added, "Ally...she wouldn't like that. Social services and all."

"No, I'm sure she wouldn't, but...There's nothing I can do."

Maria turned and walked rapidly across the room. Kate could see into the small galley kitchen as Maria rummaged in a drawer. She soon returned holding up a key. "Ally's place...it's right across, over there," Maria pointed through her still-open door to one directly opposite.

"Thank you. I'll bring the key back." Kate started toward the door, then paused, turning to look back at Maria with confusion written on her face. "When does Glory come home? Isn't she too young to be in school? Besides, it's summer. Is there school in summer here?" The questions fell from her mouth in a jumble of disconnected thoughts.

Maria threw up her hands. "Two o'clock. It's a special school. To help her learn to talk."

"She doesn't talk? From what I understood...I thought... Shouldn't she be talking?"

"No, no talking."

"Not at all?"

"No, I don't think so."

"Why?"

"I don't know. Ally didn't know."

Kate frowned. She started to turn away but then swung back yet again. "Maria, exactly how old is Glory?"

"Four, I think."

"Four."

"*Si*...yes"

Kate turned away once more and, lost in thought, walked across the landing to the opposite door.

Ally's apartment was very small, just one room, a tiny kitchenette, and a bathroom. Kate stood just inside the door and took in the worn-looking futon, its bedding piled together at one end, the rickety card table with a pair of kitchen chairs, one with a booster seat, the small, unfinished bookshelf with a few books, secondhand toys, and children's DVDs stacked neatly in it, and finally, the scratched bureau with some folded clothes and a lamp on top of it. There was also a slightly newer-looking television with a built-in DVD player on a small portable stand, with a few more children's DVDs scattered on the bare wooden floor in front of it.

Kate felt uneasy as she glanced around, feeling as though she was intruding on someone's private space and that the residents (her daughter?) might return at any moment. Certainly, it looked as though whoever lived here had left with every intention of returning. Kate walked over to the kitchenette and looked in the small refrigerator at milk, butter, a few eggs, some hot dogs, and leftover macaroni and cheese sealed in some kind of storage bowl. There was fruit in a storage drawer and some frozen vegetables and meat in the tiny freezer section. Looking in the cabinets, she found what looked like secondhand dishware and the inevitable Cheerios, bread, and peanut butter. There wasn't much else, though, and Ally had no stove, just a hotplate, toaster, and small microwave oven. And a sink, next to which were a few dishes in a drying rack.

Kate moved on to the bathroom, an old-fashioned affair with a pedestal sink and a claw-footed bathtub. There was no real shower, just a spray attachment, she noted with a wry smile, wondering how Ally, who would take long, hot, wasteful (or so Kate thought) showers back home, had liked this arrangement. A few bath toys, including a rubber duck, along with shampoo and soap filled a metal rack hung on the side of the bathtub. On the sink stood a cup with two toothbrushes, one large and one small and pink in color, along with a nearly empty tube of toothpaste. The sight of those toothbrushes brought tears to Kate's eyes as the reality of Ally's death rushed over her once again, and she sat down abruptly on the wooden toilet seat and sobbed for a few minutes.

When she had once again pulled herself together, she decided she should have a look in Ally's medicine cabinet. Bracing herself slightly, she opened the small, mirrored door. Children and adult Tylenol, tampons, Band-Aids, antibiotic ointment—nothing odd or illegal. What had she been expecting anyway, she asked herself crossly. Ally would have been furious and the old argument over "illegal substances," or even legal ones, would have sprung up, Kate knew, as if it had been yesterday and not ten years ago.

Kate closed the cabinet with a sigh and moved back toward the main living area. It occurred to her that she wasn't really sure just what she was looking for except, perhaps, some sense of who her daughter was and what she had become because she knew that, in reality, Ally was a stranger to her. However, this tiny, poorly furnished apartment was telling her very little; at least, nothing of any consequence. Kate stood in the middle of the room and scanned again its meager contents. Her eye fell on the old bureau and she walked over to it and opened the top drawer. Pint-size underwear, socks, and pajamas, neatly folded; next to them were adult versions of the same. Each of the other drawers contained neatly folded clothes divided in half in the same fashion. Tee shirts, knits, sweaters, shorts, and jeans.

As Kate was closing the bottom drawer, she noticed what looked like paper sticking out from one of the piles. Extracting it, she saw that it was a small photograph of a young woman, maybe in her late twenties, with black hair, brown eyes, and soft caramel skin tones. She was casually dressed in jeans and an unadorned tee shirt, a hint of a smile on her lips. The picture looked as though it had been taken in one of those photo booths you find in a mall or a fair. There was nothing to indicate who she was on the back, and Kate was sure she had never seen her before. She fingered the photo for a moment wondering why Ally put it in a bottom bureau drawer under her clothes. Maybe she had just misplaced it, Kate told herself. With a slight shrug, she put the picture down on top of the bureau, noticing as she did so the narrow door next to it. Kate opened it and found a rather small closet with a couple of dresses, jackets, and raincoats on a rod and a few more clothes, cold-weather things from the look of them, on a narrow shelf along with some boxes.

Impulsively, Kate reached up and took down a box that looked like an old shoe box and brought it over to the table. Sitting in what must have been Ally's chair, she contemplated the box, feeling again that sense of sneaking around, of privacy violation. How often had this been a source of the bitter fights with the teenaged Ally; Kate slipping into her room when she was gone, trying to uncover any evidence of drugs, diary, or computer entries that would reveal some wrongdoing or sexual activity. But, Kate told herself, biting her lip against the pain, it was different now. Ally was gone, and she wasn't coming back. Someone would have to go through her things eventually and more thoroughly than she was doing now. Kate reached over and pulled off the top of the shoe box and peered at the contents inside. At first glance, it appeared to be a hodgepodge of papers: bills, notes, newspaper clippings, a few more photos.

Kate looked at these first. One was a picture of Ally as she remembered her at the time she left home for good. The defiant teenager stared at her with a challenging smirk, standing on a city street somewhere, dressed in a tight, low cut black tank top that ended above her navel, tattoos on full display, earrings dangling from her multiple piercings, the sun glinting off the stud in her nose and the ring in her navel. Her hair was still long in this one, streaked with red and held back in a gaudy hair clip. Kate had never seen this picture before though and wondered exactly where and when it had been taken. Probably after she left home, she mused, feeling free of all restraints and out to conquer the world from the look on her face. In a way, seeing this made Kate feel better, reminding her of how horrible those last few years with Ally had been. *I made mistakes*, she told herself, *but I wasn't the only one. Then again...*

Kate shook off those thoughts and returned to her perusal of the box. She lifted out another, obviously more recent, photograph of Ally, thinner than she had been as a teenager, her hair cut short and framing her small face. Her face and eyes were smiling, however, and she held a child on her lap who looked to be three or four, a solemn little girl with dark hair in braids and big brown eyes, wearing a Winnie the Pooh sundress and sandals and clutching a pink stuffed animal of some indiscriminate type. The photo appeared to have been taken at some type of carnival, Kate thought. Ally was seated on a bench dressed for summer in shorts and a tank top; behind her, Kate could see what looked like a boardwalk amusement park with an old-fashioned wooden roller coaster in the distance. She gazed at it, fingers lightly tracing the image of her daughter and the child in her lap who looked so much like her, wondering who had taken the picture and where. The photo looked like it had been taken with an old film camera; after a few minutes, Kate turned it over and saw "*Glory and me*" written on it in Ally's familiar scrawl with a date only a few weeks earlier. The sight of that writing brought tears to her eyes again, and she hastily put it down on the table and returned to the contents of the box. There were only a couple of other photographs, but they were less interesting, even puzzling, as they seemed to be just pictures of empty fields somewhere, a road going off into the distance. A ranch of some sort, or maybe a farm?

Kate laid the photos aside and sifted through the other papers. She pulled out a stiff, parchmentlike paper that had been folded in half. Opening it, she saw that it was a California birth certificate declaring that Glory Allison LaRue was born in Los Angeles four years ago to Allison Kate LaRue, father unknown. The certificate open on the table before her, Kate considered this revelation. So four years ago this summer Ally had been living in Los Angeles. Kate had been there once, many years ago when she was still in college. She and a friend had flown out for spring break, mostly checking out Hollywood and the Southern California beaches.

Moving back over to the bureau, she picked up the photo of the unknown woman again and set it down on the table next to the birth certificate. Kate looked at the photo, considering the possibilities. Perhaps this was someone Ally had known in Los Angeles, someone she had confided in, who knew the story of where she had been and what had happened to her. *It won't matter*, Kate told herself despairingly, *if I don't know who she is.* The birth certificate gave a street address for Ally that meant nothing to Kate, but she carefully wrote it down in a small notebook she carried in her purse, and then considered whether she could simply take the photos and the birth certificate with her. Maybe just to copy, at least.

Suddenly, she heard a soft sound behind her and, hastily stuffing the photos and the carefully folded birth certificate in her purse, she twisted around in her chair to look out the open door behind her. A small child dressed in jeans and a stained pink top stood in the doorway, looking at her with huge brown eyes that suddenly seemed blank with fear. Kate's heart stopped for a few seconds as she and this tiny, living, breathing image of her daughter stared at each other across the room. Then Glory turned and ran, dark brown braids swinging out behind her.

"Glory!" Kate called after her as she leapt up from her chair, overturning it in the process. "Come back!"

Maria appeared in the open doorway across the hall and scooped Glory up as she came barreling through. "Shh, shh, little one," she murmured to the sobbing little girl in her arms. "This is your *abuela,* your grandmother." Glory buried her face in Maria's shoulder, clinging to her as if she'd never let go.

"She is very shy, this one," said Maria apologetically. "Don't take it personal."

Kate smiled as she fought back her tears and shook her head.

"No, I understand. Glory was expecting to see her mother, and I'm a stranger." She paused hesitantly, searching for something else to say. "Well, perhaps I'd better go. I'll just lock up for now." Kate walked back across the hall and into Ally's little apartment. There was no one else to whom any of this belonged except, of course, Glory. It wasn't as if a crime had been committed, so surely she could take what she wanted. Kate absentmindedly straightened the chair she had knocked over and reached for the shoe box. She wanted to look at some of the other things in it later, back in her motel room, or even at home, where maybe her heart wouldn't feel like it was about to break. With one last glance around the tiny apartment that had been Ally's home, Kate turned and walked out, locking the door behind her. Maria's door was still open, and Kate ventured in long enough to drop the key on the table with a quick thank you and reassurance that she would return. Kate crouched down to look at her granddaughter. "Good-bye, sweetheart, I'll see you soon," she whispered softly, but Glory, clinging to Maria's skirts as she worked in the kitchen, never looked up.

CHAPTER 6

Back in her motel room Kate contemplated the situation over a fast-food hamburger, having felt too emotionally drained to sit in a restaurant long enough to order and eat a full meal. The shoe box sat on the small motel table in front of her, its contents having been explored once more. She now knew more about Ally's private life, having looked at pay stubs from a local diner where Ally apparently worked "mother's hours" at minimum wage with a little extra earned as tips, she knew what she received in food stamps and government aid, and what her last tax return looked like. Kate saw what she paid out in bills and knew that Ally had virtually no money in her bank account. She didn't even have a phone of any kind. As sad as that was to Kate, in some ways what the shoebox told her about Glory was even more disheartening. Notes to and from teachers at the special education preschool she attended, discussing the small steps she took toward meeting the goals they had set for her. One tightly folded progress report that laid out in depressing detail just how little language Glory seemed to have, at least expressively, and just how anxious and socially withdrawn she was. Some of the newspaper and magazine clippings were about autism; clearly this possibility was being considered. There was also some information jotted down on notebook paper, seemingly taken from the Internet as well as library books, apparently on other psychological problems that were being considered. Some of these, such as selective mutism and post-traumatic stress disorder, raised even more questions for Kate.

An overwhelming urge to cry engulfed her once again, and, when her tears had dried, Kate thought about how much she longed to rewind the last few days, to go back to what had at least been a familiar, if not completely happy and satisfying, life. *And much happier and calmer than I ever realized,* Kate thought. What was she going to do with a four-year-old who could not, or would not, talk? Three days ago, Ally was still alive, even if Kate didn't know where she was, she didn't know she had a grandchild, and she wasn't faced with a decision that would turn her life upside down. No matter what she decided now, she could not return to that former life. Kate thought about her conversation with Jerry Stafford back in Yarmouth Port earlier in the afternoon. She'd poured out the whole horrible story to him, her best friend and business partner, a man she had known for nearly twenty years. So long, that he remembered the teenaged Ally as well as the sweet, lovable little girl who had preceded her. He'd again been very sympathetic and understanding, assuring her that everything was under control at the store and to do whatever she thought necessary. They'd discussed some business details and certainly everything sounded okay. Kate trusted him implicitly, but she longed to be there, to see for herself that all was well, that this piece of her life had not changed radically.

Well, it didn't matter because there was no going back anyway, no undoing what had already been done. After Ally left, she had told herself that many times, and in some way, it had helped her get through the days and nights. Tomorrow she would finalize the arrangements for sending Ally's remains home, as well as talk to the local children's services and maybe the school about Glory. She would have to stay for a week or more, like it or not, in order to close out Ally's accounts, pack up the apartment, and find a way to get Glory to accept her. As Kate again fingered the photographs, she thought about her decision to try to find people Ally knew here in San Francisco and to see what she could learn about Ally and Glory's lives here. Kate couldn't help feeling she was missing something, something big, something important that would help her understand how her daughter and granddaughter came to be here in this time and place. Something that she needed to know and there was someone out there somewhere who could tell her the answer, she was sure of that. Kate just had to find him or her.

The little preschool classroom where Kate now sat was a world of miniature tables and chairs, kitchens, and play spaces. Feeling decidedly out of place, she looked on as Glory's teacher, an impossibly young woman to her mind, along with her even younger aide, coaxed the small group of preschoolers into sitting in a semicircle on the floor. In front of them was a wall whose gaily decorated calendar with its numbers, letters, and pictures was to be the focus of this particular lesson. Glory sat cross-legged on the floor with the others, her wide brown eyes taking in everything with a kind of vigilance that suggested she would be ready to bolt in a second if she felt it warranted. It was the end of the school day, and Kate had spent it observing the efforts of Miss Cathy and Miss Lori to engage and teach this eclectic little group of children. Some of the children had been curious and friendly with their "visitor," others had ignored her, looking through her as if she weren't there. Glory, for her part, knew she was there all right, but she had maintained a still-fearful distance, saying not a word to Kate or anyone else all day.

As she watched the children and their teachers go through their end-of-the-day ritual, singing a little good-bye-see-you-tomorrow ditty, Kate's mind wandered over the last few days and what she had accomplished. This included the arrangements for Ally's remains and the cancellation of her lease, in addition to meeting with children's services and beginning the process of assuming custody of Glory. There had been so many business and just bureaucratic details to deal with that she had not begun the process she most wanted to do—unravel the mystery of Glory and Ally.

When the children had been "dismissed" and helped into jackets and sweaters, their backpacks secured, Glory's teacher let her assistant lead them out to their buses. Somewhat wearily, she sat down at her desk, beckoning Kate over to a nearby chair. Kate smiled sympathetically. "They're quite a handful. Ms. Roberts, right? I can only admire your energy and commitment. I could never have done this type of work myself."

"I love working with these children, but it isn't easy, believe me." Cathy Roberts paused, collecting her thoughts as she brushed her short blond hair out of her eyes. "Mrs. LaRue, I want to tell you again how sorry I am about your daughter. Sorry for you and for Glory. This is having a terrible impact on her."

"What do you mean?" Kate shrugged apologetically. "It's hard for me to tell what Glory is thinking and feeling. She's so..." Kate hesitated, trying to think of a word that described Glory's singular affect.

Ms. Roberts placed her arms on her desk, looking toward the far wall, her eyes thoughtful as she considered her answer. "Well, to begin with, she's regressed completely over the last week or so." She shifted her gaze to Kate. "You saw her today. No communication at all, won't do any work or play with anything, the hypervigilance."

Kate leaned forward eagerly. "She does talk, then?"

"Yes, but it's very inconsistent. She has said a few words, and she will use the picture books and schedules, gesture, point to things, laugh. Receptively, she understands a lot. However, she's very fearful, very anxious, and I think the lack of expressive language has more to do with that than anything else. She was just beginning to feel a little safe, I thought, before her mother got sick."

"But what is she so afraid of? I must admit, she hardly seems like a child who's just shy around strangers."

Ms. Roberts nodded. "I agree." She paused for a moment, biting her lower lip. "I don't know precisely, but I would guess there was some trauma in Glory's life. I received the impression that Glory and her mom came to San Francisco to escape a bad situation somewhere. Maybe your daughter was in an abusive relationship."

Seeing the question hovering on Kate's lips, she continued hastily, "Of course, I'm not certain of this; it's just an impression I picked up."

"Well, what made you think that?"

"Certain things Ms. LaRue said, the way she responded at times.

Glory's behavior just seems so traumatized. I've had some experience with this working in a women's shelter, so I recognize the signs. As a matter of fact, I understand Ms. LaRue and Glory lived there for a while when they first arrived in the city."

"Perhaps you could tell me where it is. You see, I'm trying to find out what happened to my daughter and granddaughter. I know so little and I want to understand."

"Of course. I don't know if they will talk to you, though."

"Is there anything else *you* can tell me?"

"Not really. Your daughter didn't confide in me. I do think Glory needs a stable environment and a lot of support. Life seems to have been very difficult for her thus far."

"Difficult?"

"Yes." The teacher's light green eyes looked into Kate's, measuring her. "You know, I really do believe your daughter was afraid of something or someone, but of what or whom, I don't know."

CHAPTER 7

The little seafood restaurant Kate had chosen for dinner was surrounded by wide picture windows that overlooked the San Francisco waterfront. Twilight was gathering over the bay, and Kate could just see the Golden Gate Bridge from where she sat, spanning the mouth of the bay where it connected San Francisco to Marin County. It was a lovely view, and Kate had enjoyed looking at the boats and the water as she downed fresh steamed crab and white wine, a desperately needed break from fast food in her sterile little motel room. Now she sipped some after-dinner coffee as she contemplated her day.

As Glory's teacher had suggested, the shelter had not been forthcoming about Ally and Glory's stay there. The woman who was overseeing it that day, neatly dressed with dark blond hair pulled back in a knot at her neck, looked young and somehow out of place in that setting. Nevertheless, she had been both kind and sympathetic and, while she had nodded slowly in recognition when Kate showed her the photo of Ally and Glory at the amusement park, she would not part with any further information. The only thing Kate had learned was they had not been there long and, if anyone was still living there who remembered them, she was not going to tell her who they were.

After the shelter, Kate had stopped by the diner where Ally had worked, located in the same rundown neighborhood where Ally had lived. It was tucked away behind a narrow storefront and featured, at most, two dozen well-worn metal and Formica tables sitting on cracked linoleum and a lunch counter with stools covered in some type of red faux leather with stuffing sticking out of several of them. It might have possessed some retro appeal had it not been so battered looking, dirt and dust hiding in the corners. No one there was willing or able to tell her much either. Apparently, Ally had come in two or three days a week, whenever she was scheduled, worked her shift, and gone home. The manager, a tired, middle-aged woman dressed in a stained uniform, had given an indifferent shrug to Kate's questions and said only that Ally kept to herself and didn't socialize with the other waitresses. She did her job, nothing exceptional, nothing unusual.

After an Internet search at the city library, Kate had also managed to find a telephone number for the address in Los Angeles given on Glory's birth certificate, thinking that, if this line of inquiry proved fruitful, she could take a quick side trip down the coast. Much to Kate's frustration and bewilderment, no one there had remembered Ally, not even the manager of the apartment where they were supposed to have lived.

Lastly, Kate had called Maria Carlos and made arrangements to come by for a visit the following day. Kate had been very grateful that, for the sake of stability, Glory had been able to stay with Maria temporarily until the custody arrangements were straightened out. She also hoped that Maria would be able to tell her *something* about Ally and Glory. Ally certainly seemed to have lived a friendless existence here. Kate thought about the photo of the young woman from the shoe box and wished she had thought to bring the picture with her today. She must have been a friend of Ally's or surely Ally wouldn't have kept her picture. Maybe someone would have recognized her. Then again, with any luck, maybe Maria would know who she was.

With some reluctance, Kate paid her bill and headed out into the pleasant summer evening. Not feeling ready to return to her bare, silent motel room on the other side of the city, she decided to walk through Fisherman's Wharf and enjoy the sights and sounds of this legendary piece of San Francisco. People thronged the area, stopping to check out the open-air fish markets, buying loaves of fresh sourdough bread from local bakeries, and wandering in and out of the gift and souvenir shops.

Farther down the wharf, Kate mused, was the wax museum and an amusement park ride that traveled through the 1906 earthquake. Kate remembered it well from that visit she and David had made here years ago, before Ally was born. Actually, it was just before she became pregnant with Ally, and she had always thought Ally may have been conceived on that romantic holiday. A long time ago, Kate told herself, a different lifetime altogether. David was so handsome and charming and so very masculine, or so he seemed to Kate's young and, she had to admit, besotted mind. He could be a tender and gentle lover, but he had a tough and aggressive side, and he liked to be in charge. She remembered the edge of excitement his love of fast cars, high-risk sports and hunting had provided, at least at first.

David was the first person she'd known who owned a gun, and he often went to firing ranges to practice shooting. They were very different people, she understood that now, with really very different backgrounds. She, the sheltered young woman from a quiet suburban town, educated by the nuns in Catholic schools, on her own, more or less, for the first time while she attended college in the big city. David, on the other hand, was from a much more working-class family from one of the outlying Massachusetts cities, growing up in a slightly down-at-the-heels neighborhood that had once been one of the "little Canadas" populated by French Canadian immigrants. That had attracted her too, she reminded herself, that variation in culture and even language, as David had a passing familiarity with the Canadian French his grandparents had still spoken. Most of all, Kate had deeply admired his ability to be self-sufficient in so many ways all his young life.

Nevertheless, despite everything that separated them, they had been happy together, so why did it all have to change? Well, she reminded herself, I changed, for one thing, and certainly having a child had changed things. Kate remembered how David's interest in guns and hunting seemed much less fascinating and attractively masculine when Ally was a toddler and how much they argued over his decision to keep guns in the house. Then there were the financial problems after David had lost that lucrative job. Kate tried to shake off these thoughts, telling herself once again how useless it was to dwell on what went wrong.

A light breeze picked up, bringing with it the salty scent of sea air. Kate paused, looking out across the dark water to the lights on the bridge and the more distant lights of the cities across the bay as well as the darkened rock that was Alcatraz sitting midway. Nearby, fishing boats and pleasure boats rocked at anchor together in the marina. Seeing them, Kate felt suddenly homesick for Cape Cod, for its Bay and the Sound and her own home and the Sea Witch, even for one of her favorite iced mocha lattes. Time to go back, she told herself resolutely, then, impulsively, she decided to ride a cable car to Market Street.

Kate quickened her pace, retracing her steps back to where the great turntable waited at the bottom of the hill to bring the cable cars around for the return trip. Looking ahead, Kate could see a crowd of people gathering in the hopes of boarding the next car. She slipped in among them, groups of tourists laughing and talking, loaded down with purchases, others quiet, tired, but looking satisfied with their day in the city. Kate glanced up to her right and saw the car approaching, gliding down the hill on its underground cable, loaded with people out to explore the Wharf and environs on this exceptionally fine San Francisco evening. The crowd backed up, waiting their turn as the cable car, having deposited its passengers, entered the turntable and came around to face the city for the return trip.

Once they began boarding, Kate felt fortunate to get near the front of the crowd and secure a seat along the side of the car while latecomers clung to poles as they stood on the running boards. As the car was pulled forward heading back up the hill, Kate gazed back at Fisherman's Wharf dropping away below her. What had made Ally decide to come here? Kate wondered, raising her gaze to the black waters of the bay. After a few seconds' reflection she turned away, looking toward the lights of the city. "I suppose I'll never know," she whispered into the night, "and maybe it doesn't matter anyway."

CHAPTER 8

The following afternoon, Kate found herself once again on the sidewalk outside Ally's former home. Glory's too, Kate reminded herself as she made her way up the steps. Maria must have spotted her because she heard her light, accented voice call down to her as she reached for the buzzer. "Come on up, Mrs. LaRue." Kate climbed the stairs to where Maria waited, her youngest in her arms, and this time with Glory peering around her skirts.

"Look, sweetie," Maria whispered to Glory, reaching around with one hand to pull her forward. "Your grandmama is here."

But Glory stayed determinedly where she was and Kate just smiled and said, "Hi, honey." No use forcing her, she told herself. "I have something for you."

"Ooohhh," Maria smiled broadly, eyes widening in encouragement as she met the flicker of interest in Glory's gaze. "Come on, *niña*, let's see what it is."

Once in the apartment, Glory quickly climbed into the one big-cushioned chair, wrapping her arms around her legs. Kate rummaged in her purse for a few seconds and pulled out a small rectangular object wrapped in white tissue paper.

"Here you go. I hope you like this." As she offered the packet to Glory she felt a twinge of doubt. *I hope I'm doing the right thing,* she thought worriedly, *I don't want make her cry or feel angry or hurt.* After a few seconds, when Glory didn't take the proffered gift, Kate placed it on the arm of the chair and backed away a few steps. "It's right there, sweetie." Glory looked at it for a few seconds before unwrapping her arms from around her legs and, gently picking up the gift, opened it slowly and carefully. Maria watched over

Glory's shoulder and drew in her breath as she saw the small photograph of Ally and Glory seated on the bench with the amusement park rides in the background now encased in clear plastic. "Ahh," she sighed softly while Glory stared at the image for a few seconds before lightly touching Ally's face with her small fingers.

"Have you seen that picture before?" asked Kate, relief and pleasure over the apparent success of her gift filling her.

"No, but, Ally and Glory, they went to Santa Cruz, to the boardwalk, with Glory's school, just a few weeks ago. I remember, so nice for them, to do that. They must have taken the picture there." Leaning over Glory's shoulder, Maria said, "Look, *niña*, it's Mama and you at the beach." Glory glanced from Maria to Kate, then returned to her contemplation of the photo, curling herself into a ball on the chair.

Once Maria had settled her two children, the older one with a snack and a DVD, the younger with a bottle and playpen toys, she joined Kate at the well-worn table, coffee and cookies in hand. She smiled at Kate apologetically. "I don't know what I can tell you, Mrs. LaRue, I didn't know Ally all that good. I just helped with Glory some, sometimes Ally helped with my little ones, but..." She shrugged expressively.

"I understand, but I know so little, there must be *something* you can tell me." Although she already knew the answer, Kate decided to try something easy for an opener. "When did Ally come here?"

Maria thought a minute. "Seven, eight months ago, maybe."

"And she was living in the shelter before then?" Kate asked, thinking about what she had learned the day before.

Maria looked blank. "I guess."

"Did she say anything about where she was living before she came here?"

Maria shook her head. "She did talk about when she was a young girl some. One day she came over so I could show her how to cook some Mexican dishes; she liked Mexican food. I told her about my mama teaching me to cook, and she talked about, well, that she and you didn't get along so good and how she kind of just left home and hadn't seen you since."

Not feeling up to hearing what Ally had to say about that painful time, Kate hastily changed the subject. Thinking back to what Glory's teacher had told her, Kate asked, "Maria, did Ally seem afraid to you?"

"Afraid? Of what?"

"Well, do you think there was someone or something in her past maybe that was worrying or frightening her?"

Maria looked doubtful. "She never said anything about that. She was worried about Glory and why she was like she was. Why do you ask that?"

"Because of something Glory's teacher said. She thought maybe Ally had been abused by someone, maybe Glory's father. Even if she never talked about it, did she *act* frightened?"

Maria considered this. "I don't know. Maybe. She was kind of uneasy about people knowing too much about her. I think she didn't like having to give out her name, to tell anyone where she lived or Glory's name. She liked using those phones you can throw away, too. She wanted to help Glory, but she didn't like telling the doctors stuff. 'They ask too many personal questions,' she said. And she watched people, paid attention to who was on the street when Glory came home from school. I don't know if any of that means she was afraid, though, at least not of anyone special; maybe just real careful and private. She was that, you have to be." Maria gave a sweeping gesture of the street.

"Or maybe she thought someone might be looking for them? Like Glory's father?"

Maria shrugged. "Like I said, she never said anything at all about that. I don't think she got any money or anything from Glory's daddy, and he never came around. Or anyone else. Ally and Glory kept to themselves."

Kate was silent for a minute, sipping the strong sweet coffee and nibbling a sugar cookie.

"When Ally and you were together, what did you talk about? Besides me, that is," she added hastily.

Maria smiled. "Mostly about Glory and kids, you know, generally.

Ally took Glory to some special doctors, and she talked about that. And Glory's school and what they did there and what they told her."

"What did the doctors tell her?"

"Well, some of them thought she had autism." Maria glanced at Kate as if to check that she understood what that meant. Kate nodded slightly, and Maria continued, "and they did some tests, you know, in case she had something she got from Ally or the father," shaking her head no to Kate's inquiring look, "and they checked her hearing and that was fine."

"Does she have autism?"

Maria shrugged. "I guess no one's sure. I think some doctors thought she was just not talking because she was scared to. Mutism, they called it." After a pause, Maria added, "I don't think Ally liked any of their ideas about what was wrong, but it upset her most to think that Glory was too scared by something to talk. Because then, you know, it might be something she did."

"Did she say that she thought there might be something?"

"Noooo, but I think she did have something in mind. You know, Mrs. LaRue, Ally didn't have much, and she felt bad about that. I do think she had a real hard time, but that's more of a feeling I got. Maybe Glory had a hard time too."

"Maria, I found some other pictures in Ally's apartment besides the one I gave Glory. Would you look at them and see if they mean anything to you?"

Maria nodded, and Kate produced an envelope with the photographs from the shoe box in Ally's apartment. She handed her the two photographs of the lonely country road winding through the fields first. Maria studied them for a minute, and then shook her head. "Not around here, that's all I can tell you," she said.

"How about this one?" Kate offered the photo of the dark-haired young woman with the enigmatic Mona Lisa smile.

Maria considered this one with more interest. "She's pretty. Looks maybe Navajo. Who is she? A friend of Ally's?"

"I don't know who she is. Why do you think she looks Navajo?"

"She just does. I used to live in Arizona when I was a kid, knew a lot of Navajo kids." Maria gestured toward the first two pictures. "That place could be in Arizona, I suppose."

Kate bit her lip in frustration. She hadn't really expected Maria to know her, but she couldn't help feeling disappointed. Then, out of curiosity, Kate showed Maria the photo of Ally as a teenager. "This is how Ally looked about the time she left home."

Maria smiled broadly at the sight of Ally with her dark hair streaked with red, her jewelry and tight clothes, and the defiant look on her face.

"You know, Mrs. LaRue," she said gently, "I think Ally wanted to come home. She needed you. But maybe she was afraid. Yes, I think maybe she was afraid she couldn't go home after all that time."

Kate swallowed hard, trying to keep back the tears that had filled her eyes. "I'm sorry if she felt that way," she whispered, struggling to keep her voice under control. "I didn't know where she was or..."

"I know, it's okay; please don't cry." Maria patted her arm anxiously. "Just remember, Ally would be glad to know Glory has her grandmama to take care of her now that she can't."

With that, both Kate and Maria looked over at the big chair where Glory had snuggled herself into the cushions. She was sound asleep, her head on the arm of the chair, the photograph of herself in her mother's arms clutched to her small chest as if she would never let it go.

Kate smiled at the sight of her sleeping granddaughter. "Maria, who were these doctors Ally took Glory to see? I think I need to talk to them next."

CHAPTER 9

Dr. Tenley's office was elegant and well-appointed with a wide, polished mahogany desk, deep dark blue carpets, and two large, upholstered wing chairs. Comfortably ensconced in one of these, Kate closed her eyes briefly, mentally rehearsing what she wanted to say. Dr. Tenley was the last of the doctors on the list Maria provided and whose names Kate had discovered in the shoe box. Kate's time was limited and most of the specialists Ally had consulted were not willing or able to meet with her on such short notice. As it was, Dr. Tenley, a developmental pediatrician, or so Kate had learned, had only promised a brief consultation at the end of the day. Kate had gratefully accepted this and had ridden the Muni, as San Francisco's above ground public transportation system was known, across the city to the University of California medical complex to make this hastily scheduled appointment. Now she sat in this richly furnished, air-conditioned office looking out over the city and Golden Gate Park trying to relax and compose herself. One appointment and she wanted to make the best of it; not only to understand Glory's past but also to help her try to make the best of her future.

As Kate was once again mulling over her many questions about Glory and Ally, the door suddenly opened and a man of decidedly middle age with close-cut light brown hair and a pleasant expression came in and walked over to Kate, hand outstretched. "Mrs. LaRue?" then "No, don't get up" as Kate started to rise from her chair. "I'm Dr. Tenley." Kate and Dr. Tenley shook hands briefly, and then Dr. Tenley turned and walked briskly to his desk. He picked up a file and quickly perused it. "I'm sorry to hear about your daughter's death, Mrs. LaRue, and I can understand you must have a lot of questions, but I have to admit, I only met Glory once."

Kate nodded wearily. "Yes, Ally and Glory were only here in San Francisco briefly. No one knew them well. Whatever you can tell me will be of help." Kate tried to keep the frustration out of her voice but didn't succeed. Dr. Tenley looked up from the file he held in his hands and gazed intently at Kate. Kate lifted her head, meeting his gaze with a determined one of her own. After a moment, he put aside the file and said, "What, exactly, do you think I can help you with?"

"Well, I'd like to know what diagnosis you gave Glory and why."

Dr. Tenley nodded. "All right. Actually, I do remember her, so perhaps we should begin with why your daughter brought her to see me to begin with." Dr. Tenley seemed to consider how to continue. "As you probably know at this point, as a developmental pediatrician, I evaluate and treat children with a broad range of developmental disorders, including the autism spectrum disorders, attention deficit, learning disabilities, and so forth." He glanced at Kate to see if she was following this and, satisfied that she was, went on. "Often there is referral from a child's regular pediatrician, but Ms. LaRue brought Glory in herself. Her concerns were primarily around Glory's lack of language. Or, rather, language regression, because Ms. LaRue said Glory had been talking but had stopped about the time they came to San Francisco. Now, you must understand that as part of any evaluation, in order to make an accurate diagnosis and appropriate recommendations, a thorough history of the child and the family needs to be taken."

"And Ally refused to provide that."

Dr. Tenley again fixed his intent gaze on Kate. "She was certainly reluctant." He shrugged slightly and went on. "Ms. LaRue insisted she had no idea as to the identity of Glory's father and therefore no information to provide. Her own family history was presented as very benign as far as any history of speech, language, learning problems or other developmental disabilities was concerned." He again looked at Kate who made an affirming gesture. "As a single parent, she reported herself as having been solely responsible for Glory's care and had seen her as developing normally until coming here. I questioned her about this, and she was evasive and uncomfortable, unable to tell me, for example, when most developmental milestones had been reached and seeming to guess at what would be appropriate times for others."

Dr. Tenley paused again, and Kate took advantage of this to ask a question. "Did you think she wasn't telling you the truth?"

"Well, it occurred to me that perhaps Glory had a longer history of problems than her mother was willing to admit. Why that might have been the case, I don't know, and any effort to pursue the subject with Ms. LaRue at the time was unproductive, to say the least. I examined Glory as well, of course, and found her extremely withdrawn and unresponsive to my efforts to engage her. No eye contact, and certainly no language spoken in my presence."

"Were you thinking of autism then?"

"I considered it. However, Glory did not present with any of the atypical behaviors you generally see with children with autism spectrum disorders, and there was a quality to her behavior that suggested fear, a response to some type of trauma. So I decided to give it a rule out." Seeing Kate's confused look, he added, "I decided I needed more information before I could rule an autism spectrum disorder in or out as a diagnosis."

"I see. So what diagnosis did you give her?"

"Well, one possibility that I considered was some variation of mutism; that is, a refusal to talk. The usual diagnosis is selective mutism, which means that the child does speak in certain settings, usually the home, but not in others. Clearly, this situation was different and could not be so easily defined. The only potential explanation that occurred to me at that point was that Glory had experienced some type of trauma. However, when I questioned your daughter about the possibility of some traumatic event that may have led to Glory becoming mute, she insisted quite vehemently that nothing of the sort occurred and that there must be another explanation."

"Did you believe her?" Kate could sense the tension in her

own voice as could Dr. Tenley because he gave her another quick, searching look.

"As I said, I thought that there was more to this than Ms. LaRue was willing to admit. Glory appeared to be in reasonably good physical health, although small for her age and a little underweight. There was nothing to indicate any ongoing abuse or neglect. I suggested some additional evaluations, including a psychological assessment, but I don't know whether she followed up on them."

"Ally did take Glory to see some other doctors, including a neurologist and an audiologist to get her hearing tested. She even took her to see a geneticist but, from what I understand, he found nothing wrong with her."

Dr. Tenley looked at Kate curiously. "I'm not really surprised. Mrs. LaRue, if you are going to take Glory, I would suggest a psychological assessment with recommendations for intervention and therapy when you return home. I can provide you with some referrals in your area if you will just check with the desk on your way out."

Dr. Tenley came around his desk and offered his hand again. "It was nice to meet you, Mrs. LaRue. I wish you luck with your granddaughter."

Kate reluctantly stood up, shook his hand as she murmured her thanks, and let him guide her out the door. A few minutes later, Kate found herself standing on the sidewalk, suggested referrals in hand, thinking that, for all her efforts, once again, she had come away knowing little more than she started out with.

CHAPTER 10

Kate was alone amidst a swirl of rushing people coming and going through the sliding doors that led into each airline's departure lounge at San Francisco International Airport. It was hard to believe that this day had finally come, the day when she could finally go home to Yarmouth. She had so longed to be in her own home, driving her own car, sleeping in her own bed. She had longed to walk through the Sea Witch, seeing and touching all the lovely crafts and pieces of art crowding the aisles of her beloved store. Now the time had come and, in a few hours, she would be home. She had done all she could here in dealing with the aftermath of Ally's death and trying to untangle the mystery of the last years of her life, Kate thought. She wouldn't be leaving it behind, though; it was coming with her, most definitively in the person of the little girl she could see approaching now, tightly held in Maria Carlos's arms and accompanied by a social worker from California's Child Protection Services. Kate sighed, feeling a wave of apprehension sweep over her even as she regarded that solemn little face with tenderness and affection. She noted with some relief that Glory was looking around with some interest and curiosity. At least she was not hiding her face in fear as had so often been the case lately. At least not yet. Kate had no idea how Glory was going to handle getting on an airplane with her grandma and leaving Maria and everything familiar behind.

As she watched the trio approach, Kate considered how Glory's recent acceptance of her grandma had come about. In the days following her gift of the photograph of Glory and Ally on the boardwalk in Santa Cruz, the little girl had refused to be separated from the picture, holding on to it asleep or awake, at school or at home, so much so that it was interfering with her school activities and therapies, among other things. Phone calls had been exchanged about how best to deal with the problem until Kate came up with a solution. She found a silver framed picture locket with an engraved cover that Glory could wear around her neck on a matching silver chain, and, as she told Glory, therefore keep her mama close to her heart and see her whenever she liked. Thankfully, this seemed to satisfy the child and allowed her to participate again in school and other activities of daily life a little more. It had been gratifying to everyone, Kate especially, to see her come out of her shell a bit after this. Kate had yet to hear her speak, however, and this worried her. And what was she going to do if moving across the country caused Glory to regress even further?

As the little group reached her, Kate offered her granddaughter a welcoming smile and held out her arms. Glory allowed herself to be passed from Maria's arms to Kate's, her small hands tightly clutching the locket that hung around her neck, as the adults exchanged greetings and moved on through the doors and into the airport. Kate felt her heart quicken as they approached the security checkpoint. Sensing Kate's apprehension, the social worker—what was her name again? Kate wondered—smiled and said reassuringly, "I'm sure everything will be just fine. You have, I think, all the necessary referrals to assist you, Mrs. LaRue, and, more than that, I know Glory will be in loving and capable hands."

Kate smiled weakly and murmured, "Thanks" while Maria hugged and kissed Glory good-bye. "Bye-bye, little one. Be good for Grandmama and come see Maria again sometime." Glory's dark eyes widened and a familiar look of fear flickered there. Kate struggled to quell her own anxiety. They had tried to prepare Glory for this, but who knew what she understood? Kate hated to take another person out her life, someone who had become a second mother to her in the months since she and Ally had arrived in San Francisco, but what else could she do?

"Thanks so much for all you've done for Glory and for Ally,

Maria. I can't begin to tell you what this has meant to me and to my daughter and granddaughter."

Maria shook her head. "No, no. I'm just glad everything worked out in the end. You will be good for Glory, and Glory will be good for you."

The Child Protection Services social worker looked at her watch. "You should get going, Mrs. LaRue."

"Yes, of course," Kate replied hastily and, turning to Maria, said, "Thank you again for everything." With that she took a deep breath and headed toward the security gates, Glory's face buried against her shoulder.

CHAPTER 11

Eight exhausting hours later, Kate climbed the steps to her small house with its weather-beaten gray shingles, white shutters, and simple white door, a sleeping child in her arms. The sight of home with its welcoming soft light from the lantern-styled outside lamps gently illuminating the gathering dusk comforted Kate, bringing a sense of resolution to what had been a lengthy and painful experience. It seemed like a lifetime ago that she had hurriedly descended these steps, suitcase in hand, on her way to San Francisco and to Ally.

With some difficulty, Kate managed to unlock her front door, Glory balanced on one hip. Once inside, she made her way to her bedroom and placed Glory down on the small trundle bed that had once been part of Ally's bedroom set and was now placed next to her own bed. "God bless Jerry," she intoned softly. After numerous conversations back and forth by cell phone, this man, who had been her business partner and, when she came to think of it, her only close friend for so many years, had offered to come to her house and get things ready for her return with her granddaughter. All that along with running the store single-handedly while she was gone. How would she ever find a way to repay him for all he had done for her and for the Sea Witch during all this, she wondered. Well, the Sea Witch was his too, Kate reminded herself, but as for the rest of it...

Kate looked down at her little granddaughter, still wearing the jeans and tee shirt Maria had dressed her in that morning, and contemplated how she was going to get her undressed and settled for the night. She must be hungry, Kate thought, thinking back to the long flight and how Glory had refused any food, even some favorite snacks specially prepared by Maria. Glory had been quiet but wide awake and clearly frightened, not wanting to be held or touched, so much so that Kate had worried that someone might think she absconded with the child. It wasn't until long after they had landed at Logan, headed down the expressway and crossed over the Cape Cod Canal that Glory had finally relaxed into sleep, clearly exhausted. "Perhaps it's better to just let her sleep as she is," Kate said to herself as she covered Glory with a light blanket and adjusted a night-light she had purchased before leaving San Francisco so that it would provide a soft light should Glory wake.

Once that was done, Kate wandered out to the kitchen and made herself a cold supper of sliced ham and potato salad from the supplies Jerry (*bless him again*, Kate thought) had provided, and then brought it out onto the small screened porch on the east side of the house just off the living room. From here, on a summer evening like this one, you could look out over the small side yard to the white rail fence covered in Cape roses and bordered with blue hydrangeas and watch couples and families out for a walk or returning from a day at the beach, sticky with saltwater and sand. It was one of the little pleasures of life in Kate's Yarmouth neighborhood, and she had missed it these last few weeks.

Settling herself with her food, Kate considered what lay ahead of her. One of the first things she needed to do tonight, she told herself, before anything else, was to call David and tell him what had happened. It was a call she was dreading, all the more because she had put it off far too long, and now it was certain to be a very painful and angry conversation. A breeze came up and as the warm air washed over her, scented with the sea, Kate felt herself relax despite her worries and concerns, happy just to be home.

By the time Kate had eaten her last bite of potato salad and swallowed the last of the sweet iced tea, night had descended, wrapping the little porch in a cloak of darkness punctuated by streetlamps and the occasional lighted windows of neighboring houses. Nevertheless, she could still hear the soft rustle of the nearby pine trees as well as occasional footsteps and muted laughter from the street. Kate would have loved to sit in one her cushioned wicker rocking chairs, her feet up, with another glass of iced tea or even some wine or a cold beer and just immerse herself in the lovely night. *Not this time,* she thought. *I've put this off long enough.* She walked back through the living room turning on some lights as she went. She paused for a quick peek into her bedroom before depositing her dishes in the kitchen and was relieved to see Glory still sleeping, curled under the blanket, her soft breaths audible in the silence.

Phone in hand, Kate punched in the numbers, mulling over the fact that she still remembered David's phone number after all this time. As she listened to the distant ringing, she couldn't help but hope he wouldn't be home and she could put the inevitable off once more. Just as Kate was thinking that might really be true, a tired, impatient male voice abruptly said, "Hello?" in her ear.

Kate took a deep breath. "Hi, David, it's Kate."

"Kate. Well, I haven't heard that name in a while."

"No, you're right, it's been long time. How are you, David?"

"I'm okay."

"And Jill and the children?"

"They're fine. Although the children aren't really children anymore."

"That must be true. How old are they now anyway?"

"What's this about, Kate? I can't believe you bothered to call me after all this time just to get an update on how we all are."

Kate paused, measuring the irritation in his voice. This wasn't going to be pleasant. "Yes, I do have a reason for calling. There's no easy way to tell you this, so here it is." Kate took another deep breath and plunged in, the words tumbling out of her mouth almost as fast as she could think them. "Our daughter Ally is dead. She died three weeks ago in San Francisco, of peritonitis and sepsis following a ruptured appendix. I brought her ashes home, David, and I think we should plan a memorial service. I've already looked into burial arrangements, and I have a funeral home. They have her ashes now." Kate paused again, uneasy about the silence on the other end of the line.

After a long pause in which Kate could almost hear her heart thumping in her chest, David sighed slowly and heavily. "Ally died three weeks ago and you brought her ashes home, found a funeral home, and made burial arrangements. You've been busy, Kate. I'm impressed it took you only three weeks to let me know." Kate could hear the tightness in his voice under the anger, as if he was holding back tears.

"I'm sorry, David, I know I should have called you sooner. It was wrong not to, but I'm calling you now, and I need your help and support. There's something else. Ally had a child, David, a little girl. Her name is Glory, and she's four years old. She has a lot of problems."

A sharp intake of breath, then, "Yeah? Where is she?"

"Glory's here with me, David. She's our granddaughter, and she has no one else."

"Where's the father?"

"Ally didn't know or wouldn't tell anyone. Some people I talked to thought he might have been abusive and that Ally was trying to get away from him."

There was another pause before David replied, his voice rough. "Well, this is just great, Kate. I knew when I heard your voice it couldn't be anything good. My daughter's dead, and you brought home her kid, and now you want my help. Let's see, what could that mean? I'm done with child support, done a long time ago. I have other kids that I'm going to have to try to put through college."

"Yes, well, I thought you might want to be a part of her life; after all, she's your *grandchild*."

"Goddamit, Kate, don't start this shit."

"Look, I know it's a shock, all of it, but—"

David cut her off. "I can't help you. I wasn't even consulted on this, so you're on your own. Let me tell you something *you* don't know. I heard from our darling daughter, I don't know, a year ago maybe, maybe not quite that. She called out of the blue, wanting me to send her money, no questions asked. Or answered. I wasn't about to just hand over a lot of money to her without knowing *something*."

"Oh my God, David. Ally *called* you?" Kate felt her voice rise with shock and anger.

"I just said that, didn't I?"

"Why didn't you tell me?"

"Probably the same reason you didn't tell me she was dead," he answered, bitterness underlining every word. "Although, unlike with you, there was nothing to tell, anyway. She never said anything about a kid, that's for sure."

"At least you knew she was alive!"

"Yeah, at least I knew she was alive." David's voice was thick with emotion, whether pain or anger, Kate couldn't be sure. "Do whatever you want, Kate, just like you always have. Memorial service, cremation, burial. Raise a four-year-old with a lot of problems. You did so well raising her mother, after all."

"That was uncalled for," Kate said coldly, but David probably didn't hear her before slamming down the phone.

Kate slammed the phone down herself. "Damn you!" she screamed, tears making her voice tremble. In the darkness behind her she heard a small shuffling sound and turned in alarm, only to see Glory's small form huddled against the wall.

"Oh, sweetie, I'm so sorry. Did I wake you? You must have been scared. I'm sorry I yelled." Kate gently wrapped her arms around the little girl and picked her up, carrying her, unresisting, to the big wooden rocking chair in the living room, a relic of Ally's infancy. "It's okay, it's okay," she murmured into Glory's soft hair, the slow rocking of the chair soothing them both. *That didn't go well*, Kate thought, as she leaned back against the chair's headrest, closing her eyes. *I really should have called him sooner, not left him out of the picture that way. That was my fault and I can understand he's angry. I would be too, but he knew she was alive. He knew, and he never told me.*

The soft light of a summer morning had already filled the room when Kate finally opened her eyes, feeling sweet relief at the sight of the familiar walls and furniture rather than the institutional feel of her motel room. She stretched, looking over at Glory still asleep on the old trundle bed. It had been a long night after the call with David, as Glory was unwilling to relax and go back to sleep for more than three hours. Kate herself spent a long time lying on her bed, unable to sleep, watching the changing patterns of reflected light from the street on her wall. Wondering if indeed she had made a mistake taking on a four-year-old with a lot of problems. Wondering how she was going to do it alone.

But now Kate threw back the brightly colored handmade quilt and swung her feet to the floor, wiggling her toes against the soft rag rug covering the polished hardwood floor. There was something to be said for the old adage that things will look better in the morning, for just the sight of her own bedroom on this lovely morning made Kate feel better and ready to take on whatever life had to offer. She left Glory sleeping and walked out to the kitchen, pulling on a robe as she went. She yawned as she took the coffee filters out of the cabinet, wondering what to make for breakfast. It worried Kate that Glory had barely eaten since leaving California, but she had no idea what might tempt the child. *She must be hungry,* Kate thought. *I could make scrambled eggs or maybe some pancakes.* She looked at a box of Cheerios sitting on the counter. *Of course, maybe she'd rather just have cereal.* Cheerios were always a big favorite with Ally when she was little, and Kate recalled seeing a box in Ally's apartment. *Well, Cheerios it is, then, at least for the first offering,* thought Kate.

Once that decision was made and with a cup of freshly brewed coffee in her hands, Kate walked back out onto the sunlit side porch. She settled herself on a wicker love seat with brightly flowered cushions, her feet up on a small wicker coffee table. Kate was very fond of this set which included the two matching rocking chairs, something she had acquired some years ago at a yard sale along Route 6A. She breathed deeply, inhaling pleasantly cool morning air that carried hints of later, much warmer temperatures, overlaid with the aroma of coffee.

It was fairly quiet, the street empty, the neighboring houses not yet obviously astir. *A little early for the beachgoers*, thought Kate. Most people are probably just getting up, getting breakfast, getting dressed. She considered the possibility of a brief beach visit herself, wondering what experience, if any, Glory had with the ocean. Kate had always loved the ocean herself, and when Ally was small, it had been a favorite destination for her as well on hot summer days. Looking out over the sun-dappled yard, the pine trees stirring slightly in the morning breeze, Kate wondered how the Sound looked this morning, how big the waves breaking on the beach were. It was so tantalizingly close, only a short walk away, that Kate could almost convince herself she could hear them. *Well*, she told herself, *we can certainly head down to have a look but whatever else we do today, the first order of business must be a trip to the Sea Witch. Jerry is more than competent*, she reminded herself yet again, *but no matter how much he insists business has picked up, I need to see it for myself. Besides, much like being home, it will make me feel like things are normal again, even when they aren't.* As if on cue, Kate heard the soft shuffle of feet in the living room and a small frightened sob.

"I'm out here, Glory," Kate called, setting down her coffee and heading back into the house. Glory stood in the center of the room, her long, dark hair tousled, eyes still bleary with sleep, clad in pink pajamas, and clutching both a stuffed pink cat and the picture locket. Kate smiled at her granddaughter, thinking again how much she looked like Ally when she was small.

"Good morning, honey. How's my girl today?" Kate held out her hand and Glory took it, allowing herself to be led into the kitchen. "You must be soooo hungry. Will you eat some Cheerios for Grandma?"

Kate saw some interest in Glory's dark eyes at this last question. She guided her to the round oak table and helped her climb onto one of the wide straight back chairs, then pulled back the matching oak louvers that covered the lower half of the window overlooking the street. Kate glanced out briefly at the quiet street with its row of summer cottages, peaceful under the morning sun. Turning back to the kitchen, she quickly busied herself with bowls and cereal and milk. Much to Kate's relief, Glory dove in like she hadn't eaten in days. "Well," Kate said, smiling at her hungry granddaughter, "we'll have to make sure to get plenty of *that* next time we go to the supermarket."

After the second bowl was drained of milk and cereal, Kate coaxed Glory back down the hall to dress. She led her past her own room and into the corner bedroom where the suitcase Kate had purchased for Glory's clothes stood waiting. It was no longer the teenager's bedroom it had once been; gone was the dark, moody atmosphere and the posters of punk and heavy metal rock bands that had been the decorating preferences of the teenage Ally. Some months after Ally left, Kate had packed all that away, unable to bear looking at it. Now the room was bright and airy but impersonal, Ally's old twin bed covered with a patchwork quilt she had used as a younger child, new flowered curtains at the windows.

"This was your mama's room, Glory," Kate said to the child at her side as they stood together in the doorway. "Now it belongs to you." Glory took a few steps forward, eyes wide and taking in the bed, the wood floor with its colorful rag rugs, and the light blue walls with their paintings of Cape beach scenes. Encouraged, Kate walked in and, going over to a box behind the suitcase, opened it and dragged it over to Glory. "Look, here are all your toys and books. We'll put your clothes in the closet and the dresser. Later, we can buy you some new things, new clothes and toys, maybe some furniture, make this room special, just for you."

Glory gazed at Kate for a moment, then sat down on the floor next to the box and pulled out some of the contents until she came to a book with puppies gamboling on the cover. She looked at it briefly, then brought it over to her grandmother. Kate smiled slightly, nodding her head. "Okay," she said ruefully, "but just this *one*." With that, Kate seated herself in the comfortable wing chair in the far corner she had once used for storytelling with Ally, pulled Glory onto her lap, opened the book, and began to read.

CHAPTER 12

The Sea Witch looked as it always did to Kate, its welcoming charm a balm for her stressed mind and heart, the familiar windsocks and whirligigs, already out on display, bright and cheery in the morning sun. Jerry Stafford looked up from the cash register sitting on one of the glass-topped counters as Kate and Glory came through the door, chimes ringing pleasantly. Kate smiled at her best friend and business partner, a slender man of average height, fair skinned with neatly cropped blond hair and sea-green eyes, who looked younger than his forty-five years would indicate. Jerry returned the smile warmly, the lines in his windburned face deepening; he had the look of a man who spent more time in the sun than he probably should have. Kate made her way past the in-store displays leading Glory by one hand, the other holding an iced latte, as she took mental notes of any changes, stock sold or rearranged, since she had left for California. She whistled softly to Captain Ahab, the store's bright green and gold parrot, who was sitting on a perch in his floor-to-ceiling cage. Ahab whistled back, ruffling his feathers.

"Hey, good to see you. And you must be Glory." Jerry had come out from behind the counter and was leaning down, hands on his neatly pressed pants, to look at the little girl who leaned into Kate, dark eyes fixed on the hardwood floor. "Hi, there, Glory. I'm Jerry; it's nice to meet you." Glory continued to avoid his gaze and shrank closer to Kate.

Jerry turned to Kate, eyes full of concern and sympathy. "How's it going, Kate? Doing okay?"

"As well as can be expected, I guess. Talked to David last night. It didn't go well."

Jerry grimaced. "I can imagine." With a nod to the summer sales help, he gestured toward the back of the store. "Come on back and I'll get you caught up on business. And you can tell me about David if you want to."

This brought a smile from Kate. "You've been great, Jerry. I can't begin to thank you for all you've done these last weeks."

"Well, I needed to keep you going so you'd come home and get back to work."

Once in the tiny, crowded office, Kate pulled a couple of battered Golden Books out of the large cloth bag she had been carrying over her shoulder and sat down at her desk with Glory on her lap. Fingering the child's soft dark hair with one hand while she savoring sips of her coffee with the other, Kate listened as Jerry went over the books and recounted an encouraging tale of acquiring the works of a talented local artist they had been courting for months.

"Okay, so I guess you haven't been lying to me all this time about everything going well just to get me back to work. Maybe I should go away more often."

Jerry laughed. "No, I don't think so. Business just really picked up these last few weeks—it had nothing to do with you."

Kate nodded and looked down at Glory, who was no longer looking at the books and was scribbling with some magic markers on a pad of paper taken from the bag, concentration evident in every line of her body.

"She's a real cutie." Jerry said, following Kate's gaze. "She has Ally's eyes and hair."

Kate smiled wistfully. "She does, doesn't she?" The smile faded. "David was really angry when I talked to him last night."

"You weren't surprised by that, were you?"

"No. I know I should have called him when this all started. What did surprise me was that he said he had received a phone call from Ally about a year ago; I'm guessing it was probably around the time she moved to San Francisco. She needed money, and he refused to send her any without an explanation. I just wish I'd known. Or that she had called me instead."

"What would you have done if you'd known? Or if she'd called you?"

"I don't know. But it would have been nice to know she was alive. And I'd like to think that if she'd called me, I'd have helped her, not just cut her off."

Jerry shook his head. "Kate, you know you'd have never sent her anything without some accounting for where she'd been and what was going on."

"Well, maybe. But I keep thinking about how pretty much everyone who knew Ally in San Francisco thought she was afraid of something, that maybe she'd been abused in some way. She was trying to get away, to escape, and she was looking for help."

"Did she tell David any of this?"

"He said not."

"Then she wouldn't have told you either, that would be my guess."

"Okay, okay, I suppose you're right. But I want desperately to know what happened to Ally. I want to know what she was so afraid of, where she was all this time, what she was doing. I want to know who Glory's father is."

Jerry looked at her as if considering what to say next. "Are you sure about that, Kate? Given everything you've told me so far, I don't know, maybe I'm wrong, but I think there could be some things you're better off not knowing."

Kate stared at him for a minute, uncertain how to reply, her hand still on Glory's hair while Glory scribbled furiously, seemingly oblivious.

Jerry shrugged and cleared his throat. "How much do you think she understands?" he asked, nodding in Glory's direction.

Kate looked down at her, tears welling in her eyes. "I don't know, really. She seems to understand more than she's willing—or able—to express. Last night when I was talking to David she was asleep, or at least I thought she was, and then all of a sudden she was there, trembling and sobbing. I'd been yelling, and I probably woke her up. It was just like it was with Ally all those years ago when David and I would fight, and she would wake up frightened and crying. And David...he said I'd screw it up with Glory just like I had with Ally."

Jerry groaned, throwing up his hands. "How many times have we been through this? You didn't screw up with Ally, Kate."

"There are just so many things I should have done differently. I know, I know." Kate waved Jerry off, seeing the familiar words hovering on his lips. "But I feel like I need to redeem myself somehow, that I owe Ally something. I need to take care of Glory, and I need to somehow bring, well, closure to Ally's life."

Kate laughed a little as Jerry rolled his eyes at her use of the word *closure*, a word they both hated.

"Fine. Just be careful and think this through. You may be sorry if you dig something—or someone—up you don't want. And you may very well find nothing at all and waste a lot of time and energy better focused elsewhere." Jerry gave another shrug. "But I know you, and you'll do what you want regardless of what anyone else thinks."

"That's what David said."

"Oops. Sorry about that." Jerry spread his hands and looked at her appealingly.

Kate smiled a little, shaking her head. "It's all right. I guess it's true. Time to get back to work, anyway. Until I get Glory into school, I'm going to be somewhat limited in what I can do, Jerry." Kate's eyes strayed back to the computer screen.

Jerry turned before heading out the office door. "Yeah, I know. I do have a suggestion for you, though."

Kate looked up at him. "What's that?"

"If you're looking for some child care help, Kevin's niece Jen may be available for a few hours a week, maybe more. She has some background in working with special needs kids, and she's only working part time this summer. Lives in Falmouth with her mom."

"Okay, I'll think about it. Thanks, Jerry."

Driving back across the arm of the Cape with Glory happily entertained with a CD of children's songs in the backseat, Kate reflected on her visit to the Sea Witch. For all her fears that her precious store would be in trouble without her constant presence, it was clear that business was quite brisk at the moment. Kate had stayed long enough to peruse the books on her own, overlook the stock for herself, and greet and talk to a few customers as well as to one of her suppliers who had come by to discuss a sale. Glory had been her usual quiet if clingy self, and Kate considered the possibility of being able to bring her to work with her, at least part time. Maybe she could create a little play area for her in the back of the office. *The store may not be in trouble,* Kate thought, *but I need to be there, if only for my own mental health. Besides, Jerry shouldn't have to do everything. Of course, what with school and maybe some babysitting...well, it will work out somehow.*

With this thought, Kate pushed the Sea Witch from her mind, realizing she was nearly home and remembering her morning resolution to make a visit to the beach. Glancing back at Glory, Kate announced cheerfully, "Let's go check out the beach." This brought a look of interest and curiosity from the little girl, making Kate wonder if the child was familiar with the ocean. Ally had loved the beach, after all, so maybe she had taken Glory to beaches along the Pacific. San Francisco had a beach and, of course, they had visited Santa Cruz.

Kate pulled into her driveway and unbuckled Glory from her car seat and set her on the ground. Surveying the child's cotton shorts and tee shirt, it occurred to Kate that Glory did not yet have a swimsuit. "We'll have to take care of *that* problem," Kate murmured to herself.

"Ready? Come on, this way." Kate took Glory's hand, and they headed off down the street, smiling at a stream of wet, sandy beachgoers, seemingly on their way back home for an early lunch and a break from the hot, late-morning sun. Kate waved and paused to chat briefly with a few neighbors who were relaxing on their porches or doing a little yard work, smiling at a suddenly frightened Glory and offering sympathetic looks and shaking their heads over the sad story of Ally's last days.

Eventually, though, they reached the narrow road that led to the beach and soon stood at its edge, looking out over the expanse of sand and saltwater. The creamy white sand was dotted here and there with shells and piles of coiled seaweed, dried to black in the sun, as well as brightly colored beach towels and umbrellas. The Nantucket Sound, sparkling blue and green in the sunlight, rolled in on soft waves that broke over wet sand turned brown from the lapping water, and then retreated just as quickly. Kate inhaled the salt-laden air, her favorite scent. She pulled Glory close as she removed the little girl's socks and shoes as well as her own sandals, feeling the warm breeze caress her bare legs under her light summer dress. With Glory's hand in hers, they began picking their way gingerly over the sand.

"Oooh! Hot, isn't it?" Kate smiled down at her granddaughter, the pleasure of the moment lighting her face, but, as she did so, Glory broke her grip on her hand and began to run across the scorching sand toward the inviting seawater. "Wait! Glory, no, come back!" Kate struggled across the sand in pursuit, feeling as if it was dragging her back while Glory seemed to skim across it like a bird. At the water's edge, she stopped, squealing with delight as a wave broke over her feet and ankles. Kate pulled up short at the sound, as she realized how seldom she'd heard any vocal indication of pleasure from the child. Kate reached for her, an admonishing "Glory" on her lips, but the child wriggled away and down the beach toward the jetty.

"Oh, God, stop," wailed Kate. It was far easier to catch up with her on the flat, wet sand along the breakers, however, and Kate managed to lift her into her arms only a few feet from the rocks. "Don't do that again. You could get hurt. Listen to Grandma when I tell you no!" Kate felt her own heart pounding and her breath coming far more quickly than she would have liked.

After a few seconds, Glory stopped struggling, and Kate set her down, hand held firmly in hers. She gazed at the sharp rocks extending out into the Sound, and the image of Ally at the end of the jetty in her oft-repeated dream appeared before her. A chill ran through her body despite the hot midday sun and the perspiration that covered her after her unexpected run through the sand. She gave Glory's small hand a tug, pulling her away from the rocks. "Come on, sweetie. Let's see if we can find some pretty seashells, and then we'll go home and have lunch."

With Glory tucked into bed and finally drifting off into sleep, Kate curled up in her favorite rocking chair, soothing music wafting out from her living room CD player, a second glass of cool white wine beside her on a small tiled end table. *It's going to take a lot to get myself to relax and get to sleep tonight*, she thought. She kept seeing Glory racing toward the jetty, every line of her body reminiscent of her mother's at that age, running defiantly into certain danger, so much so that Kate felt as though reality and her dream were intermingled. She hated that dream, the helplessness she felt, the despair when Ally disappeared off the end of the jetty, and Kate was certain that if she let herself go to sleep, the dream's return was inevitable. *On the other hand*, thought Kate grimly, *I can't stay awake all night. It's just a dream, anyway, the result of too much stress and worry. It will get better once I get my life—and Glory's—settled again.*

With a sigh, Kate leaned back against the chair's headrest and closed her eyes. Breathing deeply, she focused on the flow and rhythm of the music and letting some of the tension seep from her body. Several years ago, Kate remembered, when she was still struggling to deal with the reality of Ally's disappearance and the realization that she might never come back was sinking in, she had gone on a retreat to a meditation center up in the mountains in Vermont. The views had been breathtaking, the air clean and bracing, and the social environment warm and supportive. But most of all, the break from the terrible stress of her life at that point had been absolutely critical. Of course, in the end, she had to come home to her empty house and the Sea Witch, but she had learned a few things while she was there that helped her get through the worst of it.

Kate continued to breathe deeply, focusing on the word "peace" and visualizing the valley filled with wildflowers in full bloom she had visited while in Vermont's Green Mountains. She felt her body respond to this calming imagery, her muscles relaxing, and her heartbeat falling into a slower rhythm. Nevertheless, after a few moments, her mind began to wander, images and thoughts of her home, the Sea Witch, and the Cape passing through her awareness. Kate let these go, careful not to hold on to any of them, until an image of Ally appeared, slender, pale, with close-cropped hair and dark shadows under her eyes. She seemed so sad that Kate wanted nothing more than to hold her and tell her everything would be okay, much as she had when she was little and had hurt herself or thought some child at school didn't like her. But as Kate tried to reach out to her, Ally's eyes suddenly focused on hers with a desperate intensity that made Kate draw back, and, in an instant, the image was gone and Kate found herself looking at the walls of her living room as tears filled her eyes.

CHAPTER 13

The last wisps of fog were still clinging to the trees as Kate's car rolled to a stop on the gravel road that stretched out between the rows of gravestones, many of them decades, even centuries, old. The sunlight was just beginning to break through what had been ominous clouds only an hour or so ago, glinting softly off the wet grass and the newer grave markers in this part of the little cemetery. A half dozen other cars had accompanied the hearse, lining up along the grassy edge. As they all exited their cars and climbed the little knoll to the grave site, Kate couldn't help taking some mental notes on who was there: David, first of all, surprisingly alone and looking considerably older since Kate had last seen him, Jerry and his longtime partner, now husband, Kevin O'Malley, a tall, athletic man whose red hair and freckles gave him the look of a mischievous little boy, Kate's longtime next-door neighbor Fran Jackson, who Ally had never liked because she was always scolding her for being too loud, getting her toys in her yard and being rude. To Kate's surprise, there were a couple of other neighbors that she knew mostly in passing, as well as one of the artists whose work she had long sold in the Sea Witch and who had told her, touchingly, that she remembered Ally being such a sweet little girl. So few people, Kate thought. There had been no time, really, to get the word out. A small obituary in the *Cape Cod Times* and a few phone calls. Kate's sister Maggie had sent flowers and her apologies for not being able to make the trip on short notice. Who knew whom David had called in his family, if anyone. Ally had been gone too long to have friends here anymore, and Kate hadn't been sure how to get hold of her old high school friends.

The little group had reached their destination by the time Kate had finished her mental inventory, clustering around the open grave with the funeral director at its head clearing his voice to offer a short prayer and a poem Kate had selected. As he began, Kate picked up Glory, who had been clinging to her dress ever since they exited the car. Kate wished she could have left her home but that just wasn't an option at this point. Kate rocked gently, shifting Glory's weight as she attempted to soothe her. The words rolled over her as the little service proceeded, prolonging a detachment that had allowed her to get through these last few days without the tears and pain she had felt in San Francisco. Suddenly it was over, people wandering away, a last hug or pat and murmured sympathies before heading back to their cars and home. Kate saw David crossing the now sun lit grass toward her, and Jerry, who had taken a step in her direction, now took Kevin's arm and walked back to the road with a quick nod and a "See you tomorrow."

Oh, well, Kate thought as she watched David approach. He had always been an attractive man, nonetheless so for the streaks of gray now threading his thick brown hair. Broad shouldered and tall, he was imposing and more than a little intimidating at times. Today, though, his face looked lined and drawn under his tan, his shoulders hunched under his suit jacket. Putting Glory down, Kate stretched out her hand and offered a conciliatory smile. To her surprise, David took it and, leaning forward, brushed her cheek with his lips.

"A nice service, Kate, but why no priest, no Mass?"

"Oh, for heaven's sake, David, you know Ally wanted nothing to do the Catholic Church when she was still living here, and I doubt that changed over the last ten years. Besides, I haven't been there myself for so long, I couldn't imagine..."

Kate had been anticipating an argument over this, but David waved her off, shrugging and shaking his head.

"Where are Jill and the boys? Are they okay?"

"They're fine. They send their condolences. I just felt I needed to do this alone. Look, Kate, I want you to know that I'm sorry about the other night, but you still should have told me."

"I know. I'm really sorry, David."

"And I should have let you know when Ally called. I'm sorry about that too. I thought about it at the time, but I truly believed she'd try you next anyway, so it wouldn't matter." David took a deep breath before continuing with "Anyway, I wanted to tell you that, since I spoke with you, I've gone over that call and tried to remember just what she said, how she sounded, but it was pretty brief and I was, well, in shock, when I realized who it was at first, you know. She was making the usual polite conversation—how are you, how's the family—she asked about you too, if you were okay, if I'd heard from you lately." David paused, biting his lower lip, his eyes focused on the trees above Kate's head. "Then I kind of recovered and asked where the hell was she and what did she want after all this time. She never said where she was, we didn't get to that, I guess, but she said she needed some money and she wouldn't have called if there had been any other way of getting any. Could I help her out just this once and she'd never bother me again. I said I'd think about it, but first I wanted some answers. I told her I wanted the whole story, why she'd taken off like that, where she'd been all this time, what she'd been doing, and exactly what she wanted money for. Plus, I wanted an apology for putting us all through hell. When I was finished, she was quiet for a minute, then she said something like 'I should never have called you,' and hung up." David transferred his gaze to Kate, a mixture of pain and anger lining his face. "I never even told Jill about her call. I'm sure I could have handled that better, but I was still so damn angry with her I couldn't help myself. And she didn't sound terrified, by the way. If anything, she sounded pretty cool, calm, and collected."

Kate patted his arm awkwardly, saying, "I probably wouldn't have done any better." She reflected momentarily on her conversation with Jerry a few days before and knew he'd been right in saying she would have demanded an accounting as well.

David looked down at Glory, still trying to hide behind Kate's skirt. "So this must be our granddaughter. Did you say her name was Gloria?"

"Actually, it's Glory. Glory Allison LaRue." Kate reached around and pulled Glory forward, her arms wrapped around her to prevent her from escaping. She bent down, pushing loose strands of dark brown hair behind her granddaughter's ear. "Look, sweetie, it's your grandpa," she whispered, glancing up at the David.

He met Kate's gaze, a puzzled look creasing his face. "Glory? That's an odd name."

Kate straightened, her arms still protectively around Glory whose eyes were firmly focused on the grass at her feet. "It's a little different, certainly. I have no idea why Ally named her Glory, but that's her name."

"Well, whatever her name is, she does look like Ally when she was that age, doesn't she?" There was a catch in David's voice that sent a twinge of tender empathy through Kate. He crouched on the grass, trying to get under Glory's gaze. "Hi, Glory. It's nice to meet to you." He paused, waiting for a response, but Glory, motionless, kept her eyes down as if she hadn't heard.

After a moment, David stood up, smoothing down his suit jacket.

Kate reached out, gently touching his hand. "Glory's just a little shy, David, don't feel bad. She'll come around."

"It's all right, Kate. She's a little kid. She doesn't know me." David shrugged wearily. "This situation...I don't know what to say to you, Kate. I wish you luck? I just can't imagine going through that again at my age. I'm sorry for what I said before, and I will help you out when I can, just don't expect too much, okay? Remember, this was your choice, not mine. You never asked for my opinion."

Kate felt her lips tighten in anger, but she forced herself to stay in control. "Seriously, what would you have done, David, in my place? What if it was you they'd called to come to California? Would you have walked away from your grandchild, left her in foster care, never to have known what had happened to her?"

David didn't respond, staring once more at the trees above Kate's head, his lengthening silence broken by the murmuring voices of the few remaining people and the distant cawing of a gull.

Finally, he shifted his gaze to Kate's face, his eyes unreadable. "I don't know, but I guess I'd have brought her home too. It's not a decision I would want to have to make, in any case." He hesitated briefly as if considering what to say next. "I need some time with this, Kate. Let's keep in touch."" He looked back down at Glory still wrapped in her grandmother's arms. "Bye, Glory. Be good for your grandma."

Feeling surprised and a little confused, Kate responded somewhat awkwardly with "Okay, well, we'll keep in touch, then." She paused, struggling to think of something else to say. At a loss, she finally said, "I really do appreciate your coming today, David. Please give your family my best." As she was finishing, Kate noticed out of the corner of her eye a car pulling up and a young woman getting out. She walked a few steps toward the still-open grave and stopped, standing uncomfortably with her arms folded as if uncertain as to what to do next. The last of the little group of people were getting in their cars and driving off, and Kate, realizing it was time to leave, turned from David with an "I have to go now" and, with Glory in tow, approached the newcomer.

"Excuse me, are you here for Allison LaRue's funeral?"

The young woman met her gaze with a mixture of surprise and amusement underlining the sadness of her expression. "Yes, I'm sorry I'm late."

"I'm Ally's mother, Kate LaRue." Kate extended her free hand, the one not clutched tightly by Glory's.

"Yes, I know. I'm Chris Morgan, or at least I used to be. I'm Chris Angelino now."

"Oh, my God, I'm so sorry, I didn't recognize you." Kate quickly took in the woman standing before her and realized that this was indeed Ally's best friend and companion in rebellion from high school, but so transformed by age and time that Kate would never have recognized her if she hadn't been told who she was. Ten years ago, like Ally, Chris had sported a punk look with the tips of her blond hair dyed magenta, heavy makeup, multiple body piercings, tight black clothes, and an insolent attitude. Now, her short blond hair framed a heart-shaped face devoid of any makeup, and her clothes looked pretty conservative, a simple dark blue blouse and charcoal-colored pants. The only visible nod to her more exotic past was the series of graduated silver loop earrings that adorned both lobes.

Chris waved a hand dismissively. "It's okay. I guess I don't look much like the Chris Morgan you once knew. So, what happened? I didn't even know Ally was back, much less..." she paused, not sure how to continue.

"She wasn't. A few weeks ago, I received a call from a hospital in San Francisco that she was a patient there and very ill. I flew out immediately, but she died soon after I got there of complications from a burst appendix. Peritonitis and sepsis."

"Wow," Chris said softly, more to herself than to Kate. "San Francisco. So *that's* where she was. It's been so long since I heard anything, I had no idea."

Kate stared at her in astonishment and disbelief. "You heard from her? Chris, every day I've wondered where she was and how she was doing. Now I want to know more than ever. I want to know how she came to be in that hospital, what had happened that brought her to San Francisco. She left behind a little girl, Chris. This is Ally's daughter, Glory." Kate picked up Glory who whimpered softly, rubbed her eyes, and put her head down on Kate's shoulder as Chris looked at her in surprise. "Do you have children yourself now?"

Chris hesitated again, and then said resignedly, "Yes, I have children. A boy and a girl. And a husband, which I'm guessing Ally did not."

Kate shook her head. "Not as far as I know."

"All right, look, I last heard from Ally about seven years ago, I guess. For a while after she left, we kept in touch fairly regularly. Then she disappeared, and I didn't hear from her again. So, Mrs. LaRue, I can't tell you how she came to be in a hospital in San Francisco."

Kate drew in a deep breath. "Could you please tell me what you do know? It's important to me, and I think it's important for Glory's sake."

"Why?"

"I can't explain it; it just is."

"Fine. Call me. It's in the book or on the Net. Angelino, Jack and Christine. Now please, let me be."

Kate watched as Chris turned and walked up the knoll, then paused by the grave, hands clasped in front of her. *All this time,* Kate thought, *I believed no one knew where Ally had gone, no one had heard from her, until I received that phone call. I had no choice but to believe it because everyone denied it, no matter how much I pleaded and begged. How many people had heard from her, corresponded with her, knew how to find her all this time? And how can I find them now and make them tell me?* And with that, Kate turned and slowly headed to her car, Glory weighing heavily in her arms.

CHAPTER 14

Two days later, Kate sat on a hard kitchen chair in Chris Angelino's crowded little house just over the canal in Bourne, a town divided in two by Cape Cod's distinctive canal. Kate had serious misgivings as to whether this meeting would ever take place, remembering her own dislike of the teenage Chris Morgan, someone she had considered a bad influence on Ally and whose friendship with her daughter she had done her best to break up. Chris had been well aware of Kate's antagonism toward her and of her suspicion that she knew far more than she was telling in the weeks and months after Ally left home. Apparently Kate's suspicions were correct, but she had understood that nothing short of torture would have made Chris part with the information. *Not that I wouldn't have considered it at the time*, thought Kate grimly. And Chris's mother, who Kate considered far too lenient, even neglectful, setting no limits, not providing adequate supervision and so on, refused to push Chris to get her to divulge what she knew, choosing, instead, to believe she was telling the truth. Given all that, Kate was afraid that when she had time to think about it, Chris would refuse to tell her anything or even answer her phone calls.

But here she was on this bright and sunny morning when she really should be at the Sea Witch, she thought guiltily, sipping mint tea and eating warm croissants while sitting across from Ally's high school friend at a table piled high with folded laundry and the last remnants of a recent shopping trip to the local supermarket. Chris's two children, a stocky blond boy about Glory's age and a girl with a mop of red gold curls a couple of years younger, played noisily in and around a Little Tykes fort set up in one corner of the kitchen.

Glory sat on Kate's lap, clutching her new Raggedy Ann doll and occasionally fingering the picture locket that hung from her neck. She was observing the other children with some interest although she had resisted all efforts to coax her off Kate's lap and into their game. Chris had listened to Kate's description of Glory's problems, asking numerous questions that revealed more than a passing acquaintance with child development issues.

"I have a certificate in early childhood education from the 4-Cs, you know, the Cape Cod—" Chris began telling Kate when she expressed her admiration of Chris's understanding of the issues involved.

"—Community College, yes, I know," Kate finished for her. "Well, that's great. And are you working in that field?"

"Only at home right now," replied Chris, laughing a little. "Someday, when they're older," nodding toward her two active youngsters, "I'd like to have my own preschool. But for the time being..." Chris shrugged, and then assessed Kate with a penetrating look. "I bet you thought I'd be dead or in jail by now."

Kate sucked in her breath and met Chris's gaze with one of her own. "Well, it doesn't matter what I thought, does it." Kate lifted her chin. "Obviously, I was wrong about a lot of things." She pulled Glory a little closer, playing with one her braids.

Chris smiled slightly, glancing away toward her own two children, who were now chasing each other around the fort, giggling mischievously. She picked up a rubber band from the table and began twisting it between her fingers. "Yeah, well, you know, it can be tough being a kid, especially a teenager, on the Cape. Even more so in the winter. The place was so deserted, more than it is now, not much to do, not many people to do it with. Ally and I, we were a lot alike; we were both only children from single-parent homes, our dads were remarried, our moms worked a lot. We liked the same music, clothes, art, books, whatever. We wanted to be different, to stand out. We told ourselves we weren't like the other kids. Anyway, Ally had a pretty hard time with you. She thought that you just didn't get it, and you were always in her face." Chris paused to note Kate's reaction to this, but Kate kept her expression decidedly neutral. Chris went back to her cat's cradle with the rubber band. "She was determined early on to get out at the first opportunity. Ally always wanted me to go with her, and we talked about it, all the things we would do when we left home, but she was the only one with the nerve to actually do it."

Kate looked at her curiously. "Do you regret not going?"

"No, not now, although I did at first." She paused again, considering. Her daughter ran over to her, sippy cup in her chubby hands. Chris hugged her, planting a kiss on her cheek, before getting up to fill the cup. "One summer we met some older teenagers, or maybe young adults, at a concert in Hyannis. They were musicians, singers, here on a sort of working vacation from New York City. We were so jealous of them, living in New York, with all the clubs and the concerts. They offered to put us up if we ever came to New York."

"I don't remember any kids from New York," Kate interjected, puzzled.

"That's because you never met them," Chris returned coolly. "Ally knew you wouldn't have approved." She paused, gesturing apologetically. "If it makes you feel any better, my mother didn't meet them either for much the same reason." She turned away for a moment, watching her children at play, before continuing. "Anyway, Ally began making plans with them to come to New York when she turned eighteen. Our friends were on their own too, with a place in the Village." Before Kate could ask any questions, she added, "They were struggling musicians, I guess you'd say, trying to break into the clubs. Once you and Ally had that last big fight, she decided she'd had enough. She got a room in one of the motels that first night. The next day, I took her to the bus station up by Route 6, and she boarded a bus for New York."

Chris stopped in her narrative to intervene between her son and daughter, who had gotten into a struggle over a stuffed dog. Kate watched as she slipped a DVD into the slot below a small TV in the kitchen's play corner and coaxed her children onto cushions on the floor, marveling at how deftly Chris dealt with their quarrel. Chris returned to the table and picked up her teacup. "Another cup?"

"No, thank you. I think I've had enough for today." Kate smiled at Chris, then rubbed her forehead with her free hand, the other securing Glory in her lap, who looked up with troubled eyes. "I'm okay, honey, just a little tired," Kate offered soothingly. In response to Chris's curious look, she added, "It's funny, but sometimes she seems to know what I'm thinking or feeling."

Chris nodded and said, "I'm sure this isn't pleasant for you, Mrs. LaRue. And I'm sorry about what happened with Ally. Actually, if you want to know the truth, I tried to talk her out of going that day. I was scared for her, going to New York like that, but she was determined to do it and nothing I could say was going to stop her. And as you might imagine, she made me promise not to tell anyone where she was."

"You know, I went to that bus station with her picture a few days later. No one remembered anyone looking like Ally getting on a bus."

"Yeah. Ally thought you might. She didn't look like someone you would have recognized that day. Believe me, she really planned for this."

Kate nodded in resignation. "All right, so she got to New York and stayed with these struggling musician friends. Then what?"

"She had a great time, at least for a while. She was happy. She got odd jobs waitressing and stuff like that to support herself. Rented a room in another flat. Got a false ID so that she could hang out and drink at the clubs and be part of the scene in New York."

"So what happened?"

"I'm not sure. It was a lot of fun and that was wonderful, but Ally wanted more out of life than just that. Everything wasn't just sex, drugs, and rock 'n' roll for either of us, despite what some people thought." Chris paused again to check Kate's reaction before smiling a little sheepishly. "Actually, that was something my mother kept saying."

Kate offered a smile in return, although the phrase stirred up memories of her own fears regarding just what Ally and her friends had been into back then.

"Anyway, I think the club scene just got old after a few years. Besides, Ally liked spending time in places like art galleries and libraries in addition to hanging out in the clubs. And she got interested in stuff like metaphysics and mysticism, altering consciousness in ways that didn't necessarily involve drugs."

When Chris paused again, Kate prodded, "Okay, so, what? She ran off and joined the Hare Krishnas?" Kate conjured up memories of her own youth and the orange-robed young men chanting and collecting money outside on the lawns of her college campus.

"No. Well, I don't know. All I know is she met someone, a man, at some group she went to, like a Yoga class or a meditation circle. I think she saw him as kind of a mentor, but they may have dated as well, I just don't know. You see, by that time, it had been a while since Ally left, and I was at the 4-Cs and working a lot when I wasn't in classes. I wasn't hearing from her as often as I once did, and I didn't have time myself to keep up with her. Then she just stopped calling altogether. I tried to get in touch with her but she had moved, and no one seemed to know where."

"Who was this man she met?"

"I don't know. She may have mentioned his name, but if so, I don't remember. And I don't know if she left New York with him. It's just the last thing I remember her talking about."

Kate mulled this over for a minute. "Chris, I'd like to show you some pictures I found in Ally's apartment in San Francisco. See if you can tell me anything about them."

Chris shrugged. "Sure, but I probably won't be much help."

Kate set Glory on her feet while she rummaged in her purse for the photos. Glory leaned against her, one hand on her lap. She brought out the photograph of the younger Ally, the one on the city street that she now suspected was taken in New York. Chris looked at it, smiling widely as she tenderly fingered the photo. "Yeah, that's her all right. She sent me one a lot like this once, shortly after she got to New York. I probably still have it somewhere."

Next, Kate laid out the photographs of the road through the empty fields along with the one of the young woman. Chris looked at them and slowly shook her head. "No idea."

She glanced up to see that Glory had moved a few inches from Kate, watching from a distance the Disney DVD that Chris had put on to distract her own youngsters. She picked up another pillow, smiling encouragingly. "Come here, Glory, and sit down. You can see better if you get a little closer."

The little girl glanced up uncertainly, looking to her grandmother, her big eyes questioning. "Go ahead, sit down, sweetheart." Kate smiled and nodded toward the TV. Glory advanced a foot or two before kneeling on the floor, still a considerable distance behind the other children and the proffered cushion. Chris looked at her thoughtfully for a minute or two, and then turned to Kate. "You know, Mrs. LaRue, it would be fine with me if you wanted to bring Glory over for a play date occasionally. Ally meant a lot to me, and I'd like to do something to help out with her daughter."

Kate looked at Chris, a little surprised by this offer, but then thinking maybe she shouldn't be. "Of course. That would be nice." She hesitated a few seconds, then asked, "Chris, have you stayed in touch with these friends from New York? Do you think I could speak with them, ask what they know about Ally?"

Chris bit her lower lip, eyes on Glory, sitting now on the floor, absorbed in the action on the TV. Finally, she said, "It's been awhile since I talked with any of them, and I doubt there's anything more they can tell you. But I'll see if anyone will talk to you."

Kate considered this. "Well, please tell whoever you speak to it's important. I'm not looking to blame anyone at this late date if that's what—"

Chris interrupted with a brusque, "It's not that. I'll try, but I just don't know, okay?"

Kate nodded. "Thanks, Chris. I'll appreciate whatever you can do."

CHAPTER 15

Slicing vegetables to cook for dinner, Kate let her thoughts wander over the events of the last few days, particularly what she had begun to learn about Ally. When she remembered the anguish of those early months and years after Ally's departure, it was hard even now to accept, without anger and resentment, the reality that Ally's whereabouts had been no mystery to some, even though she had long suspected it. Hard not to want to scream her anger and pain at Chris, to wish on her some measure of what she had felt all those years ago. Hard, too, not to feel some loss of the renewed tenderness and compassion she had felt for her daughter, a struggling single mother of a disabled, troubled child, dying before her time. Now, Kate couldn't help but feel the burning fire of anger and pain directed at a daughter and her friend who had known how desperately she had tried to find her but apparently did not care for anything but her own desire to be free.

Kate wiped at her eyes, putting down her knife. A faint red sprang up into her cheekbones as a sense of shame filled her. She pictured Chris holding her little daughter, giving her a kiss, Ally with Glory on her lap in Santa Cruz. No, she would not wish that pain on anyone. Besides, maybe Ally really had regretted it in the end, had wanted to find a way to come home but didn't know how. *Whether she did or not*, Kate thought*, it makes me feel better to think Ally* may *have had a change of heart. Anyway, it was long ago now, and it's no use holding on to anger and resentment*. Kate smiled sadly. *Well, it may have taken some time, but I did learn that eventually.*

Staring at the brightly colored mixture of red and green peppers, yellow squash, and orange carrots, Kate went back over in her mind Chris's story of Ally's interest in "metaphysics and mysticism" and consciousness raising "in ways that didn't involve drugs." *What was that about?* Kate wondered. She'd never known Ally to have the slightest interest in anything even marginally religious. Even when she was a child, it had been a constant battle to get her to Mass on Sunday and to religious education classes on weekday evenings and after school. *Anyway,* she thought with some amusement, *this sounds more like a flashback to the '60s. Of course,* Kate thought, *I can understand the appeal of meditation and even Yoga, but Chris made this sound like something beyond what I learned during that relaxing sojourn in the mountains.*

Shaking her head in puzzlement, Kate dropped the vegetables into a pan with a little olive oil and began to lightly sauté them. Her thoughts turned to tomorrow and Glory's evaluation with the special education department in Yarmouth. *What would they have to offer her?* Kate thought back to the school she'd visited in San Francisco. Glory had seemed to do well there, and it did give her a chance to be with other children. Then too, Kate had to admit, Glory had adapted better than she had thought possible over the short time since they had arrived from San Francisco. Kate still had not heard her speak, yet the little girl seemed to have learned to trust her, and she was eating more and sleeping better than she had those first few days, exploring her new toys and playing with those Kate had brought with them from California.

Kate smiled to herself. The best thing she ever did was to get Glory that locket with that photo of her and Ally. It clearly was her most treasured possession and seemed to provide the little girl with a sense of security. Now, if she could just get her to talk. Kate pondered this for a moment. What had happened to Glory that made her not want to talk? The more time Kate spent with Glory, the more convinced she was that this was not a matter of being unable to talk but some fear that held her back and made her unwilling to speak. Kate wasn't precisely sure why she thought this, but she intuitively believed it to be so. Special education was all well and good, she thought to herself, but if this is an emotional or psychological problem, wouldn't some type of psychotherapy be more to the point? Maybe she could revisit some of those referrals Dr. Tenley gave her, see if there was someone who could work with Glory, draw her out a little.

When dinner was ready and on the table, Kate went in search of Glory. She found the little girl in her mother's old room, lying on her stomach on the floor with an old wooden play set spread out on the floor in front of her. The late-summer light streaming through the window caught the swirling dust motes above her head as it illuminated the painted house and barn with its accompanying human and animal figures as well as cars, tractors, and wagons. As Glory seemed intent on her play and unaware of her grandmother's presence, Kate stepped back into the hallway. She watched in fascination as Glory moved the pieces around all the while murmuring under her breath in a tone all but inaudible to Kate. She had a cluster of the human figures, mostly representing adult females and children off to one side while another adult, a man with painted black hair parted in the middle and a moustache, walked as much as a legless figure could walk back in forth in front of them, seemingly lecturing them about something. After a few seconds of increasingly agitated walking and talking, Glory placed the figure in a car and drove it away, then dispersed the group around the house and barn. As she sat back on her heels, viewing the scene with a look of satisfaction, she suddenly caught sight of Kate watching from the doorway and jumped up with a little gasp. She backed into a shadowy corner of the room, dark eyes widening in fright.

"It's okay, honey," said Kate, startled by Glory's reaction. "I was just coming to call you to supper, and I didn't want to interrupt your game. You looked like you were having fun. Isn't this nice, with the house and the barn and all the people and animals. Have you ever been to a farm?" Kate flashed to the two photographs of the road and the empty fields. Wasn't it likely that it was part of a farm where Glory and Ally had once lived? Glory didn't respond but studied the scene intently from where she had retreated, her small hands clasped behind her back. Kate sighed. "Well," she said as brightly as she could manage, "it's time to eat. You can come back and play some more after supper."

Together, they walked out to the kitchen, Glory's small soft palm lightly clasped in Kate's. She helped Glory climb up into her booster seat kitty-corner from Kate's chair. While eating her own dinner, Kate watched as unobtrusively as possible as Glory picked at the pieces of roast chicken, potatoes, and vegetables, and downed a glass of milk. After five minutes or so of this, Kate said gently, in response to Glory's questioning eyes, "You can get down if you're finished." With that, Glory jumped down and disappeared into the recesses of the hall. Kate shrugged and cleared Glory's plate, remembering many such meals with Ally when the carefully prepared food would barely be touched before she would be begging to be allowed to go back to her play. At first, Kate would insist she take just one more (or two more or three more) mouthfuls before leaving, or at least eat some vegetables or some of the meat. No eating, no dessert, or no going back outside to play. But after a while, Kate gave up that struggle, and Ally never really seemed to suffer for it. *Anyway, standoffs over dinner were the least of my worries,* thought Kate.

Shaking off the memories of Ally, Kate tiptoed quietly down the hall to Glory's bedroom, peeking around the corner of the door to see her granddaughter's dark head once again bent over her little farm scene as she lined up the little wooden people in orderly rows. Satisfied that Glory was happily back to her play, she retreated to the kitchen table and her own dinner. She stood for a moment, looking out the window as the soft light of a summer early evening dappled the front lawn with leaf shadows and the last stragglers from the beach headed home, brightly colored towels draped over their shoulders, clutching plastic buckets and the odd assortment of rafts, boards, and swim rings.

Kate picked up her own plate with the thought of heading out to her favorite retreat. In the years since Ally left, she almost never ate at the table in the kitchen in the summer, preferring the atmosphere of the porch, with its pleasant sights, sounds, and smells instead. She had only taken a few steps when a series of crashes from the direction of the bedrooms stopped her. Hastily setting her plate down, she hurried back down the hall to Ally's room. Glory stood in the center of the room, her small mouth set in a familiar angry line, hands clenched at her sides, the collection of wooden buildings, figures, and vehicles scattered across the floor where she had evidently thrown or kicked them.

"Glory!" exclaimed Kate sharply. The child looked up at her grandmother, her lower lip trembling as eyes filled with confusion and fear. "Glory, sweetheart, what's wrong?" Kate's voice tone changed to one of concern. She tried to reach out to her, but Glory turned, and with sudden wrenching sobs, ran past Kate into the next room burrowing into the trundle bed. Kate followed, and then stood looking down at the little girl in despair, uncertain whether this was just sheer naughtiness or some emotional conflict Kate didn't understand. *Those referrals from Dr. Tenley are looking more and more like the way to go*, she thought.

CHAPTER 16

Kate walked down the broad steps of the large red brick school building with Glory once again in tow, feeling a sense of relief and accomplishment over getting through this first hurdle. The Dennis-Yarmouth School District had been very welcoming and accepting, and Kate's growing collection of documentation of Glory's problems seemed adequate to get this particular ball rolling. So much so that, while the school district would be conducting its own assessments in the fall, Glory was assured of a placement in a separate class that focused on children with communication and emotional problems. The only concern was that Glory would not begin until September as the optional summer program was full and Kate was left with finding adequate childcare and needed services until then. She had Dr. Tenley's recommendations, as well as some from the school district, and Kate had not forgotten Jerry's suggestion about Kevin's niece or Chris Angelino's offer of play dates. Maybe Chris would be interested in working with Glory, providing her with a little early childhood education. She seemed so knowledgeable and really very good with her own children. Surely Chris could use some extra money.

Kate helped Glory into the car and fastened her car seat safety belt. She tried to make cheery chitchat and to meet Glory's gaze, but the little girl, more subdued than usual since the last night's tantrum, didn't respond, her eyes skidding away whenever Kate tried to make contact. *I really need to get over to the Sea Witch this morning*, Kate thought, *but maybe if we do something fun later I can get her out of this mood she's in.* The day was warm, bordering on hot and sunny, the sky a pure silkscreen blue. A light breeze was blowing in off the unseen water to the south, carrying with it a fragrant whiff of salt air. It was a day to be outside, cycling down one of the Cape's scenic bike paths or renting one of the paddle boats on Swan River or just frolicking on the beach. Kate let her thoughts dwell uncomfortably on that last option. She had yet to bring Glory back to the beach since their first visit when Glory had run away from her and out toward the jetty. They pulled out of the school parking lot, windows down to catch the breeze, and headed back out onto a crowded Route 28, and then up one of the roads connecting with Route 6A.

Ten minutes later as she slid her car into the Sea Witch's parking area, tires crunching on the pebbles and crushed seashells, she was pleased to note the number of cars in the lot, including a couple with out-of-state plates. With Glory firmly in hand as she entered the store, she gave Jerry a nod and Captain Ahab his obligatory whistle before heading toward the office. Glory pulled away as they entered, climbing onto a small chair at the child-sized table Kate had brought from home (*I knew there was a reason I've never got rid of this stuff*, she had thought as she raided her basement storage area for Ally's old toys) and reaching for an old toy computer that played electronic games. Glory had been delighted by the cornucopia of toys that awaited her since arriving on the Cape and especially seemed to have taken to Kate's suggestion that this was her "desk" with its own computer as well as books, paper, pencils, and crayons so that she could "work" alongside Grandma. "She's really a smart little girl," Kate said to herself, watching Glory's expression as she followed the images on her "computer," "so whatever the reason is for her lack of speech, it's not her intelligence."

When Jerry came to the door an hour or so later, Kate was so intent on her work that she didn't see him or respond to his throat clearing or his repetition of her name until he had raised his voice enough to draw a confused and frightened look from Glory. "Sorry, honey," he offered, and then to Kate, who looked equally startled, he said, "You're the only person I know who can get that lost in business accounts."

Kate smiled at this and shook her head. "It's hard to keep up, not being here as much as I should. Not that you haven't been doing a great job here without me," she added hastily.

"Yeah, yeah. I'd like it better if you were around more too," he responded with a shrug and a glance in Glory's direction.

Kate looked at Glory who had returned to coloring pictures of Disney cartoon characters. "I know. Look, I wanted to talk to you about Kevin's niece, the one who does childcare. I had the meeting with the school today and, while Glory will be in a special education class in the fall, they don't have an opening for her in their summer program. So I'm going to have to come up with something for her in the meantime. She can't stay cooped up in here all day."

Jerry held up his hand. "No problem. As luck would have it, Kevin and I saw Jen the other day. I told her the whole story about Ally and you and Glory, and she was really interested. Thought it would be a nice opportunity for her. She really wanted to help out."

Kate smiled again. "That's great, Jerry. When can I meet her?"

"Whenever you can arrange it. I have her phone number right here." Jerry gestured toward the bulletin board on the wall above the desk where a yellow sticky bore the name Jennifer O'Malley and a phone number.

Kate nodded. "Okay, I'll get on that tomorrow. Meanwhile, let's talk about that shipment of coral we're supposed to be getting." She glanced up at the computer. "Next week, right?"

An hour later, Kate was headed back across the Cape's arm toward home, winding through streets full of mostly year-round homes and stands of pine trees, still ruminating on the Sea Witch and all she needed to do there and couldn't accomplish in a couple of hours. "Glory has been an angel about all this," Kate reiterated to herself, "but she can't be expected to spend several hours a day there. Well, maybe Kevin's niece can give me enough time so that I can get caught up, and then when school starts...Oooh, now *there's* an idea." Kate had turned onto Route 28 and, noticing a Dairy Queen up ahead, gave a quick glance to Glory in the backseat.

"Do you like ice cream, Glory?" Glory shifted her gaze from the window to her grandmother, but her expression seemed remote. Kate pulled into the parking lot, forcing a cheery, "Well, I do," and slid into a just vacated space ahead of a family from Pennsylvania. Kate climbed out of the car and released Glory from her car seat. The day had turned hot, and the cooling sea breeze had disappeared while she and Glory had been in the Sea Witch's office, leaving the air feeling like warm bathwater. Kate felt beads of perspiration form on her forehead in the time it took to get out of the car and get in line behind a group of giggling, energetic, school-aged kids and their weary-looking guardians. Glory, for her part, stood docilely by Kate's side until after they had secured a couple of soft serve vanilla ice-cream cones, and then followed close at her heels while Kate searched for a table with an umbrella.

"Hey, there, Kate! Why don't you and your little cutie come sit with me?"

Kate turned to see her neighbor Fran Jackson sitting at a table in the corner she hadn't noticed on her initial visual sweep of the patio. "Thanks, Fran, we will." Kate sat down gratefully, nodding to Glory to climb up on the bench with her. She handed Glory her ice-cream cone, watching her eyes widen as she took it gingerly from her hand. Glory licked it tentatively, her eyes fixed on her grandmother's face.

"My goodness, do you think she's never had an ice-cream cone before?" Fran's blue eyes were full of amazement as she watched Glory work her way around the cone, her eyes still glued to Kate, seemingly imitating her example of how to eat an ice-cream cone.

Kate shrugged. "Maybe not." Then, wanting to divert the subject from any possible recounting of Glory's limitations, she asked, "How are you doing, Fran? Keeping the cottage booked this season?"

Fran owned a small, picturesque white cottage complete with a rose trellis covered with pink Cape roses and complemented with the customary blue hyacinth bushes and stands of yellow day lilies. The cottage was located to the side and slightly behind her own comfortable Cape Cod-style home. Fran's parents had purchased the pair many years ago in order to have a "guest home" to accommodate friends and relatives who came to visit while the family was summering on the Cape. Fran, a slender, tanned woman now in her seventies with a cap of soft silver curls, was the last of the family; at least, of those still close enough to have an interest in spending summers on the Cape. Like Kate, Fran was a year-round Yarmouth resident. Renting out the smaller cottage to vacationers each summer provided a much-needed supplement to her retirement income.

"Well, as you know, things have been slow this season for everyone," Fran opined in response to Kate's question. "I've done pretty well, considering, but I still have a week open coming up and no takers yet. But we'll see. I think I can get it rented. Too good a location to stay vacant, right?"

"I think you're right, Fran. After all, who wouldn't want such a sweet little cottage just a short walk from the beach?"

Kate smiled encouragingly at her neighbor, then listened with relief while offering the occasional comment or understanding murmur as Fran elaborated on the problems of managing rental properties, the competition from the big resorts fronting the beaches, along with the idiosyncrasies of her current tenants. Pausing in her narrative, Fran's eyes rested on Glory, now eating her ice cream with gusto, rivulets dribbling down her small hands, her mouth encircled in white.

"What a picture!" Fran took in the little girl's neatly braided hair with its sunny yellow bows and matching yellow sundress once immaculate but now splotched with drops of melting ice cream, the silver on the picture locket twinkling when it caught the light. "She looks just like her mother, doesn't she? So sad, poor little thing." Kate could only assume that this was said in reference to Ally's death, not Glory's resemblance to her. "Still not talking?"

Kate grimaced slightly. *What is it about Fran that makes me so uncomfortable? Maybe because it's a little like being cross-examined by your teacher or mother after being suspected of some wrongdoing.* "No, but we're working on it. I'm sure Glory's going to be just fine."

"Well, I certainly hope that's true. This is quite a task for you to take on, raising a child along with running a business and all. You're no kid yourself, either." Fran shook her head, her appraising gaze fixed on Glory.

Kate squirmed inwardly, and, finishing her own cone, cast about for a reason to make a quick exit. "Yes, I've got a lot going on. I really do need to get home now. I've got some phone calls to make. It was nice to see you, Fran." Kate set Glory on her feet, scooping up a handful of napkins as she did so. "I know you'll get that cottage rented, just wait and see."

"Well, when I do, I'll send them your way, like always."

Kate smiled. "Thanks, Fran. I appreciate it."

As she and Glory prepared to exit the crowded parking lot, Kate reminded herself that Fran was a good person at heart despite her irritating manner. And she did send business her way whenever possible. "I'm going to get a lot of comments like that from well-meaning people. I suppose I'd better get used to it," Kate told herself as she merged into the long slow line of traffic on Route 28, heading toward home.

CHAPTER 17

Kate watched from a low wooden bench as Jen O'Malley pushed a delighted Glory on a swing located in a small seaside playground, Glory's braids flying out behind her, her short little legs flailing in an attempt to assist in the motion of the swing. Kate had discovered that Glory liked swings almost as much as the beach, which was a tremendous relief as she felt a lot safer in the fenced confines of the playground. Glory hadn't repeated her run for the jetty when Kate had finally worked up the nerve to try another beach visit, but the experience had shaken her, nonetheless. Kate smiled at the sight of her granddaughter, face turned up to the wide expanse of blue sky, giggles streaming forth from her small open mouth as if they were bubbles floating on the wind. Kate gave a satisfied sigh. *This is going to work*, she thought happily, watching as Jen continued to push Glory, offering a flow of comments along with laughter of her own.

Much to Kate's relief, they had taken to each other immediately, and Jen, as Jerry had suggested, was quite knowledgeable about special needs children. Kate had learned that she was considering a major in psychology and, like Chris, had taken courses in child development as well as done some work in a summer program for children with autism last year. Jen already had a number of interesting observations and suggestions about ways to engage Glory and draw her out. Plus, she'd been understanding about Kate's concerns and was more than willing to participate in some "trial runs" so that Kate could see how she interacted with Glory. Kate thought Jen was a sweet young woman who looked even younger than her twenty years with her long red hair tied back in a ponytail, wide blue eyes, and skin covered with freckles. The right outfit, Kate concluded, and she would look just like an elf or a leprechaun.

Kate watched as Jen caught Glory's swing and whispered something in her ear. The little girl wiggled free and, getting down off the swing, ran over to the playground's big climbing structure with its ladders, bridges, and slides. Glory was more cautious about playing on this equipment, but with encouragement from Jen, she clambered up on it, pushing buttons and turning wheels on a board mounted on one of the walls, then sliding tentatively down the shortest slide. Kate moved over to another one of the small wooden benches lining the playground's perimeter and sat down, stretching out her legs, and feeling the warm rays of late-afternoon summer sun on her body. Despite the lovely day, or perhaps because of it, the little playground was deserted. Kate could see a group of children silhouetted out on the beach, running in and out of the sparkling water as a beach ball arced up and onto the sand.

Glory, having finished with the slide, was heading back toward the swings, but Jen coaxed her back to a group of animals that could be bounced or rocked on, helping Glory mount a circus lion, and then to move her body to make it rock. Once this was done, Jen smiled in Kate's direction as she walked over to her, leaving Glory to rock on the lion on her own.

"She has plenty of energy, that's for sure." Jen brushed damp wisps of hair away from her face with the back of hand.

Kate smiled in return. "She most certainly does. Are you ready to head back?"

Jen glanced over at Glory, who had abandoned the lion and was already sitting on one of the swings, looking expectantly at Jen and Kate. Jen laughed.

"Well, I'll give her another ride on the swings first. It's getting late, and I need to get home. I'm working tonight." Kate knew that Jen had a summer job waitressing in one of the many restaurants lining Route 28, mostly working in the evenings.

"That's fine. It's almost suppertime anyway. You'll be able to start tomorrow around noon?"

"No problem," Jen called back to Kate as she headed in Glory's direction.

Glory settled into the swing as Jen pulled her back, and then let go, the swing moving forward and back on its own before Jen gave it another push. Kate followed its arc against the ocean, and then the sky, Glory's laughter a pleasure to hear. After a few minutes, Jen let the swing slow on its own before bringing it to a stop. Glory glanced back at her questioningly as Jen leaned forward with a cheerful "All done for today. It's time to go home and have supper."

Getting up from the bench, Kate could see the Glory's eyebrows draw together and her lips tremble. She clutched the metal chains of the swing tightly, her frown deepening, as she saw her grandmother walking toward her.

"Hey, we can come back tomorrow" Jen said soothingly, looking into Glory's troubled eyes. Kate reached her and tried to take her in her arms, but Glory stubbornly clung to the swing.

Kate looked surprised. "She's usually so cooperative."

Jen shrugged. "My fault. I should have given her some warning."

Kate turned back to Glory. "Be a good girl, Glory, and let's go home. We have ice cream for dessert," Kate added coaxingly.

"No!"

Kate stared at Glory in astonishment with Glory looking just as astonished as she glared back at Kate for a few seconds before bursting into tears. She let go of the swing and evaded Kate's grasp, heading for the gate, but Jen caught up with her before she could undo the latch. Kate picked up the sobbing child. "All right, it's all right, Glory." She looked back at Jen, a bemused smile on her lips. "Wouldn't you know it, the first word I hear her say is no."

CHAPTER 18

The office of Dr. Lawler, the child psychologist Dr. Tenley had recommended, was located in a block of medical offices on Main Street in Hyannis, not far from Cape Cod Hospital. Glory hung back reluctantly as Kate led her down a paved walkway bordered with bright summer flowers and through the door of the first of the single-story white clapboard buildings. The office waiting room was bright and cheery and filled with toys and books, but Glory, pressing her face against Kate's shoulder as they sat waiting for Dr. Lawler, refused to even look.

"Hey, come on, honey. We're just here to talk. And play," Kate added hastily, realizing that the idea of talking might be almost as aversive as the shot she imagined Glory being afraid of getting. Kate stroked the child's hair absently, thinking back to Glory's outburst at the playground the other day. She had been thrilled at what seemed to be a significant breakthrough, but afterward Glory had once again retreated into silence, difficult to engage at all, even with her newfound friend Jen. *Well, let's hope this helps, because I'm at a loss as to what else to do*, she thought.

"Glory LaRue?"

Kate looked up at the person standing in the doorway. Dr. Lawler was a short, stocky woman whose long, honey-blond hair, liberally salted with gray, was caught up in a ponytail. She looked from Glory to Kate, a smile lighting up her surprisingly youthful face.

Kate stood up, setting Glory on her feet, and offered her hand. "Hi, I'm Kate LaRue, Glory's grandmother."

Dr. Lawler took her hand with a warm "A pleasure to meet you."

"And this is Glory, of course." Dr. Lawler turned her smile toward

Glory, who was clinging to the back of Kate's Capri pants in an effort to conceal herself. "Why don't you come in to the office?" Kate, with Glory glued to her side, followed Dr. Lawler into a spacious room that was furnished with the usual office furniture as well as a child-sized table and chairs, a fully equipped dollhouse, a toy race-track and train set, and a sandbox with pails, shovels, and trucks, as well as shelves filled with toys and arts and craft materials. "Ooooh, look at this, Glory," whispered Kate, bending closer to the little girl. "See, I told you this could be fun."

"Play with whatever you like, Glory," Dr. Lawler offered, with a sweeping gesture of the room. "I'm going to talk to your grandma for a little while."

Glory, biting her lower lip, looked uncertainly from Kate to the cornucopia of toys but, after hesitating for a moment released her grip on Kate's hand and walked tentatively over to the dollhouse and peered inside. Kate let out a sigh of relief and sank into the comfortable armchair indicated by Dr. Lawler.

"I received the information you sent from Glory's doctors and her school in San Francisco, as well as from her recent school evaluation here. A very interesting young lady, your granddaughter." Dr. Lawler paused as Kate nodded acknowledgment. "I realize you don't know much about her life before she came to live with you" Dr. Lawler held up her hand as Kate started to interrupt, "but today I would like you to just tell me what you *do* know and, again, what you're seeing now with her. Plus, I'll need you to fill out an assessment." Dr. Lawler smiled again. "You're all I've got in that regard, Mrs. LaRue, you and Glory herself. To that end, while you're filling out the assessment, I'll observe and try to get to know Glory a little better."

Kate nodded and began with the call from San Francisco General Hospital in what seemed like a lifetime ago now, leading Dr. Lawler through her meetings with Maria Carlos and Glory's teacher and doctors, as well as what she had been told about Ally and Glory by Mrs. Randall and the nurses at the hospital. Kate then moved on to Glory's adjustments to the move to the Cape, finishing with the story of how she had heard her speak her first word only days ago.

"You may not realize it but you've learned quite a lot about Glory in these few weeks since your daughter died, Mrs. LaRue. You know her far better than you think you do."

"Why doesn't she talk?"

"I can't answer that right now. I do think that from everything I've seen and heard that Glory's lack of speech stems more from a psychological source rather than, say, a physical problem or cognitive limitations. But let's see how things go first before coming to any definite conclusions."

Dr. Lawler and Kate both looked over in Glory's direction. She had abandoned the dollhouse and was investigating the sandbox toys, watching as shovelfuls of sand poured through a sifter, turned a wheel, and passed into an attached container.

"For the initial few sessions I like to let the children explore the toys on their own, without any particular direction. It helps both to assess the child's level of development as far as their play is concerned and also to allow me to build a relationship with the child." Dr. Lawler smiled again at Kate. "I want to make it clear to Glory that she's under no pressure to talk until she's ready. There's a lot that can be learned from play alone, in any case."

"Okay" Kate said taking a deep breath as Dr. Lawler proceeded to explain the written assessments she wanted Kate to complete. Once Kate was occupied with these, Dr. Lawler moved over nearer to Glory, still mesmerized by the sand passing through the sifter, and watched silently as Glory continued to pour endless shovelfuls of sand.

The telephone was ringing as Kate walked back through her door a few hours later, her arms weighed down with groceries. Glory followed her in, immediately trotting off toward the bedroom. With an anxious glance over her shoulder in Glory's direction, Kate set down the bags and her purse and scooped up the phone. "Hello?" Kate questioned distractedly, the phone cradled against her ear.

"Mrs. LaRue? This is Chris Angelino."

"Oh yes." Kate straightened, her mind racing in anticipation. "Nice to hear from you, Chris. How are you?"

"I'm fine. I'm glad I caught you. I tried your cell phone, but you didn't pick up."

"Oh, yes, sorry. I probably forgot to turn it back on this morning."

"Well, anyway, I wanted to let you know I've gotten in touch with someone Ally was living with for a while in New York, one of the musicians we were hanging around with back in the day."

"Really? Oh, Chris, that's terrific. But wait, is this person willing to talk to me?"

"Yes, actually, she is. Her name is Andi Moore and she's here on the Cape, playing in Provincetown this summer with another old friend, Tim Downs. He's her husband now it seems. Anyway, she felt terrible about Ally when I told her and wouldn't mind reminiscing a bit. I think it would be best if I went with you, though."

"That would be perfect, Chris. When were you thinking of going?"

"Well, Jack has a day off coming up the beginning of next week. I'm sure he'll be willing to take care of the kids for the day. I'd really like to see Andi and Tim myself. Do you want to try bringing Glory over here? Jack's really good with kids."

Kate hesitated, weighing the options. "I have someone to do part-time child care now. Let me see if she's available first. And I'd need to make arrangements at the Sea Witch. What time would you want to leave?"

"Well, we need to get up there in the afternoon so that we can catch them before their performances. Figure on noon or so."

"I'll see what I can work out and get back to you. Thanks, Chris."

"You're welcome, but I have to say that we really got lucky with this one."

CHAPTER 19

Another lovely sunny summer day, Kate thought, driving once again with her windows down to catch the breeze as she headed out along Route 6 in the direction of Provincetown, following behind Chris Angelino's little black car. They were moving at a fast clip for this portion of the trip at least, with traffic fairly light on the Mid-Cape Highway. Kate didn't often take this route unless she was traveling a fair distance along the Cape's arm or heading over the canal to the mainland. It was, after all, a less interesting ride, if more efficient than the other two major routes crossing the Cape, with little to see but the stretches of scrub pine and oak trees on either side of the road. Driving along, eyes on Chris's fast moving car, Kate's thoughts wandered back to Glory. When Kate had left her, she was happily eating a bowl of Oreo cookie ice cream as a post-luncheon treat and was no doubt enjoying a trip to the playground with Jen about now. Kate gave a quick, automatic check to her cell phone sitting in the well next to her. "Stop worrying, Glory will be fine," she told herself sternly.

With that self-admonishment, her eyes caught the sun sparkling off the waters of one of the many kettle ponds that dotted the Cape, bodies of fresh water left behind by the glaciers that formed the peninsula thousands of years ago. The sight of water reminded Kate that it had been many days since it last rained and that, while the delightful weather was a boon for beachgoers, the dry spell would soon create its own problems if some good soaking rains didn't appear. Besides, a day or two of cooler, rainy weather tended to get the tourists off the beaches and out shopping for souvenirs and, as a result, more business for the Sea Witch. Kate couldn't help smiling to herself. Nothing kept the store out of her thoughts for long; she always came back to it. As a matter of fact, she had even managed to parlay some work into this trip to Provincetown to interview Chris and Ally's musician friends as she also had an appointment with one of the local artists to do some buying for the store.

Kate was turning over prices in her head as she and Chris reached the rotary in Orleans that signaled the end of the Mid -Cape Highway along with Routes 6A and 28. This essentially created a left turn at the Cape's elbow so that one could head north up the forearm, otherwise known as the Outer or Lower Cape. On this stretch of Route 6 the trees thinned out somewhat, replaced by motels and campgrounds, fine restaurants shouldered by lobster shanties and clam bars, as well as souvenir shacks decorated in brightly colored beach toys and flotation devices. The Outer Cape always had a sense of wildness for Kate, untamed and primitive, that the Upper Cape did not possess with its refined, cultured atmosphere on Route 6A or its trashy commercialism along certain sections of Route 28. Here, there was more a feeling of being exposed to the raw, unfiltered elements of wind, sand, and sea pulsing just beneath the surface of human habitation.

Along the way, the taillights of Chris's car always in her sights, Kate's peripheral vision slid over all the familiar landmarks: the Eastham Windmill by the turn to First Encounter Beach, the old-style general stores like the Eastham Superette and Nauset Market. Beaches with picturesque names like Sunken Meadow or Newcomb Hollow beckoned from side roads. Later on, the sign for the Wellfleet Drive-in came into view, still showing first run double features all summer. Kate had also noted the unmistakable sign that guarded the entrance to the Cape Cod National Seashore, a national park sponsored in the early 1960s by John F. Kennedy to preserve the Atlantic coastline from the ever-encroaching developers. Memories rose to mind of the many times she had walked along those beaches in the off-season, seeking the hard-won peace of the open ocean and the rhythmic push and pull of its waves, feeling the salt-laden wind in her hair and the firm sand beneath her feet, an experience the more mellow Nantucket Sound or Cape Cod Bay lacked.

Kate drummed her fingers on the steering wheel to a tune on the radio, laughing a little to herself as she reminisced about her visits to the Outer Cape and its Atlantic beaches. She was feeling good today, a sense of adventure combined with the expectation that the unknown Andi and Tim were going to be able to provide her with some of the answers to her many questions about Ally and, consequently, Glory as well. Kate had always enjoyed Provincetown. In her mind, she pictured the crowded, narrow streets that overflowed with people in the summer and were lined with picturesque houses, inns, and bed and breakfasts. Art galleries. Museums. Intriguing stores of every description. A town dominated by the Pilgrim Monument, a tall granite building built as a memorial to the Pilgrims' initial landing on the Cape that Kate had often thought looked like a lone castle tower overlooking and guarding the town. Once primarily a fishing village founded by Portuguese immigrants, Provincetown had reinvented itself as an artist colony, and then as a haven for the LGBTQ crowd, as well as a center of Cape Cod tourism. It was nothing, Kate told herself, if not unique.

She was approaching the town now, cresting the hill with the vista of sand dunes, beach cottages, and the distant bay briefly laid out before her, then descending to the straight strip of road running between the sand dunes of the Province Lands. A row of identical little white cottages with green shutters could be seen well off to her left, cottages that were the subject of many photographs and paintings sold from the Sea Witch and other stores up and down the Cape. The sea caught in the curve of the Cape's wrist lay just beyond those cottages as well as other brightly hued summerhouses in red, yellow, green, and blue. The picturesque cottages existed in contrast to the numerous gray-shingled homes of varying sizes that also lined the beach road before it all ended at the tip of this easternmost spit of land.

Kate followed Chris's car through the outskirts of the town toward the parking lot they'd agreed to use when they had made the arrangements for this trip. She and Chris had decided to drive up separately in order to allow Kate to get in some business and Chris to take in one of Andi and Tim's shows. Kate had to marvel at Jack Angelino's willingness to spend his day off taking care of his children alone while Chris spent a carefree day in Provincetown. She tried to picture the scene that would have ensued with David if she had made a similar proposition back when Ally was a preschooler and couldn't help but smile ruefully to herself. If anything, David would have seen a day off from work as *his* opportunity to go off and enjoy himself, to go fishing, pay a visit to the shooting range, play a round of golf, or even watch a game in a sports bar with a few friends. Well, maybe things were different now, or maybe Chris was just really lucky. Probably the latter, thought Kate as she pulled into a parking space.

Kate sat across from Chris and Tim Downs and next to Andi Moore at a shaded wooden trestle table overlooking McMillan Wharf. From where she sat Kate could look down the long pier filled with people perusing the sidewalk vendors' wares, walking, bicycling, and just enjoying themselves in the summer sunshine. A group of teenagers in skimpy, brightly colored swimsuits were challenging each other to jump off the side of the pier into the harbor; more than a few were responding to the challenge and taking running leaps from the other side of the pier, shrieking excitedly as they did so. Farther down, Kate could see the masts of both pleasure and fishing boats bobbing side by side, while across from them a few of the boats belonging to the different whale watch cruises sat tied to their moorings, awaiting their next set of passengers. Off in the distance, the Provincetown to Boston ferry could be seen heading out into calm blue waters of Cape Cod Bay.

Kate shifted her gaze to the remnants of fried clam and fish and chip dinners still scattered in front of them as she listened to the trio share stories and reminisce about their past. It was interesting up to a point, but also disconcerting, as Kate realized that what she was hearing tended to confirm much of what had been her worst fears about Ally and her friends. Chris, her short blond hair tousled in the wind, looked the part far more today, dressed in a tight-fitting camisole top, jean cutoffs, and sandals. Her artfully applied makeup and multiple earrings rendered her features far more like those of the teenage Chris Morgan Kate had once known than those of the young wife and mother she had more recently met. In the end, she was relieved when Andi, a sweet, energetic woman with dark hair and eyes and a complexion that Kate thought looked very Mediterranean, looked over at her and with a sympathetic smile said, "I think Kate has probably heard enough about us. She doesn't want to know what we were doing back then. She wants to know about Ally."

"You're right, thanks. I appreciate that," Kate breathed in relief, avoiding Chris's gaze and noting the appraising glance from Tim, a short, powerful-looking man, wearing a sleeveless shirt of some indiscriminate color and worn dark blue shorts, his long, light brown hair tied back in a ponytail, his face obscured by a thick brown beard. Tim leaned forward, his blue eyes holding a warm curious glint, twirling his half-empty beer glass in his fingers, a display of intricately designed tattoos covering both heavily muscled arms. Kate couldn't help thinking he seemed an unlikely match for the charming, slight woman dressed in a clean, unadorned light blue tee shirt and crisp denim shorts sitting next to her.

"What is it you want to know, Kate?" Tim asked, eyes focused intently on hers.

Kate considered this for a moment, realizing there were a good many things she may have thought she wanted to know about what Ally was doing all those years in New York, and that maybe she was better off not knowing. She took a deep breath. "Well, from what I've heard, I know Ally was living in New York for a few years starting when she first left home ten years ago. Chris says that for a while, she was working as a waitress and enjoying the clubs and the music scene, which, I understand, is how she knew both of you. At some point, though, she met someone who introduced her to Yoga, meditation, Eastern religions, maybe?" Kate scanned Andi's and Tim's faces for confirmation, got a slight shrug and nod from Andi, and continued. "I gather she got pretty involved with that and kind of dropped out of the club scene and eventually left New York. What I mostly want to know, I guess, is who this group was, or this person, that she got involved with. And when she left New York, where did she go and with whom?"

Tim shrugged and spread his hands. "The 'group,' " he began, making quotation marks with his fingers, "that she got involved with is easy enough. It's not actually a group but an organization, I guess, called The Center for Yoga, Meditation, and Healing in downtown Manhattan. It's a big place, very well-known. They offer classes in Yoga, meditation, Eastern philosophy, and religion, just about everything you could ask for, if that's what you're into, at every level of knowledge and experience. I don't know who first suggested she should check it out but it could have been anybody. I've known plenty of other people who spent some time there. Anyway, Ally took a lot of classes at the Center. I'm not sure but I think she may have even gotten a part-time job with them. She was really into it, in any case."

Andi, who had been studying Tim with a frown of concentration, looked from him to Kate and added, "I'm not sure if anyone in particular got Ally involved with the Center but she did meet someone there she had a relationship with for a while. I think he was from down South somewhere, nice guy, a bit older than Ally." Andi thought for a moment. "We never really got to know him. She tried bringing him around to the club a few times, but I don't think the club scene was really his thing."

"Who was he? Do you remember his name?" Kate interjected eagerly.

"Yeah, I think so. To the best of my recollection, his name was John McCarthy or maybe McCarty. Something like that. Anyway, I guess he had been working with the Center for a few years before Ally met him."

Chris drained her beer and looked over at Andi, a slightly puzzled look in her eyes. "Wasn't this guy some sort of teacher or mentor to Ally?"

"I'm not sure. Whether he was or not, I do think things may have gotten a little cozier as time went on," Tim answered, glancing away from Kate. "It's hard to say. We didn't see them very often."

"There was actually another guy who was more of a teacher or mentor, I think, to both of them. Remember?" Andi appealed to Tim, who shrugged noncommittally. She turned, looking back in Kate's direction and offered a shrug of her own. "I don't know. I don't really remember myself."

Kate felt her lips twist in an amused smile. "So, anyway, what next? Did Ally leave New York with this John McCarty?"

Andi glanced at Tim briefly, as if for confirmation, before turning back to face Kate. "Well, we thought so, but no one seemed to know. You have to understand, like Tim said, we weren't seeing much of Ally by that time. She almost never came around to the clubs anymore, so we didn't even know she was gone. Actually, it was Chris who called and told us she'd moved out of her apartment. I went by the Center to see if she was there but they told me she and John had quit. No forwarding addresses, apparently, or none they were going to tell me."

Kate caught Chris's see-I-told-you-so glance. She smiled at Tim and Andi. "So that's it, then, I guess. There's nothing else you can tell me?" she said.

Andi smiled back at her with a little shake of her head, seeming to be relishing the moment. "Actually, there is something else. About a year or so later, maybe a little more, I ran into this John McWhatever in a bakery in Manhattan. He remembered seeing me play so we got into a conversation and I asked him if he knew what Ally was up to." She paused for effect, aware that both Chris and Kate were staring at her. A seagull flew overhead, its abrasive call making everyone jump a little.

"Well? What did he say?" asked Chris impatiently.

"He said Ally was out west, in New Mexico, if I remember

correctly. The two of them had moved out there to join some type of group like a religious commune, one that espoused similar principles to what was being taught at the Center, apparently. John had left after a while, said he decided it wasn't for him, but Ally liked it and had chosen to stay on." Another pause accompanied by a shrug of resignation. "That's it, though. We didn't talk long; we both had places to go. I didn't see any reason to press him for any details, anyway."

Kate looked at Andi thoughtfully. "He didn't mention the name of this group?"

"Not that I recall; if he did, I don't remember. Like I said, it was really just a brief conversation."

"And you haven't seen him since?"

"No. If you're wondering if he's living in New York now, I have no idea. But I suppose you could always check out The Center for Yoga, Meditation, and Healing and see if he might be working there again." Andi looked at Kate and offered an encouraging smile.

"Yes, thank you, I will." Kate shifted her weight on the bench, reaching for her purse. "Here, let me get this. I must be going soon but I do appreciate your meeting with me." Murmurs of thanks followed as the three exchanged surprised glances. "One more thing, though, before I go. I've been showing these photos I found in Ally's apartment to everyone." Kate cast an apologetic glance in Chris's direction. "I imagine you've seen this one?" Kate put the New York picture down on the table.

Andi and Tim smiled. "Yeah, I'm the one who took that. I took a bunch of her that day. It was right after she arrived in New York." Tim shook his head, the grin on his face widening as he studied the photo.

Not sure if she wanted to pursue this memory further, Kate quickly replaced the New York photo with that of the pretty woman whose dark eyes seemed to look straight through you. "How about her? Do you know her?"

Tim and Andi exchanged glances. "No," Andi answered for both of them.

"And these?" Kate laid out the photos of the fields without much hope either of them would recognize them.

"No, sorry," Andi replied for a second time.

Tim leaned over for a better view. "I'd be willing to bet that's somewhere in the Southwest, though. Maybe wherever she was staying in New Mexico."

Kate nodded. "Yeah, I think that's a good possibility too." Glancing at her watch, she hastily stuffed the photos back in her bag and stood up. "Well, I've got to go."

Tim regarded Kate with the same look of curiosity as before, now mixed with something like pity. "I hope you find whatever it is you're looking for. We're sorry about Ally, by the way. She was a great girl, smart and a lot of fun to be with."

Kate nodded, struggling with a rush of overwhelming sadness for that lost girl. "Yes, she was. Well, thanks again." She turned and headed hastily toward the cashier, feeling the smart of her tears as they filled her eyes. Swallowing hard, she handed the young woman behind the counter the bill.

"Did you enjoy your meal?" A bright smile beamed at her from under artfully made up eyes and a cascade of blue-tinted hair.

Kate nodded with a half smile of her own, stuffing her change into her purse as she moved out into the sunshine and the throng of people crowding the wharf. "I need to focus," she told herself firmly. "I'll think about Ally and her friends later but first I have work to do."

And Provincetown to enjoy, she reminded herself as she turned onto Commercial Street, a narrow one-way road that was the focal point of the town. Kate stepped up onto one of the narrow brick sidewalks to avoid a car that was attempting to nose its way down the street, pushing pedestrians and cyclists off to the sides of the road, and eventually trailing one of the pedicabs, bicycle-driven passenger vehicles that could ferry one or two people around town for a reasonable fare.

Kate looked around with an inward sigh of pleasure at the familiar and varied sights of the town's commercial and artistic heart.

Tightly packed storefronts offered the usual variety of gifts and clothes, overlaid with a local color that included a slightly raunchy flair, existing side by side with those providing more explicit sexual themes and paraphernalia. Cabarets, musical revues, bookstores, storefront psychics; they all shared that offbeat, off-color appeal. A variety of restaurants crowded in as well, some with menus written in chalk on blackboard easels outside their doors, often featuring seafood dishes as well as some with Portuguese specialties, a nod toward part of Provincetown's cultural heritage. There were Provincetown's signature restaurants as well—the Crown and Anchor, which was also a hotel, the Governor Bradford, and the Lobster Pot. These stood alongside cozy guesthouses and upscale art galleries, at least, the ones not tucked away in little side streets and alleyways. Kate paused in a few of these, scanning paintings of Cape scenes in watercolors and oils, classic prints, crystal ware, and carefully crafted pottery.

Browsing the stores and galleries was delightful, but it was undeniably rivaled by the opportunity to people watch that Provincetown provided. The local gay community was out in full force in the summer, same-sex pairs of men and women of all ages, sizes, and descriptions strolled along together, some hand in hand, clearly enjoying the opportunity to openly express their feelings for each other as much as to simply be themselves. More flamboyant members of the community were also in evidence. Kate stepped aside for one young man roller skating through the crowd decked out in yellow body paint and a flaming orange wig. Another sashayed by in a glittering blue dress and matching blue heels, topped by a black wig and stylish "fascinator" hat. Heterosexual couples, some holding the hands of young children or pushing baby strollers, looked on with amused, or sometimes bewildered, expressions. Others seemed to barely notice. Kate smiled at the sight of one young gay couple, two slightly weary-looking women loaded down with baby paraphernalia who were pushing a double stroller occupied by a pair of identical redheaded toddlers. Both little boys were pointing and calling out demandingly for ice cream as another family passed by licking cones that were dripping in the summer heat.

I remember that only too well, thought Kate, shaking her head ruefully, *and while I would never have believed it to be possible I will be dealing with it again*. Decisively pushing that idea out of her mind for now, Kate noted that she was nearing the Provincetown Town Hall, a wooden building with a tall clock tower painted in cream and green that stood back from the street with an expanse of green lawn out front and the Monument overlooking it from behind. The sidewalk featured shade trees and benches while a small group of musicians were playing to an audience no doubt delighted by the relative coolness of the shade as much as the entertainment. Kate thought with longing of a short break from the afternoon sun under the trees but decided instead on a quick visit to the corner shop that sold the Cape's signature saltwater taffy as well as a wide selection of other freshly made candies. The store was crowded with tourists and Kate had to first fight her way past a cluster of people watching the machines pulling the taffy to the counters loaded with every imaginable flavor of the sticky candy, and then worm her way across the narrow wooden floor to counters displaying an assortment of her favorite treats—big squares of fudge. A few minutes later, she emerged victorious with a bag filled with assorted taffies and rich chocolate fudge.

Back on the street Kate decided that it was best to push on the short distance to her artist's little studio located down a tiny alleyway off Commercial Street. A minute or two later, she made the turn onto the narrow, shell-encrusted path, the crowd noises fading into the background and the close-pressed buildings on either side providing some shelter from the sun's rays. Even better was the cool air wafting off the harbor, Kate thought, feeling it penetrate the cotton of her blouse and dry the perspiration on her skin. She came to a stop under a small swaying sign proclaiming this to be the Olivia Hagan Art Studio.

Kate opened the glass-fronted door to the musical tinkle of bells and walked into a surprisingly large room overflowing with canvases, easels, racks for drying, as well as tables and benches containing an assortment of art supplies. A tall woman of late middle age, her pale blond hair neatly pulled back from her face, approached Kate with arms outflung. "Kate! How wonderful to see you!" The two women embraced, planting light kisses on each other's cheeks.

"It's great to see you too, Olivia." Kate held both her hands, smiling warmly. Olivia Hagan had been among the first artists to sell their work at the Sea Witch and, while the relationship had certainly been profitable for both sides, over the years it had also resulted in a close bond.

"Kate, you look like you need something to drink. Come and have a seat." Olivia gestured Kate over to a round wooden table next to a small kitchenette. Kate sank down gratefully. "What would you like? Iced tea? Lemonade? Mineral water?"

"I'll take the lemonade. If I remember correctly, you make great lemonade."

Olivia laughed, the lines in her tanned face creasing. "I'll get you some."

She set a tall glass of the icy mixture in front of Kate then sat down across from her. "I was so sad to hear about your daughter, Kate. I never did get to fully express my condolences at her funeral." Olivia placed a hand over hers. "How terrible this must have been for you, my dear friend. Is there anything I can do?" Olivia's blue eyes, filled with a mixture of compassion and concern, locked onto Kate's.

Kate smiled reassuringly and gave her hand a gentle squeeze. "Thank you, Olivia. That's very kind of you and I so appreciated that you took the time to come down for her funeral. That alone expressed so much. I'm doing okay. Really."

Olivia laughed gently and shook her head. "Always the strong one! And the little granddaughter? You didn't bring her, I see, but you must the next time you come. What's her name now? I know Jerry told me but..."

"Glory. Glory Allison LaRue."

"A pretty name, I like that. And just a little different."

"Yes, it is." Kate smiled and gave a little shrug of her shoulders. "I don't know where Ally might have come up with that but it does have a nice sound to it." A shadow crossed her face momentarily and was gone but not before Olivia's appraising eye caught it.

She leaned across the table, both hands holding Kate's. "Kate, I know you always hoped to find Ally again or for her to come home. It must be hard now to accept that won't happen, that you will never have the opportunity to ask her why and where and how." Kate pulled back, startled by the turn the conversation had taken. "I may be talking out of turn here but I just wanted to say that I understand what this is like. It's not your fault, Kate. I was here all those years when Ally was growing up and I know you were a good mother to her. She was very young, but nevertheless, she made her own choices and she could have turned back at any time. She left you her little girl with the pretty name, though. She knew you would take good care of her, of Glory. She knew she could trust you to do right by her. If she didn't truly believe you were a good mother, she never would have done that."

Kate stared at Olivia for a moment, at a loss for words. "Well, thank you for saying that." She paused, trying to gather her thoughts. "You're right, of course. It has been hard all these years, wondering where Ally was and if she was okay. I don't know much more now than I did before but I do like to think Ally felt she could entrust Glory to me. And I'm trying to do right by her—and by Ally."

Olivia smiled. "You are, and you will."

Heading back down Route 6 toward home, with the rays of the early evening sun glinting silver and gold across the waters of Cape Cod Bay and the deal with Olivia for some lovely Provincetown land and seascapes finalized, Kate pondered both the information she had obtained from Andi and Tim and her conversation with Olivia. A certain sadness and pain bookended both sides of her day, she realized, but nevertheless, Andi and Tim had given her some hope and direction while Olivia's support and understanding had lifted her spirits.

Kate's turned her thoughts back to what she had learned from Ally's friends. It was more, certainly, than Chris thought she would gain, she thought smugly. Hopefully, this John McCarty was back at The Center for Yoga, Meditation, and Healing and, if so, could tell her just who he and Ally had gone to New Mexico to see. A religious commune, Andi said. Kate sighed. It was so hard to imagine her rebellious, irreverent daughter as part of any religious group. What had been the big attraction that kept her there even when this John guy, someone she supposedly had a relationship with, decided to leave? New York seemed so much more her style than New Mexico. And then there was the big question: Was John Glory's father? Kate contemplated this but decided probably not. No, the most likely answer to this question was she had met some new man from this group, a man with whom she was having a child, until, Kate surmised, at some point something went wrong. But why go to San Francisco? Why not back to New York where she had friends to help her? No one had said anything about Ally calling them for money. Not that they probably had much. *Ah, well*, Kate thought, *my next problem is figuring out how to go about finding this John McCarty and getting him to talk to me*.

CHAPTER 20

The sun was sinking just below the horizon, lacing the soft fluffy clouds in pink and orange, when Kate arrived home to find that Glory, exhausted by an afternoon on the playground and at the beach, had eaten an early dinner and was fast asleep in her trundle bed, a halo of dark brown hair all that could be seen of the child from under the blanket. Once Jen had given her enthusiastic report of the day's activities and headed for home, Kate was left to contemplate her evening. *A light dinner and an early bedtime sounds good to me too,* Kate thought, realizing that the day had been draining, given the long drive to Provincetown and back and the tension and stress of dealing with Ally's unknown past. Kate was considering warming up some leftovers from last night's dinner when the silence was broken by the sudden ringing of the telephone. She looked up in mild irritation, then started in surprise at the identifying name and number on the screen.

"Maggie? This is a surprise! How are you?" Kate's mind raced, wondering what would prompt her sister to call, and then realized, of course...Ally. Maggie had sent those flowers to the funeral, along with a note that had suggested she'd call soon, but Kate had forgotten with all she had been dealing with lately. Maggie lived in New Jersey with her husband of the last thirty years, Bill, a high-priced corporate lawyer. Their three children were grown, the youngest still in college, the older two out on their own. As a child, Kate had idolized her older sister. Both smart and attractive with a lean athlete's body, honey-colored hair, and large hazel eyes, Kate had always thought of her as the antithesis of herself, with her shorter, chunkier frame, dark hair and eyes, and what she perceived as her greater struggles to achieve.

Maggie had met her husband while in college and married shortly after graduation, retiring to the suburbs to raise children and be the epitome of the successful wife and mother, the precise area in which Kate felt she had failed most spectacularly. Maggie had tried to be supportive of Kate throughout the years in which her marriage was failing and Ally was at her most difficult. However, after Ally disappeared, Kate couldn't deal with the well-meaning advice and sympathy any longer, and after a few high-intensity arguments, Maggie had retreated to her comfortable and, apparently, happy life, their ongoing contact primarily through birthday and Christmas cards and the rare phone call.

"I'm fine, Kate. We're all fine. I just wanted to call and tell you how sorry I am about Ally. I wish I could have managed to get to the Cape for the funeral, but Beth had gone into labor early, and I couldn't leave her."

"I understand, Maggie. Please don't worry about it." Kate tried to remember if this was Maggie's second or third grandchild that her daughter Beth was expecting. Beth, if Kate remembered correctly, had married pretty much right out of high school to the only son of a prosperous local businessman who was poised to take over his father's company when he retired. *The great American success story, that was Maggie's family*, thought Kate resignedly. *You couldn't make this stuff up if you tried.* "Is Beth okay?"

"Oh yes. The doctor has everything under control, and she's home now, on bed rest. I'd have still come up to see you, but I've been helping out some with Nathan. He's her first, you know, only just turned two."

"Yes, of course, I remember." *So only the one,* Kate thought, *since Bill Jr., Maggie's oldest child, was not yet married, unless there's something I've missed.*

"So what happened, Kate? This is an awful shock. Did Ally come home? Your message was so brief, I have no idea."

The last comment roused feelings of guilt as Kate had indeed left only a short, late message for Maggie, relieved at the time that she had avoided this very conversation. Kate took a deep breath and, wearily, launched into the story beginning with the phone call from San Francisco and finishing, to her own surprise, with the day's visit to Provincetown, especially since she hadn't planned on telling Maggie any more than the basics of Ally's brief reappearance and sudden death. Maggie listened silently until the end with only a gasp of "Oh, Kate" when she related how she came to learn of Glory's existence.

"So what are you going to do now, Kate?" Maggie voice was quiet with a touch of resolve that made Kate think she probably was about to offer her own suggestions on what to do.

"I guess I'll have to get in touch with the Yoga center in New York and see if this John McCarty is there, and if he'll talk to me. See if I can find out more about this group they joined out in New Mexico."

"Hmm. Okay, but, Kate, I really think you should be careful about this. It may very well be that Ally did want to get away from someone, possibly Glory's father. Are you sure you want to find him? If this person was her father, he could take Glory away from you, you know, and if he was abusive—"

"Believe me, I've thought about that possibility. I'm well aware that if I found her father, he could take her away, and I might never see her again. Nevertheless, I feel Glory's father should know where she is, that he has a right to be a part of her life if he wants to be. And I don't *know* that he was abusive or that Ally was trying to get away him. I don't know why Ally did what she did. I just don't think I should take anything for granted. I think both Glory and I will be better off knowing the truth instead of hiding from it."

"Well, maybe. I mean, in principle, that's true. But there's something about all this that doesn't sound right, Kate."

"Yes, I know what you mean, but there's no other way to find out the truth. Anyway, I just think this is what Ally would want me to do." Kate tried to keep from sounding overly stubborn, not wanting Maggie to feel a need to remonstrate with her difficult little sister.

"Okay. Well, as I said, I understand your point, but I still want to remind you that sometimes the truth is better off hidden." Kate could almost see Maggie shaking her head in frustration. "Look, Kate," Maggie added impulsively, "if you're going to come to New York, you and Glory should stay with us. I'd like to meet my grandniece. And it would be good to see you again. I know Bill won't mind."

For a moment, Kate was too startled to reply. It hadn't occurred to her that Maggie was within easy commute to New York. "Um, thanks, Maggie, that's very nice of you. I'm not sure exactly what I'll do, but I'll think about it. Thanks."

"Come anyway, Kate. I'd come there, but Beth really does need me right now."

"I know. You're where you should be, Maggie. We'll get together sometime soon. Really. I've got to go now. It's late, and I haven't had dinner yet. I'll call, though, I promise, and let you know."

After they had said their good-byes, and Kate had taken out the container of stew and warmed it up in her new microwave oven, she sat at the table with her dinner in front of her and let it slowly grow cold as she ruminated over the phone call and her memories of her sister and growing up together in the Boston suburbs. Margaret and Katherine. Two good, Irish Catholic names for two Irish Catholic girls, like those of many of the girls they knew in their largely Catholic neighborhood. It had been a happy childhood for the most part and having just one sister, unlike most of her friends who came from larger families, had its advantages. Maggie, two years older, had been her mentor and her pal, the big sister who tried things out first, and then guided Kate through the pitfalls. Which was not to say they didn't fight from time to time as Maggie sometimes lost patience with Kate's tendency to follow her wherever she went, something Maggie found especially trying once she developed an interest in the opposite sex. Since there was enough money for whatever they needed and a few luxuries besides, like a summer home in Yarmouth, there was also less they had to share.

It was all rosy until the winter their father died of a heart attack, the first winter Maggie was away at college and while Kate was still in high school. Even then, they were still financially solvent, thanks to good planning and careful investment by their father, but life would never feel so secure and protected again. Kate had always been convinced that Maggie had decided to give up any idea of an independent life after that and just find someone who could take care of her the way Daddy had. This theory was met with considerable scorn from her sister when she broached it one night shortly after she and David had separated, and Maggie, full of advice and remonstration, had come by to visit. In time, Kate herself had come to realize how much her attraction to David LaRue was grounded in the loss of father. David had always seemed such a strong person, someone who knew all the answers and could provide the guidance and direction Kate lost when her father died and Maggie left.

Kate toyed with her fork, pushing the meat around the plate as she remembered those years in high school home alone with her own mother. They had not been especially close, and Kate had long believed that Maggie had been her mother's favorite, anyway, but it was nothing like her own years alone with Ally. Kate smiled at the thought. She had been much too afraid of her mother, too much the good Catholic schoolgirl for that. Nevertheless, Kate would always be eternally grateful to her mother for her acceptance of the divorce from David and for her subsequent help both in acquiring the Sea Witch and buying out Maggie's share in the Cape house. That was without mentioning helping in every way possible to get through the business courses in the local community college and, later, the University of Massachusetts. It was hard for Kate to imagine what her life would have been like otherwise. In some ways, her mother's death from a fast-growing cancer when Ally was in her early teens was even more traumatic than her father's death a quarter century before. Kate was just grateful that Mom hadn't lived to see what had happened between herself and Ally or her granddaughter's premature death and illegitimate child.

Illegitimate. Yes, that is how Mom would have seen it Kate told herself as she picked up the plate of uneaten stew and, taking it to the sink, sent its contents down the garbage disposal. Then again, she mused as the last of her dinner disappeared into the drain's black hole, Mom always did come through for me, didn't she? Why would this be any different? She would have understood, loved her little great-granddaughter no matter what the circumstances. Kate sent up a silent prayer. *I just wish you were here, Mom. Tell me what I should do.*

CHAPTER 21

Main Street in Hyannis is certainly the place to be this morning, thought Kate as she and Glory wove their way through the crowds of people enjoying one of the village's street fairs. This had long been the shopping center of the Cape, or at least until the Cape Cod Mall had been built, a street lined with one-story shops that sold clothing, shoes, gifts, books, and novelties. Restaurants were interspersed with the stores, as were a number of churches with signs encouraging people to come in to pray and to hear the Word of the Lord. Hyannis lacked some of the quaintness and charm of the other town centers, but it had its appeal, particularly today, Kate thought. The stores had many of their wares out on the sidewalks, artists offered caricatures or face painting while street musicians played only a few feet away. Children carried balloons and cotton candy, clinging to their parents with sticky hands.

In the little park just up ahead, Kate spied the merry-go-round surrounded by groups of eager children, the calliope music barely audible over their shrieks and laughter. She paused, glancing at her watch. She and Glory were due to see Dr. Lawler soon, but Kate told herself, we should have enough time for at least one ride. She leaned down, looking into Glory's dark brown eyes, round as silver dollars.

"Would you like to ride the merry-go-round, honey? Remember when you and Mama went to beach? I bet they had one there." Kate lightly touched the locket around Glory's neck as her fingers came up to grasp it. "See it over there?" The little girl's eyes followed her grandmother's finger. She watched for a moment and looked up with a tentative smile. "Come on, I''ll go on with you. It'll be fun." Kate threaded her way through the cluster of children and parents to the ticket booth and, once the tickets were firmly in hand, joined the line waiting their turn. Kate lifted Glory up into her arms so that she could see the flying horses better and, feeling the warmth of the child's skin against hers, reached up to push her damp hair back from her face and plant a light kiss on her cheek. *She's hot,* Kate mused. *Well, one ride, and then we'll be at Dr. Lawler's where we'll have air-conditioning.*

As they watched, the ride slowed to a stop, one group of children scrambling to get off, others to get on. Kate guided Glory through the crowd and lifted her onto a handsome black horse with a brightly colored saddle. As soon as the seat belt was fastened, the music began again and Kate wrapped her arms around Glory. "I'm right here sweetheart," Kate murmured in her ear. But Kate needn't have been concerned because Glory rode like a carousel pro, her small hands clutching the silver pole, delighted giggles bubbling up from her throat, tendrils of dark hair lifted by the flowing air. Feeling the cooling breeze on her own face Kate listened to her granddaughter, thinking how much she enjoyed hearing that happy sound, and realizing too how much Glory sounded like another long ago little girl whose small body Kate had once held on a merry-go-round's flying horse.

Kate sat on one end of a long leather sofa in Dr. Lawler's spacious waiting room, her laptop computer on her knees. Nothing like a well equipped, modern waiting area she thought to herself, especially one that came with a wireless Internet connection for waiting parents or, in her own case, grandparents. The air-conditioning, she told herself, goes without mentioning. Glory had departed with Dr. Lawler to the playroom/office with relatively little resistance, buoyed by reassurances that Grandma would be nearby if needed, as well as the pleasurable aftereffects of her carousel ride.

Once Glory had disappeared from sight, Kate logged on and ran a quick Google search for The Center for Yoga, Meditation, and Healing in Manhattan. Within seconds, she was viewing a colorful home page extolling the virtues of Yoga and meditation and its beneficial effects for mind and body. The site included numerous pictures of the facility and its location, and featured students and instructors in any number of yoga positions with relaxed, peaceful expressions on their faces. Kate found a faculty list and ran a quick search for John McCarty that came up blank as did a run through with similar names, just in case Andi's memory had been further off than she realized. Well, the chances were it wouldn't be that easy, she told herself philosophically. Kate noted the address and phone number, as well as the hours of operation, and considered whether she wanted to send an e-mail but in the end decided not to, thinking it unlikely that anyone would give her the kind of information she was hoping for that readily. Kate studied the photographs more closely, wondering how old they were and if any might include Ally, but, not surprisingly, that drew a blank as well.

Kate drummed her fingers on the edge of the computer considering what to do next. After a moment's consideration, she tried another search typing in "religious communes" and "New Mexico." An array of possibilities greeted her and with some determination, Kate began checking through the sites. She soon realized religious communes were actually more common than she would have thought in New Mexico. The 1960s and '70s had been the high point for these, not surprisingly; however, there were a few left over that were still functioning, as well as some newer groups trying to gain a foothold. Kate disregarded those that appeared too far removed in philosophy from the Eastern-influenced Center for Yoga, Meditation and Healing in New York, and focused on one or two that had some promise. As she was perusing one interesting possibility, the familiar musical notes of her cell phone sounded from the depths of her purse. She took a quick glance at the screen and saw the Sea Witch's number.

"Hey, there," Jerry's voice sounded cheerfully in her ear.

"Hey, yourself. What's up? Everything okay?" Kate cradled the phone against her shoulder, eyes still on a Web page featuring a commune in New Mexico with an Eastern-sounding orientation.

"Everything's fine. We've already got that order from P-town you arranged the other day. Olivia's paintings are just magnificent. When do you think you'll be in?"

"We should be done here soon." Kate glanced at the clock and realized Glory had already been in with Dr. Lawler for about forty minutes. "Figure a half hour to an hour, tops. I'm bringing Glory today because Jen has some prior commitments and can't babysit. By the way, have I thanked you and Kevin enough for suggesting her as a child care provider?"

Jerry laughed. "Yes, Kate, more than enough."

As soon as the good byes were said and the cell phone safely tucked away back in her purse, Kate saw Dr. Lawler approaching from the hallway.

"You can come in, if you like. We are just finishing up."

Kate closed her computer, remembering to save the page she had been investigating. "How did it go today, Dr. Lawler?" Kate looked up anxiously as she gathered her belongings together.

"Quite well. Glory seemed to relax and enjoy herself fairly quickly. She engaged in some nice play with the dollhouse and the farm sets. Interestingly, I also noticed her moving her lips at times while she was playing, at least until she realized that I had seen her, and then she stopped."

"Really? Could you understand what she was saying?"

"No, it was more subtle than that. But I feel confident that Glory is capable of speech, and that she has an inner dialogue going. Remember, we're still at the assessment stage of therapy. I'm not attempting any intervention just yet. Perhaps next week I'll introduce the dolls and puppets I use in therapy and see what she thinks of them."

Computer and purse in hand, Kate followed Dr. Lawler back down the hall to where Glory stood at a table covered with a roadway map, driving a schoolbus filled with wooden figures of children and adults around the streets. Dr. Lawler and Kate both paused in the doorway, listening to Glory's soft, unintelligible humming as the bus veered precipitously around the curves, teetering on the edges of the table. After a couple of close calls, the bus hit a wooden bridge and came to a stop, tumbling its passengers out onto the road. Glory was regrouping them in orderly lines under the gaze of one of the adult male figures when she caught sight of her grandmother and ran to her, arms extended. Kate picked her up awkwardly, trying to balance her purse and computer, and gave her a kiss. Glory buried her head on Kate's shoulder, giving Dr. Lawler a sideways glance from under a stray lock of hair.

The psychologist leaned over to smile at Glory as Kate set the child on her feet and took hold of her hand. "I'll see you next week, my friend." She straightened and exchanged good-byes with Kate, watching thoughtfully as Kate bundled Glory out the door to the waiting car and the ride to the Sea Witch.

Kate and Jerry gazed admiringly at the Provincetown paintings he had unloaded from their crates earlier in the day. She thought they looked even better today here in her store than they had in Olivia's studio in Provincetown.

"As always, you have a great eye for this stuff, my friend," Jerry commented, shaking his head in amazement.

"Thank you, I appreciate the compliment." Kate glanced around her, noting a couple of customers poring over some prints of the National Seashore and a few more looking at some pretty pieces of cranberry glass arrayed near one of the windows. Captain Ahab looked in their direction, suddenly calling out, "Pretty things, see the pretty things." Several customers turned around startled, then laughed. Kate smiled indulgently. "How were sales today?"

"Not bad. We could use a few not-so-good-beach-days, though."

Kate nodded, well aware that the lovely weather was likely keeping away some potential buyers. She sighed. "Come on in the office, Jerry. Let me update you on a few things while I check on Glory."

"Uh-oh. I sense another trip coming."

Kate looked back at him as they walked single file down the connecting hall and smiled apologetically. "Yes, I probably have to go to New York for a few days. No big rush, really, but I have a lead on someone and someplace Ally was associated with while she was living there."

"Is this something you learned from the musician friends up in P-town?"

"That's right."

"Okay, a few more days shouldn't be a problem. Just let me know when you plan to go so I can make the necessary arrangements."

"Jerry, you lived in New York for a while, didn't you?"

"Yes, but that was quite a long way back. Why do you ask?"

"Any chance you were familiar with The Center for Yoga, Meditation and Healing?" Kate and Jerry were at the door to the office where Glory could easily be seen kneeling on her chair at the table coloring pictures in an activity book, a sea of crayons spread out in front of her, seemingly oblivious to their presence.

Jerry brought his eyebrows together in a frown. "In Manhattan, right?" Kate nodded in surprise. "I've heard of it. Very well known, very popular with those interested in that sort of thing. It has a good reputation. Why? Was Ally hanging out there?"

"It would seem so. She met someone there, a man named John McCarty who she then went to New Mexico with."

Jerry glanced over at Glory. She had finished one picture and quickly moved on the next, her crayon pressed hard against the page.

"Do you think he might be..." Jerry lifted his chin in Glory's direction.

Kate shrugged helplessly. "I don't know. It's possible, of course." She gave Glory a sideways glance before turning her gaze back to Jerry. She paused, biting her lip. "You know what? I'm really starting to wonder if I should do this. Everyone I've talked to has told me not to. I love her, Jerry. She's my granddaughter. I don't want to lose her like I lost Ally; I don't want to go through that again. But it just seems wrong somehow to not even try..." Kate's voice trailed off.

Jerry looked at her, searching for something to say. "Kate, I don't know what you should do. I will tell you this, though. You'll do the right thing when the time comes. I know you, and I know you have good judgment, Kate." Jerry's expression became thoughtful. "It's possible Kevin might still have some connections at the Center. I'll ask him. I think he took a class or two or knew someone who did. Years ago, though, so don't get your hopes up too much."

CHAPTER 22

The wind was whispering through the pine trees, their branches outlined in black against the faded peach-colored light that still illuminated the evening sky, when Kate brought her wine and a light snack of sweet cheeses and crisp, salty crackers to the porch. Stretching tired muscles, she relaxed into the comforting warmth of the night air and her favorite rocking chair. Kate hadn't much time for this soothing ritual the last few days and she couldn't help thinking guiltily that she should be doing something more constructive, even if it was just continuing her Internet research into possible communes or other groups Ally could have been living in out in New Mexico. Sipping her wine, one ear cocked for any sounds to indicate Glory was awake and out of bed, she reminded herself of the need for relaxation, for calming rituals such as her summer evenings on her porch.

She smiled to herself, picturing Glory asleep in her bed, one hand still clutching the locket with the photograph of her and Ally, her small face serene and peaceful. She was really a pretty good sleeper, thought Kate gratefully, one who engaged in the bedtime routine of bathing and getting into her pajamas without protest and who inevitably drifted off to sleep before Kate could finish a second bedtime story. Actually, so was Ally at this age Kate reminded herself. It wasn't until later that bedtime became a battle, when she was too old for stories and wanted to stay up and watch TV. And could never seem to get her homework done in a reasonable time frame. Kate sighed, telling herself not to waste time worrying too much about what life was going to be like five, ten years down the road, when Glory was nine or ten. Or fifteen. And she was, what, sixty or more?

Feeling her blood pressure rise and fighting an impending sense of panic, Kate closed her eyes and focused her mind on her breathing. After a few minutes, she could feel herself relax again as the breeze picked up, bringing the scent of the ocean. Kate visualized the waves breaking on the beach, creamy foam illuminated in the moonlight, the dark water reflecting stars. She was imagining herself walking down to the water's edge and picking up seashells and pebbles that sparkled in the cool light when the images were chased away by the abrupt ringing of the house phone.

"I don't think I've had as many phone calls in the last six months as I've had in the last six weeks," Kate mumbled as she pushed herself out of the rocking chair, hastily picking up the living-room phone before the ringing could wake Glory. Once again, she felt a wave of surprise and astonishment at the sight of the caller's name.

"David?" she offered, the doubt in her voice audible.

"Hello, Kate. Yes, it's me."

Yes, it certainly is, thought Kate, hearing that thread of impatient irritation, unchanged over the years.

"What a pleasant surprise," she tried to sound cheerful but could tell it came across forced. "How are you?"

"I'm fine. Yourself?"

"I'm fine too. Um, so, is there something I can help with? Any particular reason why you're calling?" Kate cursed silently, wishing she could have phrased that better.

David paused for a few beats. "No, not exactly. Well, actually, I guess there is. I was...concerned about you and, um, Glory. Wondered how things were going." Another awkward pause.

"Well, we're doing okay." It was Kate's turn to hesitate, surprised. *How much does he really want to know? And what do I want to tell him* she thought. Finally, feeling a little desperate, Kate added, "Do you want to see her?"

Another few seconds of silence that suddenly made Kate think of long-distance calls bouncing off satellites, resulting in a brief delay in transmission. Except that David was less than an hour away in Plymouth. "Maybe later. Actually, I want to see you, if you don't mind."

"Me?" Kate knew David could hear both the alarm and the astonishment conveyed in that one word.

"Yes, you," responded David, the irritation back in his voice. "Do you think you could meet me for lunch? Coffee?"

"I suppose so, but why?"

"Oh, for God's sake, Kate. I just want to talk. I've been thinking a lot about Ally lately. Is that really such a surprise? And by extension, you and my...granddaughter."

"Okay, well, that's great, David. We can talk. What did you have in mind?" After a few more minutes of discussion, they settled on lunch in a small seafood restaurant overlooking the harbor in Plymouth, pending childcare arrangements. Kate hung up the phone and walked slowly back out onto the porch, considering this unexpected turn of events as she looked up at the night sky, watching the pinpoint light of the stars appearing and disappearing behind swiftly moving black clouds.

"What does he want, do you suppose?" Kate asked the black bowl of the sky above her. She let the silence stretch out but the stars only winked at her, the quiet of the night uninterrupted. "Well, after all this time," she mused, "and all that passed between us, I don't know if we can have any working relationship at all, especially over something as important as this."

Still gazing upward, Kate addressed the silent sky once more. "I have to admit I was wrong about at least one thing, though, because I never expected him to call."

The air was heavy with moisture as Kate crossed the Sagamore Bridge into Bourne, the canal far below gray and choppy under the overcast sky, the pavement slick from the light misty rain that had fallen the night before. *Far less than what we really need*, thought Kate, but the shift in weather had at least brought a slight uptick in business over the last few days. Glancing in the rearview mirror, Kate could see Glory lean forward, straining against the shoulder harness of her car seat as she craned her neck to get a better view of the bridge and the canal below.

"Do you remember coming across the bridge before, honey, that time we went to visit Chris?" Kate called back to her. Glory's eyes met hers for a moment, enough to make Kate feel certain that Glory indeed remembered that earlier trip. "Well, I think you'll have fun with Chris. And with...Mark and Gina." Kate had to reflect for a moment to bring to mind the names of Chris's two children. Between sips of her latte, Kate kept up a patter of conversation, listing what she could recall of the toys, games, and DVDs Chris's family possessed and the good times to be had with all of them as they descended the bridge and turned onto the stretch of Route 6 that ran parallel to the canal.

Ten minutes later they were pulling into the driveway next to Chris and Jack Angelino's converted summer cottage. As soon as the car rolled to a stop, Chris's two preschoolers came running down the front steps, banging the door of the screened-in front porch behind them, closely followed by a slender young man of average height and build, clad in jeans and a tee shirt, his light brown hair looking sun bleached, dark blue eyes standing out in his tanned face. Grabbing the small hands of his two youngsters in each of his, he smiled and nodded in Kate's direction. "You must be Mrs. LaRue, and you, of course, must be Glory." He bent down to smile at Glory in her car seat, then straightened up and smiled again at Kate. "I'm Jack Angelino, Chris's husband."

"A pleasure to meet you." Kate took him in, noting the dirt-smudged clothes, paint flecks spattered across his tennis shoes.

"Doing some work around the house today," he offered, following her gaze. "Chris is out at the moment, picking up a few things at the supermarket. She'll be right back. Come on in." Once Glory was liberated from the car, the two of them followed Jack across the unkempt front yard, picking their way around tricycles and toys with little Mark and Gina leading the way.

"Have a seat." Jack gestured broadly around the house once they were inside. Kate hesitated. She was anxious to get back on the road for this lunch with David but, at the same time, she knew she couldn't just drop Glory off here. Better to wait for Chris anyway. There was no telling how this was going to work out and for the thousandth time she found herself wishing Jen had been available to stay with Glory today. In the living room a wide-screen TV featured an animated children's movie and several toys were scattered across the well-worn carpet. Thinking Glory might find the more passive activity of watching TV easier to handle, Kate settled herself resignedly on the sofa as Glory, predictably, climbed up next to her, leaning her head against Kate's arm. Jack had vanished into the kitchen, but Mark and Gina remained in the living room and now regarded their younger visitor with curious eyes.

"Glory's shy," Kate explained. "You'll have to give her some time to get used to being here again."

At that, Gina turned and trotted off into the kitchen but Mark came over to the sofa and reached for Glory's hand. "We made cookies for you in the kitchen," he said in a voice meant to convey the irresistible appeal of these culinary masterpieces. "Come on, you want to have some." With one meaningful look back at Kate, Glory slid off the sofa and allowed Mark to tug her along into the next room. Kate followed, feeling a flicker of hope that this might work after all.

Back on Route 3, heading north in the direction of Plymouth, Kate smiled to herself as she reflected on the sight of Glory sitting at Chris's kitchen table with the two other children and their father, warm chocolate smeared across her face and a look of blissful delight in her brown eyes as she savored her cookies. It was a sight Chris had shaken her head over with an annoyed "for God's sake, Jack" when she returned home soon after with a shopping bag full of food intended for their lunch. In the end, Chris had shooed Kate off with reassurances that she would call if there were any significant problems and, anyway, Glory had seemed content enough once an afternoon playing on the swings in the backyard had been promised.

Pushing Glory out of her mind, Kate returned to mulling over David's unexpected request to meet with her. Until she had been forced to call after Ally's death, it had been years since she'd even spoken to him. Her last meetings with him had been screaming matches in which they'd blamed each other for Ally's disappearance. Before that, they'd fought over child support payments, visitation, and who was to blame for Ally's attitude and behavior, all of which was nothing compared to the divorce and the fights that led up to it. It was enough that the very idea of meeting with David made Kate want to run for the Alka-Seltzer—or a stiff drink. Of course, she had to acknowledge that he probably felt the same way about her.

It was hard to remember now but she had really loved David once. Kate let her mind wander through an assortment of memories. Going on dates to the movies or out to dinner, occasionally dancing. Playing miniature golf together in the summer after a day at the beach. They had both loved the Cape, swimming in the Sound, sailboating, kayaking. Kate chuckled as she thought about the first time she watched him race motorcycles in New Hampshire, so very young and in love, worried he'd get hurt but feeling the thrill of living on the edge, even if just a little bit. And afterward, the passionate lovemaking in the cheap little motel room they'd rented, an intense arousal fueled by heat, excitement, and testosterone. It was when life got so serious that it all fell apart. She and David did far better with the thrill of a secret tryst, a stolen night together, than the mundane daily grind of work, domesticity, and childcare. Kate shook herself out of her reverie, suddenly realizing that cars behind her were honking at her because the light had changed.

"I'm almost there anyway; time to leave that behind and return to the present," Kate told herself sternly as she wound along a street thronged with tourists there to see Plymouth Rock and the *Mayflower II*. "What I need to be concentrating on is finding a parking space." Just ahead someone pulled out of a space in a long row of metered parking spaces, and Kate was able to quickly slide her little Toyota into the spot, beating out a harried-looking father with a car crammed with kids. Kate could feel the sun beat down on her uncovered head as it broke through the clouds, adding another dimension of heat to an already hot and sticky day. Sprinting across the road in an effort to avoid being mowed down by some overeager sightseer, Kate caught sight of David standing by the door of the restaurant, inhaling deeply on a cigarette held to his mouth.

"Oh, my," Kate murmured softly. "I thought he gave that up years ago." David quickly discarded the cigarette once he saw her approach and pushed his hands into the pockets of his lightweight, tan pants, focusing his gaze on the horizon.

"Hi, David, I know I'm a little late but Glory..." Kate let loose an anxious stream of words as she reached him but to her relief he brushed her intended apology aside with an "It's fine, Kate, let's just get some lunch." Once inside the small and comfortably cool restaurant, Kate was grateful to see it was largely empty, allowing them to be seated immediately. A pleasant young woman in jeans and a tight-fitting T-shirt approached, announced her name to be Sally, and offered them menus and took drink orders. Kate and David studied their menus silently, relieved of the need for further awkward conversation. Nevertheless, once their orders had been placed and their waitress had departed with a cheery "thank you," Kate and David were left staring at each other across the expanse of the table.

"Sooo, David..." Kate began and then ended, searching fruitlessly for something meaningful to say.

"Look, Kate, this is difficult for both of us. Why don't we just dispense with any small talk and get right to the heart of the matter. You could start by telling me what exactly happened out there in San Francisco. I'm sorry I cut you off the night you called, but Ally was my daughter too. I think have a right to know whatever you know."

Kate looked at him with some compassion, noting the sadness and pain beneath the determined gaze. With difficulty, she swallowed the tart reply that rose to her lips, reminding herself that she needed whatever support he was willing to provide. *Don't blow this* she mentally scolded herself.

"Yes, David, I guess you do have a right to know." Kate paused, pulling her thoughts together and once again launched into the tale, beginning with the call from San Francisco General Hospital. David was a far less attentive listener than Maggie had been a few nights earlier, breaking into her narrative with frequent questions, many of which she could not adequately answer. Even so, it was when the conversation turned to the more current situation that tension became significantly heightened.

"Exactly what is this Dr. Lawler, a child psychologist if I understood you correctly, doing to help Glory start to talk?" David queried, a frown forming on his features. "Wouldn't something like speech therapy be more appropriate?"

"The doctors who saw her in San Francisco as well as Dr. Lawler think this is a psychological problem of some sort, not a problem with her ability to speak. If she needs speech therapy once we get her talking, then we'll do that, but first we need to find out why she doesn't want to speak." Kate cast about for something else to say, knowing that this answer was not going to be satisfactory for him.

"And you're telling me the way to do that is to *play* with her?" David replied, a note of sarcasm slipping into his voice. "Hell, Kate, you could do that. How much is this play doctor costing you anyway?"

"All right, David, that's enough," Kate responded, her voice firm. "Whatever you may think of the idea of play therapy, please keep in mind I'm not asking you to foot the bill. It's an accepted form of psychotherapy for children and Dr. Lawler is a respected child psychologist and not some crank."

David leaned back in his chair raising his hands in surrender. "Okay, fine, you're right. It *is* your money, do what you want. I'm sure it can't hurt, anyway."

"Here we go." Kate and David both started slightly as Sally set down plates of steamed clams in front of each of them. "Is there anything else I can get you?" she beamed. David shook his head, quickly waving her off. She gave them a practiced smile and assurance that she'd be back to check on them later.

“Do you have any idea what this problem Glory has might be?” David looked up from the clamshell he was opening to study Kate’s face.

“Well,” Kate paused, slipping a clam into her mouth as she considered her answer, “I think she had a traumatic experience at some point, maybe while she and Ally were in New Mexico with this religious commune Ally was involved with.”

David looked up at her, his face lined with suspicion. “Yeah, what’s that all about anyway? Are you really saying you think Ally was involved with some type of cult? Our daughter? You can’t be serious.”

“I told you, I met with these friends of hers—”

“Who are likely to be addicts or worse—”

“David, they knew her; she lived with them for a while, they kept in touch, at least until she left New York. They knew she was interested in Yoga and meditation.”

“I don’t think there are any Yoga cults out in New Mexico, Kate.”

Kate sat back in her chair, weighing the sarcasm in his voice. They looked at each other for a long minute before Kate answered in measured tones. “I don’t know enough about this group to say exactly what their belief systems were. There’s no reason to think that she didn’t go to New Mexico at some point. After all she ended up in California. Her friend Chris isn’t a drug addict, by the way. She’s married with a couple of kids. She has a degree in early childhood education from the 4-Cs and wants to have her own preschool some day. Glory likes her. As a matter of fact, she’s there now, eating home baked chocolate chip cookies and playing on their swing set.”

David put his fork down, regarding Kate coolly. “You’re letting *Chris Morgan* babysit our granddaughter?”

“Yes, weren’t you listening? She isn’t eighteen anymore. She’s a responsible mother with a husband who is a good father to their two children.”

“And you know this because?” David’s voice rose, loud enough that Sally cast an uneasy look their way.

"Lower your voice, David." Kate leaned across the table, lightly touching his hand. "I've been in her house, I've talked with her, watched her with her own children and with Glory. I've also met her husband and observed *him* with the children. If you're really that concerned, you can meet them yourself but I think you have to trust my judgment here."

David pulled back, an emotion Kate could not identify passing over his face. "I just hope you're right about her." He looked down at his plate, spending some time opening another clamshell, spearing the clam with his fork, and then slowly eating it. "So you're going to follow up with this Yoga place in New York?"

"Yes, I think that's my best hope to find out where she went and who she went there with." Kate paused. "I'm also hoping to find out who Glory's father is. It seems like the right thing to do but not everyone agrees with me."

David looked back up at her. "It seems the right thing to do to me. If this were my child, I'd want to know what happened to her. Why shouldn't he know where she is?"

"Because he may have been abusing Ally or Glory or both of them. Maybe that's why she ended up in San Francisco alone with Glory."

David pointed to Kate with his fork. "Is *that* what you think?"

"I don't know what to think. Maybe."

Sally suddenly materialized at their table, ready to collect their dishes. "Are we ready for some dessert?"

"No, we're fine. Just the check," David said as Sally scooped up the plates and left with a "Sure thing!" tossed over her shoulder. David turned back to Kate. "Look, I need to get back but...I would like to see Glory sometime. I just don't know when or how to make that work. Besides, I don't know how to talk to a little kid who's shy or scared and can't or won't talk back."

Kate looked surprised. "Okay, well, I'm sure we can think of something and don't worry about connecting with Glory. She...You just need a little time, that's all." Kate quickly collected herself. "Oh, by the way, before you go, David, there's something I want you to have." She rummaged in her purse until she came up with an envelope containing the two photographs of Ally. She handed the Santa Cruz picture to David first and watched his expression as he held it, staring at the young woman who had been his daughter, looking so much the same and yet so different, a panolopy of emotions flitting across his face. Then Kate placed the second photograph on the table in front of him, watching as he picked it up and looked at the teenage Ally standing on the streets of New York. "Sometimes I look at that one when I'm feeling particularly sad and I want to remind myself just how difficult Ally could be."

David continued to look at it for a moment a slight smile on his lips. He pocketed both pictures with a sincere "Thank you, Kate. I really appreciate that."

At least, thought Kate later as she headed back toward Bourne, *David did not reiterate his earlier statement about how I'm on my own in this, even if he made no firm offers of assistance*. And while she might have disagreed with the sentiments he expressed about Dr. Lawler and Chris Angelino, it was clear that they were based on concerns for Glory's well-being. He'd even expressed an interest in seeing Glory despite his uncertainty as how to communicate with a mute four-year-old. Kate could empathize with that one. There was no question that David had been grateful when she'd offered him the photographs.

So maybe it was worth it after all Kate thought. *Anyway, compared to David, reestablishing contact with Maggie should be a piece of cake.*

CHAPTER 23

Glory ran into Kate's arms as soon as she saw her, leaving the swing she had been on swaying crazily behind her. Chris followed, her own two children trotting over curiously from where they had abandoned their tricycles.

"How did it go?" she asked, pushing strands of damp blond hair away from her face with the back of her hand, her eyes focused on the children rather than Kate.

"Not bad, not bad at all. David just needs a little time to get used to everything that's happened, but it will be fine, I think. How did Glory do?"

"Good. She does love those swings. We did some other things too, though." Chris hesitated. "She painted a picture. Want to see it?"

"Sure." Holding Glory, limbs tightly wrapped around her body, Kate followed Chris through the back door and into the house with Mark and Gina dutifully bringing up the rear. Once inside the kitchen, Chris walked swiftly over to a group of brightly colored sheets of paper pinned to a clothesline and, selecting one, brought it over to Kate. She took it awkwardly, peering at it over Glory's shoulder. What appeared to be a house stood on a line of grass surrounded by stick people with circles for faces. The faces, most of them, had dots for eyes but no other features. What drew Kate's startled "Oh!" however was the red, yellow, and orange halo that surrounded the house.

"I thought it was pretty interesting myself," offered Chris. "I tried to ask Glory about it but once she finished it, she didn't want anything to do with it; tried to throw it out, as a matter of fact."

Kate nodded. "She scribbles a lot, but this is the first time she's done something that's actually representative."

"You might want to show that to her therapist. The idea about Glory being traumatized—"

"I know." Kate wanted to head off this conversation. She'd had enough of discussing Glory's potential trauma for one day. "By the way, I wanted to thank you again for contacting Andi and Tim. This is really important to me and to Glory. As a matter of fact, I'm thinking of taking a trip to New York to look up this John McCarty and the Yoga center. Glory and I will be staying with my sister," Kate added hastily, seeing the question in Chris's eyes.

Looking away for a few seconds, Chris chewed her lower lip. "Well, good luck with that. I hope you'll bring Glory over again sometime soon. I enjoyed having her."

"I will. And thanks again." Kate unwrapped Glory's arms and legs from her upper body and set her on the ground. "Time to go, sweetie. Wave good-bye to Chris." Glory shyly imitated her grandmother''s wave, to the delight of Chris. "This is new." Kate smiled proudly. "Her child care provider Jen got her to start doing this."

"That's great," said Chris, returning the wave. "Mark, Gina, come say good-bye." The pair quickly appeared from an adjoining bedroom and enthusiastically waved good-bye as Glory and Kate made their exit amid promises to come back soon.

The car wheels crunched over the seashells as Kate pulled into the nearly empty parking lot of the Sea Witch about twenty minutes later. She sighed despairingly as she glanced in the rearview mirror at Glory sound asleep in her car seat. Jerry looked up as she entered, carrying the still-sleeping child and, smiling, called over, "Need some help?"

"Thanks, but I can manage." Kate carried Glory back to the office, Captain Ahab's squawks following her as she went, and settled her on an old love seat-sized sofa.

"Long day?" asked Jerry. He was leaning against the door frame, arms folded across his body.

"Yeah," Kate sighed, looking down at Glory, her little face flushed in the oppressive late afternoon air, Kate's own expression clouded.

"Didn't things go well with David?" he asked, eyes scrutinizing Kate's troubled face.

"No, no. It's not that. David is coming around, I think."

"Something else bothering you?"

"No...yes...I don't know, it's just that there's so much going on. Too many changes, you know? A couple of months ago my life was so much simpler. Now I'm dealing with people I haven't heard from in years and doing things I wouldn't have dreamed of only a short while ago." Kate held up her hands in a gesture of futility. "I don't know, don't mind me, I'm rambling."

"Give yourself a break, Kate. Given what you've had to deal with, I don't think anyone could have done better."

"Thanks. You've really been a tremendous help, though, Jerry. You've done far more than you should have to under the circumstances."

"Yeah, yeah, I know. You're welcome to any help I can give. After all, it's not as if you've never done anything for me. This is allowing me a little payback, you know?"

"Jerry..." Kate interjected.

He waved her off. "No, Kate, listen to me. You were the one who supported and encouraged me when I first came out to my parents."

"Yes, and then they disowned you," she added bitterly.

"It was the right thing to do, Kate. And then you stood by me when my relationship with Jason broke up, remember?"

"Of course, I remember," she replied. "I also remember that you started drinking too much afterward. Actually, you and Jason were drinking too much even *before* you broke up."

Jerry laughed softly. "Yeah, you never did have too high an opinion of Jason. I might add that when my drinking started getting out of hand it was you who pushed me into going to AA and who encouraged me to stick with it. I may never have gotten together with Kevin if I hadn't."

Kate smiled. “Well, I can’t take credit for Kevin.”

“Maybe not, but you did take a chance when you brought me in as your business partner for the Sea Witch. You couldn’t have been sure I’d stay sober.”

“Okay, Jerry, I get your point. We’re friends; I help you, you help me.”

“Yes, but you need to give yourself more credit here. You’ve done this on your own, Kate. You’re very self-sufficient, you know, sometimes too much so. I think it’s hard for you to let other people be supportive because maybe it makes you feel like you’re too needy. You like to be the one giving the help, not receving it. It’s okay for you to need assistance once in a while too, you know. After all, everyone needs a little help sometime. I did, and now you do too. Did I upset you?” he added, seeing Kate’s startled look.

“Uh, no, it’s okay.” Kate paused uncertainly. “Is my...um...reluctance to accept help something you’ve given a lot of thought to?”

Jerry laughed. “No, I wouldn’t say that. But I’ve known you for a long time now, and I can’t help making some observations.”

Kate looked down at Glory, watching the rhythmic rise and fall of her chest, seeing her small hand clutching the locket hanging around her neck as another child might clutch a favorite doll or blanket. “What else have you observed?”

“Oh, Kate...”

“No, really, I want to know.”

Jerry regarded her with some exasperation. “Fine. You know, Kate, having Glory around has been good for you. If nothing else, she’s forcing you out into the world a little more where you have to talk to people, get to know them, ask for help, admit you don’t know everything, can’t do everything yourself. Maybe even admit there’s more to life than the Sea Witch.”

“You really think I believe that, that the Sea Witch is all there is to my life?”

“Pretty much, yeah. What do you do for fun, Kate? Who do you see, where do you go?”

“Okay, so I’m no social butterfly. And I haven’t wanted to date, to deal with all that goes with that. I can't imagine being married again. I like being on my own. But I have interests other than the Sea Witch. I like to read, I go to movies. I like to swim and take long walks on the beach."

Jerry smiled. "And browse the antique stores, the art shows, because you never know..." He smiled more broadly, as Kate shook her head, laughing softly.

"So I love my work, what's wrong with that?"

"Nothing. Except it's the only thing you love."

She frowned. "I don't think that's true, not at all."

"Okay, okay. What do I know?" Jerry started to turn away, then looked back at Kate, another smile playing on his lips. "Oh, by the way, Kevin and I are having some people over for a cookout Sunday. We'd like to invite you and Glory. Jen and her family will be there, plus a lot of other interesting folks you probably don't already know. And you can talk to Kevin about that Yoga center in New York."

Kate stared at him for a minute, then smiled sweetly. "Fine. Sounds great. We'll be there."

"Glad to hear it." Jerry called back over his shoulder as he headed back into the front of the store. "Come around 2 or so for drinks and appetizers."

Kate continued to stare after him for a minute or two before sitting down heavily on the old wooden office chair. She picked up a pen, twirling it in her fingers as she turned over in her mind what she had just heard. What a strange conversation that was! she told herself. Yes, it was true that she didn't have much of a social life, pretty much none, if she was being honest with herself. But she'd never seen it as a shortcoming. Oh well, who was she kidding? She'd been too badly hurt, first by David and then by Ally to want to ever put herself in that position again. Nor did she want sympathy or pity, she'd told herself. It was just easier to be alone and she was fine with that, once she got used to it. The Sea Witch kept her more than busy.

Glory stirred, mumbling under her breath. Kate listened intently, but heard nothing intelligible. Well, she thought, she was in a relationship now with plenty of potential for hurt. With another sigh, Kate gazed down at Glory's closed eyes, her long dark lashes clearly defined against her pink cheeks. Not, she told herself, that she was really looking for an out. Chewing her lower lip, Kate considered Jerry's cookout invitation. This was hardly the first such invitation she'd had and, as Jerry well knew, she always found some polite way to decline them. The idea of making conversational small talk with a group of people she didn't know wasn't her idea of recreation. After all, she did it enough as part of her job. But if she had turned him down, it would have looked like he was right. And maybe he *was* but... Kate gave a mental shrug. At least, as Jerry had said, she would have an opportunity to talk to Kevin about The Center for Yoga, Meditation, and Healing. And with that thought, she reached over and gently shook Glory's shoulder. If I don't wake her up now, I'll never get her to sleep tonight, she reminded herself.

CHAPTER 24

It's going to be another hot sunny day on the Cape Kate noted wearily, her eyes focused on the shimmering sidewalk outside the window of Dr. Lawler's air-conditioned waiting room. She and Glory were ensconced in one the big chairs listening to the usual soft, pleasant, nondescript music while they waited for Dr. Lawler. Kate hummed along unthinkingly while her mind wandered back to the Sea Witch, yesterday's conversation with Jerry replaying itself in her head. *Jerry can think what he likes* Kate told herself, *I really should be at work and not because this is all there is in my life.*

"Well, hello, Glory, Mrs. LaRue, how are you this morning?" Kate looked up, slightly startled, to see Dr. Lawler standing before her. Glory promptly buried her face in Kate's shoulder, arms wrapped around her neck.

Kate smiled apologetically. "I'm afraid I was a bit lost in thought. Dr. Lawler," she struggled to stand, her little granddaughter still clinging to her side, "Glory's not feeling too sociable today. She and I didn't get much sleep last night. She had a busy day yesterday, and I let her take too long a nap."

The psychologist waved her explanation aside, steadying Kate's elbow as she did so. "Don't be concerned, I understand. Why don't you both come on in and we'll see if there isn't something Glory might enjoy doing today."

Kate followed her down the hall with Glory still in her arms. Over her shoulder, Dr. Lawler said to Kate, "I think we're ready today to begin introducing Glory to the puppets and, since Glory is feeling a little extra shy today, why don't you come in for a while too, Mrs. LaRue, at least until she's feeling more comfortable." And then, with a smile to Glory, who was peeking out at her from under the lock of hair half covering her face, she added, "I bet you'll like this. The puppets are fun to watch and play with."

Once they entered the expansive playroom, Dr. Lawler gestured them over to a corner where a small puppet stage had been set up with a few cushions for seating. She pulled up a hard plastic chair for Kate who sat down gratefully, Glory still attached to her side. The psychologist took out three hand puppets from behind the stage and brought them over to Glory. Putting them on her own hands one at a time, she introduced them to her. "Glory, this is Bunny; Bunny, this is Glory." She held out a gray and white rabbit puppet with big floppy ears, a pink nose, black button eyes, and sporting a red bow. Bunny hid her face under her paws, peeking out at Glory much as she had done moments earlier at Dr. Lawler. Curious, Glory moved away from Kate toward the puppet. "Bunny's shy, like you are sometimes," Dr. Lawler whispered confidentially. She enacted the same scenario with the other two puppets, a small pink pig with a big smile and, Kate noted with amusement, what could be described as a porkpie hat named Peter Piglet, and a brown and white duck with a green band around her neck named Mrs. Mallard. Both of these puppets offered a cheerful "Hi, Glory, nice to meet you!"

"Glory has come to play with us today," Dr. Lawler announced to the assembled puppets who, with the exception of the shy Bunny, jumped up and down enthusiastically calling, "Yay! I want to play!" Entranced by this, Glory sat herself down on the cushions, her hand going automatically to the picture locket around her neck. She watched intently as Dr. Lawler had the pig and duck puppets try to get Bunny to say something similar to Glory with Peter Piglet going so far as to try to pretend to talk for him using a funny voice, which made Glory giggle, much to Kate's surprise. Finally the puppets gave up, saying to Glory, "Oh well, don't worry, Bunny will talk someday when she wants to."

The little show moved on with the puppets passing around a

whistle, each blowing it, even Bunny, with some assistance from Dr. Lawler, who had her own, and who then passed the puppets' whistle on to Glory. She gave it a tentative hoot before handing it to her grandmother, laughing when Kate made an awkward squawk on her first try. With this portion of the session over, Dr. Lawler handed out stickers all around, including Kate and the puppets, and then offered a much more relaxed Glory free choice among the plethora of toys while she and Kate retired to her desk in the corner.

"I think that went very well for the first treatment session," Dr. Lawler commented, a warm smile lighting her face.

Kate returned the smile somewhat tentatively. "She certainly seemed to enjoy it, I will say that. And you think listening to the puppets talk about it will help Glory talk herself?"

"It can be very effective, Mrs. LaRue. As I said before, Glory needs to feel she's not under any pressure to talk. Nevertheless, she also needs to believe that it is safe to do so. The puppets can help demonstrate how someone who can talk but is holding back can be encouraged and supported in doing so and that good things will result when that happens."

Kate mulled this over for a moment. "Okay. But...Do you have any diagnosis for this yet?"

"Well, one possibility I've considered is elective mutism."

Kate nodded in recognition. "Yes, that was mentioned in San Francisco."

"Right. However, Glory's presentation does not precisely fit the diagnostic criteria. While a refusal to speak when the child is able to do so is certainly the principal symptom, most children do so only in certain situations such as school. The child will speak at home and perhaps with close friends and other family members. As a result, it is often seen as a type of social anxiety disorder. Glory, of course, is not speaking at all and, from what you have told me, apparently was not speaking at home with her mother for some period of time."

"So what else do you think it is?" Kate asked uneasily.

"I've also considered posttraumatic stress disorder which is often called by its initials PTSD. As you know, PTSD was also considered by Dr. Tenley back in San Francisco. That diagnosis requires a specific traumatic event that sets off the problems. In Glory's case, we don't know what that would be or even if there is one. Certainly, her mother's death would be a traumatic event, especially for such a young child, but apparently Glory was not talking before that happened. Anyway, the refusal to talk is not a typical symptom of PTSD."

Kate gazed over at Glory who was happily engaged in building a tower of some sort with Legos. Her thoughts wandered back to the painting that seemed to be a building on fire.

"What kind of traumatic event would we be talking about, Dr. Lawler?"

Dr. Lawler sighed. "Well, I know you don't want to hear this but some type of abuse is often a cause in children."

Kate stiffened.

"Mrs. LaRue, there was no physical evidence of abuse noted with Glory. None of the doctors who saw her in San Francisco reported that. Of course, I suppose something could have happened earlier. This could have resolved itself so that overt physical evidence was no longer present when the doctors examined her. In any case, I think physical abuse is unlikely." Dr. Lawler paused. "What I *do* think is that for some reason Glory is afraid to talk; that whatever happened to her made her feel that talking was somehow unsafe. I have to add that I agree with her previous doctor that your daughter knew what happened but didn't want to admit it. Hopefully, if we help Glory feel that no harm will come from speaking, even that it will make things better for her, she will talk and perhaps tell us what happened."

Kate hesitated, turning over the possibilities. She knew she really did not want to believe Glory had experienced some type of severe trauma, especially physical abuse. Nevertheless, she could not help seeing images of religious cults and flaming buildings in her mind. Jonestown. David Koresh and the Branch Davidians. Just what *had* happened in New Mexico?

"Well, thank you, Dr. Lawler." Kate abruptly turned and called to Glory, "Time to go, sweetheart." Glory dropped the Lego block she was holding and headed toward the door, looking expectantly at Kate.

"Good-bye, Glory; Mrs. LaRue. We'll see you both next week," Dr. Lawler said behind her. Kate glanced back at the psychologist, who was regarding her with an expression of interested curiosity.

Kate gave her a brief smile. "Yes, next week."

As she and Glory walked back out into the hot summer day, Kate ran it through her mind once again and wondered why she didn't want to tell Dr. Lawler about Glory's painting. After all, maybe it was nothing, just a child's imagination. *I'll tell her later*, she thought, when she knew something more. When she was more certain.

CHAPTER 25

Kate had always loved the town of Wellfleet for its classic Cape Cod ambience that included a plentiful supply of exceptional art galleries, upscale restaurants, and charming little gift shops. With Glory ensconced in the backseat, she turned off Route 6 and headed into Wellfleet Center on her way to Jerry and Kevin's cookout, soon winding down Commercial Street through the center of town. Kate cast quick admiring glances at the beautifully maintained old houses fronted by gardens festooned with roses and sporting elegant carriage lamps at the end of paved walkways, some crowned with widow's walks looking out to the harbor. She passed Wellfleet Marketplace wth its offerings of fresh produce displayed in rows out on the narrow sidewalk and wondered if she might have time to stop off on her way home for some fresh fruit for tomorrow's breakfast. Kate drove out to the harbor to point out to Glory the fleet of fishing boats, charters, and private craft of all sizes filling the water surrounded by hills and sand dunes.

They turned back, Kate searching for the familiar Wellfleet landmark known as Uncle Tim's Bridge that was her checkpoint for Jerry's house. Soon after passing the long wooden footbridge that spanned Duck Pond Kate found the little side street on which Jerry and Kevin's elegant home was set. The two story house, with it's dark blue paint accented with a white trim on rows of double-paned windows and the paneled front door, looked warm and inviting under the dappled shade of an old maple tree. Kate hadn't been there often, but she couldn't help admiring its Cape Cod grace and style whenever she saw it and marvel at Jerry's good fortune to have a partner so well connected and prosperous that they could afford such a place. Kevin practiced real estate law, working out of Barnstable, with an office in another classic eighteenth century Cape Cod house located along Route 6A. As she understood it, the firm had been started by Kevin's grandfather some fifty years ago or more and inherited by Kevin's father. Together with his father and another partner, Kevin had continued the family tradition of making a small fortune out of the legal issues inherent in the high priced real estate market on Cape Cod.

Kate breathed a sigh of relief when she found a place to park not far from the house. Once ensconced in the spot, she lifted Glory from her car seat and began the walk back along the tree shaded street. Kate looked down at Glory, who was clutching her hand apprehensively, round dark eyes focused on the unfamiliar house.

"Don't worry, it will be fun, honey. Remember, I told you Jerry will be here and so will Jen. Besides, I'm not going anywhere."

Glory looked unconvinced but trotted along obediently at Kate's side as they skirted the house, heading toward the backyard and the covered patio Jerry and Kevin had added for summer cookouts and outdoor parties. It's amazing, Kate thought, how Glory's grown these past weeks, noting that the pink shorts and sleeveless floral knit shirt she was wearing, bought for her in California, were almost too small for her already. They won't last the summer at this rate, she mused. As Kate was pondering the possibilities of trying to find her additional summer clothes this late in the season, they encountered Jen as she exited the screened kitchen door, arms laden with platters of uncooked hamburger patties, sliced tomatoes, thick cheddar cheese, and shredded lettuce. Glory's troubled face brightened immediately and, releasing her grip on Kate's hand, she raced toward Jen with a squeal of delight.

"Glory, don't!"

"Watch out, sweetie!" Jen lifted her arms out of way somewhat awkwardly and braced herself as Glory reached her, throwing her arms around Jen's hips in an enthusiastic greeting.

Kate, close on Glory's heels, quickly pried her loose, scolding her as she did so.

"Glory, listen to Grandma when I tell you no. You could have hurt Jen or knocked over all that food." Kate glanced up at Jen. "Sorry about that," she added apologetically.

"No harm done." Jen looked over at Glory, now standing quietly beside Kate, her expression downcast. "Don't be sad. We're going to have fun today. Look over there." Jen thrust her chin toward the backyard where a small moonwalk was set up, quivering under the weight of several children whose outlines were clearly evident through the screens as they bounced around the interior. Glory followed her gaze, but her expression was more one of confusion and trepidation than gleeful anticipation.

Kate followed Jen's gaze as well, then dropped hers to examine Glory's face. "It's possible she's never seen one of those."

"Well," called Jen over her shoulder as she headed for the patio with the platters of food, "if all else fails, there is a swing." She again gestured with her head and Kate noted the single wooden swing hanging from the branches of an old oak.

Jerry, seeing the trio approach, rose from where he was sitting conversing with a small group of guests and headed in their direction. "Kate, welcome," he said and, taking her hand, leaned forward and planted a light kiss on her cheek. Before she could respond, he turned to Glory and, tugging gently on one of her braids, said, "You too, Glory. Glad you came."

Glory offered a shy smile in return, to Kate's relief. She'd been pleased to see that Glory was showing more and more small signs of communication recently, if not outright speech but, Kate had noted, she was much shyer around men, even Jerry, who she saw frequently and seemed to like for the most part.

"Didn't think I would come, did you?" Kate met his gaze challengingly but with considerable amusement in her eyes, nonetheless.

"Let's just say I wouldn't have been at all surprised if there had been a last minute phone call saying something had come up."

Kate lifted her chin. "Well, then, you don't know me as well as you thought."

Jerry smiled and shook his head as Kevin came up behind him, their golden cocker spaniel Duncan trotting along at his side. With a wave in Kate's direction and a perfunctory "Hey, good to see you," he turned his attention to Jerry, whispering in his ear, and then gesturing for him to follow. Jerry called back, "We'll catch up with you later" as the two of them made their way across the wide wooden floorboards toward a group standing around a makeshift bar, Duncan bounding after them.

Jen had disappeared in the direction of the outsized barbeque grill. Kate found herself standing alone with Glory in the midst of the laughing, chattering guests, uncertain what to do next when she heard a voice off to her left call out, "Mrs. LaRue? Would you and Glory like to have a seat with us?" Kate turned to see a heavyset woman about her own age with short auburn hair and warm green eyes looking up at her from her seat at a large wooden picnic table. Across from her was a man whose smiling visage looked like a slightly older version of Kevin O'Malley's. Kate's puzzlement quickly dissolved once she realized this must be Jen's mother and father, Kevin's sister-in-law and older brother. Kate smiled, searching her memory to come up with the names when Jen materialized at her side. "Oh, Mrs. LaRue, this is my mom Colleen and my dad Roger O'Malley. Mom and Dad, this is Glory's grandmother, Kate LaRue. They've already met Glory," she added as an aside. Kate smiled gratefully at Jen's parents and, with a nod of acknowledgment to Jen, slid onto a chair next to them. Jen, leaning down, took Glory's hand, and after a quick exchange with Kate said "Come on with me, honey" and the pair headed back toward the kitchen.

"It's a pleasure to meet you at last, Kate. I have to tell you that Jen has really been enjoying working with you and Glory." Colleen O'Malley propped her arms on the table and fixed an open, friendly gaze on Kate's face. "Roger and I were hoping to meet you before the end of the summer. Such a sad story about your daughter but thankfully your little Glory has her grandmother to take care of her." Kate smiled again and said something perfunctory, hoping this wasn't going to be a lengthy discussion of Ally's sad story as well as Glory's, but Colleen had already moved on to a narrative of Cape Cod summers and the unusually dry weather they had been having. Roger O'Malley interrupted briefly with an offer to obtain drinks for everyone, an offer Kate gratefully accepted, already feeling parched in the summer afternoon sun. By the time he returned carrying a tray of drinks, his brother following on his heels with a basket of popcorn, Colleen had moved on to talking about the high price of college tuition and how proud she was of her daughter's academic record despite needing to help contribute to the costs.

"I just want you to know, Kate," began Kevin as soon as he caught the drift of the conversation, "I've offered to help with Jen's tuition a number of times, but Colleen and Roger won't hear of it. There's no need for her to have to pay her own way." Noting the irritated expression on Colleen's face and how Roger, setting down the drinks, rolled his eyes in frustration, Kate decided this was the perfect opportunity to ask Kevin about The Center for Yoga, Meditation, and Healing.

"Kevin, I'm thinking of taking a trip to New York to check out a place called The Center for Yoga, Meditation and Healing. Jerry told me you're familiar with it, is that right?"

"Yes, I know it. Jerry mentioned that you were interested in the Center. Wasn't Ally taking some classes there or something like that?" Kevin looked at Kate curiously as he placed the popcorn on the table, then pulled up a folding chair and sat down next to her, popping a few kernels into his mouth. Duncan reappeared, apparently having tired of wrestling with one of his chew toys, and propped his chin on Kevin's lap while he rubbed his head.

"Yes, something like that," Kate agreed. "I was hoping to talk to someone who knew Ally while she was there, particularly a man named John McCarty."

Kevin considered this for a few seconds before shaking his head. "Doesn't sound familiar. Of course, it's been awhile since I was there. It was back when I was in law school, after all. Learning Yoga and meditation was a bit of a lifesaver, given the stresses of trying to get myself through law school." Kevin cast a meaningful glance at his sister-in-law. Colleen had relaxed and been following the conversation with considerable interest but now was clearly ready to respond with a sharp retort until Kate hastily added, "Oh, I didn't really expect you to know *him*. I was hoping that you might still know someone there who could help me get in touch with him. You see, I have reason to believe he's in New York and that maybe..."

"Mmm..." said Kevin through a mouthful of popcorn. "Well, I think Nick Maxwell is still there. Last I heard he was an associate director or something of that sort. Did this guy you're looking for work there?"

Kate shrugged, her expression uncertain.

"Huh. Well, Kate, I haven't spoken with Nick in a while so I can't promise anything. I'll try giving him a call, see what he says."

"That would be great, Kevin, thanks." Out of the corner of her eye, Kate could see Jen and Glory emerging from the back door, Jen carrying a platter with hot dogs and sausages, Glory clutching an oversized bag of potato chips. As they approached across the grass, Glory elevating her speed to a quick trot to keep up, Kate turned to Colleen and Roger with a smile and added, "Jen has really been great with Glory. You have a wonderful daughter." Colleen smiled proudly. "Yes, we've been very fortunate with our children. It helps that we've taught them responsibility early on, to take nothing for granted, and that they need to work for what they want." Colleen cast a glance at her brother-in-law as she said this, causing Kate to groan inwardly, anticipating another exchange over Jen's tuition costs. Much to her relief, Kevin tapped her arm, saying, "Come on, there are some people on the other side of the patio I think you'd like to meet."

Taking her leave of Jen's parents, Kate crossed the patio in the wake of Jen, Glory, and Kevin, Duncan running ahead of them with an occasional excited bark. Taking Kevin's elbow, Kate whispered in his ear, "Whom did you want to introduce me to?"

He shrugged. "No one in particular. I just wanted to get out of another debate over Jen and her tuition. Colleen and Roger are great parents, no question, but I do think they're being a little myopic about this."

Kate laughed heartily. "Well, *I* think it's great that you want to help out." She paused as they reached the grill where Jerry stood enveloped in a cloud of smoke, flipping steaming burgers onto a platter. He waved to Kate with his spatula. "Hamburger or cheeseburger? I can do hot dogs but they'll take longer."

"Two hamburgers. One for me, one for Glory." Kate pushed a wisp of hair away from her face, her eyes on her granddaughter standing at a nearby table pouring the chips into a bowl with Jen's assistance. Jerry handed her a couple of thick paper plates, a hamburger and bun on each. Glancing toward his partner, he called out, "Hey, Kevin, why don't you take Kate over and introduce her to Sam Ritter?" Jerry turned back toward Kate. "Sam is a friend of our next-door neighbors. I'm told he owns a gift store called the Sandpiper out on Long Island."

Kate raised a quizzical eyebrow.

Jerry smiled and waved his arms. "Nice guy. Good looking, unattached, in the business. Bats for your side, sad to say, or I might be interested myself." Jerry's grin widened mischievously. "Looks like he might be into Yoga."

At that, Kate frowned and pursed her lips. "Jerry!" she hissed. "You know how much I hate setups like this."

"Hey, just kidding! You might enjoy talking to him, though."

"I need to get Glory her supper. I don't have time for either business or socializing right now." Kate beckoned to Glory, who was happily munching potato chips while Jen chatted with an older woman whose face bore an unmistakable resemblance to the O'Malleys. Seeing Kate juggling hamburgers as she reached for Glory's hand, Jen smiled and called out, "Oh, Mrs. LaRue, why don't you let Glory eat with me? I don't mind."

"See?" remarked Kevin at her elbow. "Sam's a great guy. I'll get a burger and join you."

Kate sighed in resignation and, turning over one of the hamburgers to Jen, followed Kevin to a picnic table under an arbor. Sam, she admitted to herself once introductions were made, was an attractive man about her own age, friendly and charming with dark brown hair just starting to turn gray and warm blue eyes. As was generally the case when she met someone "in the business," as Jerry had put it, she found it easy to make pleasant business small talk.

Once their burgers were gone, along with some cold beers, they fell into an animated discussion of the comparative virtues of Cape Cod versus Long Island while the shadows lengthened across Jerry and Kevin's carefully manicured lawn and the sun dropped behind a cluster of old oak trees.

"I was planning to head back home tomorrow," Sam was telling Kate, whose eyes were straying toward Glory, walking in the direction of the moonwalk, her hand tightly clutching Jen's, "but I'd like to drop by the Sea Witch before I go."

"That would be fine," Kate replied somewhat absently.

"Is that your granddaughter?" Sam asked, following her gaze to where Glory stood peering into the interior of the moonwalk with Jen bending over next to her, seemingly trying to encourage her to climb into it.

Kate looked back at him, startled. "Yes, how did you know?"

"Lucky guess," Sam shrugged, smiling. "Well, maybe, not *that* lucky. Jerry told me a little about the situation when he was telling me about you and the Sea Witch. She's a pretty little girl. What's her name?"

Kate smiled somewhat wearily, not wanting to get into a conversation about Glory's "situation" and wondering just what Jerry had told him. "Her name is Glory." She paused, not wanting to say more but anticipating the inevitable question about the origin of Glory's unusual name.

Sam just smiled, looking at Kate curiously. "That's an interesting name," he said noncommittally.

Kevin, who had long since excused himself and headed off in the direction of the grill, now strolled back in their direction trailed by Jerry, both bearing slices of watermelon, Duncan once more tagging along at their heels. As they approached, Kate smiled at Jerry and said, "Sam would like to visit the store tomorrow," and then to

Sam, "I'm sure Jerry can show you around if I'm not available." She stood up. "It's getting late so I think Glory and I are going to head out. Thanks so much for a lovely day," Kate added quickly, seeing the protest rise to Jerry's lips. "Sam, it was nice to meet you. Maybe I'll see you tomorrow."

Sam stood and offered his hand. A little bemused, Kate held out her own, which Sam then gently squeezed between both of his. "A pleasure. I do hope I'll see you again, if not tomorrow, then perhaps you'll stop by the Sandpiper next time you come to New York. You have my card."

Kate nodded, patting her purse and avoiding Sam's intensely curious gaze. She turned and walked quickly in Glory's direction, feeling the scrutiny of the group behind her as she did so. To her relief, the little girl ran happily over to her as soon as she saw her, even pulling her eagerly in the direction of the front of the house. Clearly Glory had enough partying for one day as well.

CHAPTER 26

On the long ride home in the gathering late summer twilight with Glory dozing in her car seat in the back of the car, Kate ruminated on the events of the day. She was going to have to call Maggie when she got home and work out a time when she and Glory could visit. Then she would have to make sure Kevin got in touch with his friend Nick Maxwell at The Center for Yoga, Meditation, and Healing before she left.

Kate let her thoughts dwell on Sam Ritter for a moment. A nice man and certainly good looking, as Jerry had indicated, tall, well built with those clear blue eyes, well defined cheekbones, and dark hair threaded with gray. She had enjoyed hearing about his store and the trials and tribulations of running a business on the south coast of Long Island. "And I'd much rather talk about that than get into anything personal," Kate mused. *If* she ever wanted to have a relationship again, Sam would be the kind of man with whom she could have one. But in all the years since her divorce from David, Kate had seldom dated and when she did, the experience had always been uncomfortable and strained. At first, she thought it had been because she was too wounded from the bitter breakup of her marriage, her self-esteem and confidence having taken too much of a beating to want to even consider another relationship. Not only that, she had been so busy with getting the store off the ground and being a mother to Ally. Then, later, after Ally left, well...it just seemed safer to retreat into the narrow little world where she'd been something of a success and stay there. Besides, independence had its virtues. With no one to answer to she could come and go as she pleased, choose what to spend her money on, and how she wanted to live her life.

By the time Kate pulled into her driveway and parked under the carport, night had fallen. She was glad she had thought to leave the outside lights on, even though when she left she had been convinced she would be back long before dark. As she helped a sleepy Glory out of the car, she exchanged greetings with Fran Jackson, out for an after dinner walk in the balmy summer night.

"How's it going, dear?" Fran called, leaning on one of the posts in Kate's split rail fence. "You and the little one out having some fun?"

"We're doing fine. We were at a barbeque out in Wellfleet today and I think Glory's pretty well worn out."

"Beautiful day for it. Hey, have you been watching the weather reports lately? There are some big storms brewing out in the Atlantic, might be tracking up here this year. That's what they say, anyway. Personally, I'm thinking we're ripe for a big hurricane this summer."

Kate looked at Fran for a moment before heading up the walk with Glory. "Yes, I've heard that too," she called back over her shoulder, "but I certainly hope they're wrong. We need rain, but a hurricane is bad news. See you later, Fran." Kate closed the door behind her, pushing thoughts of the havoc hurricanes could wreak aside for now.

With Glory asleep in the soft light of her bedroom, Kate stood in the center of her living room, considering her options. Maybe a little TV? She could catch up on those weather reports, see if there really were any significant storms potentially heading toward the Cape. Kate thought longingly of another cold beer and perhaps some cheese and crackers out on the deck. *No*, she thought, *this needs to be taken care of first.* She resolutely picked up the phone and punched in Maggie's telephone number, listening to the distant ringing as she poured herself that beer she'd been wanting after all.

"Hello, Kate?" Maggie's voice, sounding tired but nonetheless hopeful came on the line.

"Hi, Maggie, am I calling at a bad time?" Kate moved out onto the deck with her beer and bowl of soft pretzels, the phone under one ear, and settled herself once again in one of her favorite rocking chairs.

"No, not at all. I'm glad you called, I've been thinking about you all day. I just got back from Beth's where I spent the day taking care of Nathan. An active two-year-old is just exhausting for an old grandma like myself. It made me wonder how you were holding up with your little granddaughter—Glory, you said her name was, is that right?"

"That's right. And I don't know why Ally named her that, in case you were wondering."

Maggie laughed. "Who knows, right? You hear some pretty strange names these days. Glory's not bad."

"Well, Glory and I are doing fine. She's a sweetheart, really. Look, Maggie, I was thinking of taking you up on that offer to stay with you while I check out this Yoga center in New York. I've got a possible contact there. I know you're busy with Beth and I really hate to impose but I won't stay long."

"No, no, don't worry about that. I'll work something out with Beth. When were you thinking of coming here?"

Kate took a deep breath. "Maybe the first part of next week? If I can get there Sunday night, I can head over to the city Monday, talk to someone at this Yoga center, and then, if it all works out the way I want it to, I could be back here as early as Tuesday."

"Oh, Kate, why the rush? Stay a few days. Do you realize we haven't seen each other since Beth's wedding? That's five years."

Kate thought about this for a few seconds. Had it been that long? "Maggie, I would, but I have a business to run and this is still my busy season. Labor Day will be coming up before long. After that, maybe I can come for a longer visit."

"Yes, of course. But Kate?"

"What?"

"Don't forget you said that."

Kate turned restlessly onto her back once more, frustrated by her inability to relax into sleep. Moonlight threw the outlines of the trees outside Kate's open window into sharp relief against the far wall, leaves dancing in the light breeze she could feel stroking her cheek. Every effort she made to stop the images of the day replaying in her mind had been unsuccessful, and now Kate tried to remember if she had one of those pain relievers with something to help her sleep in her bathroom medicine cabinet. She didn't like the idea of resorting to drugs but she needed to find a way to turn off the video player in her head. She sighed. What was it about Sam Ritter that was making her want to visualize his strong, deeply tanned face with its high cheekbones and imagine what lay beneath that black tee shirt and frayed denim shorts?

Well, that should tell me something right there, she thought, smiling to herself in the darkness. *He is certainly one of the best looking men I've met in a long time*. That, and the shivery feeling that had run through her when he had held her hand in both of his. *The last thing I need right now is an emotional entanglement with a man*, Kate scolded herself. *But still*...She closed her eyes resolutely. Images of a young David surfaced, handsome and dark-haired, his bare skin honey colored from long hours in the summer sun. Despite everything that had happened between them, she could still feel the passion they had once shared well up deep inside her. The David of thirty years ago was still an intensely sexy, appealing man, she thought as she pushed away a sudden memory of her naked body entwined with his on a cot in a rented cabin somewhere in Maine shortly after they were married. She allowed herself to imagine again what Sam looked like without his clothes for a minute, toying with the thought of what of what it would be like to have sex with him and then, feeling again the delicious warmth spreading through her, decided she was never going to get to sleep if she kept this up.

Throwing aside the sheet, Kate sat up and reached for her robe, pulling it on and tying the sash tightly around her waist, angry for allowing herself to get distracted this way. Walking out to the kitchen, she opened the refrigerator and moodily perused its contents. Milk was supposed to have some sedative effects, she thought.

That and turkey, she remembered, but Kate decided she would have to make do with the milk and a couple of the chocolate chip cookies she and Glory had made yesterday. As she munched her cookies and sipped her milk, her eyes fell on the painting Glory had done while at Chris Angelino's. With her free hand, Kate took the paper down from where she had pinned it to the big cork bulletin board and studied the images: a simple brown square with a couple of bare spaces that might be windows, the collection of circles and lines that seemed to be people nearby, green paint that could be grass, and the elaborate multicolored halo that looked like it might be fire. Since it essentially surrounded the brown square house, it didn't seem likely to be the sun, she thought.

Swallowing the last of her milk, Kate took the painting with her into the living room, pulling out her laptop computer and settling herself into a large comfortable armchair under her favorite reading lamp. While waiting for her computer homepage to come up, she considered what she might be looking for once she got online. Newspaper or online articles from New Mexico about a fire at a religious commune maybe a year or so ago? Glory couldn't have been too much younger or she wouldn't have remembered it, Kate reasoned, but it must have been before she and Ally came to San Francisco. Once she was online, she tried typing in keywords like "fire," "commune," "New Mexico" into the search engine. After several minutes of sorting through Web pages and altering keywords, she was rewarded with a couple of small articles in a Santa Fe online news site reporting the destruction the previous autumn of a small group of ranch or farmhouses as well as neighboring stables and barns rented by a religious community called simply The Way. The articles noted that the fire appeared accidental and that no one died or had been seriously injured, but otherwise, very little was said about the group itself except that they had nowhere to go and many of them, including a number of women and children, were staying in shelters in Santa Fe. There were also a few photographs of the site, both before and after the fire, set in a landscape that certainly resembled the photographs found in Ally's apartment.

Kate stared at the pictures of the deserted, burned out buildings for a moment or two, then tried googling The Way. However, another five minutes of sorting through Web pages turned up nothing that seemed relevant; besides, the milk and the late hour were having their effects and she decided it was probably time to give sleep another chance. Shutting down her laptop, Kate leaned back in her chair and stared unseeingly at the far wall, the painting still in her hands, trying to imagine Ally living in what seemed like relatively primitive conditions on a remote ranch or farm in New Mexico—Ally, who had hated camping and any form of "roughing it" throughout her childhood and teen years.

After a minute or two of trying unsuccessfully to picture her daughter in this setting, Kate rose from her chair and, returning the painting to its place on the bulletin board, made her way through the darkened house toward her bedroom and sleep. She paused for a moment to check in on Glory, sleeping soundly in her mother's old bed, her small face just visible above the covers, partially concealed by her long, dark hair. Kate reminded herself how relieved and surprised she had been that Glory had made this transition from the trundle bed to Ally's old bedroom without any protest or difficulty. What was stored away in that little head, Kate couldn't help but wonder. What did she know that she couldn't—or wouldn't—tell? Glory's serene face, her chest rising and falling, barely perceptible below the sheets, told nothing. Finally, Kate turned and headed back into her own room and, climbing into bed, this time quickly fell into a deep sleep of her own.

CHAPTER 27

The next day was again bright and sunny, dazzling the eye as it reflected off the crushed shells in the Sea Witch's parking lot, but Kate couldn't help but sense a hint of autumn in the late summer air. She had spotted the dark blue convertible with its New York license plates as she pulled in and, heart thumping in her chest, couldn't stop herself from checking her reflection in the rearview mirror and smoothing the fabric of her wide white summer skirt trimmed in tiny flounces and embroidered blue flowers.

Both Jerry and Sam looked up with wide smiles as she came through the door, the bell above it tinkling lightly. She noted wryly the amused look in Jerry's eyes and, blushingly, the appreciative one in Sam's.

"Well, good morning, Kate," called Jerry. "Sam just got here about ten minutes ago. I've been giving him a quick tour of the place."

Sam smiled in Kate's direction. "What can I say? It's absolutely delightful. Great stock. A terrific location. The very essence of Cape Cod. Plus, the parrot is a nice touch." Everyone laughed, Captain Ahab joining in with some raucous ha-has of his own.

"Thanks, I'm in love with the place myself, as Jerry will be glad to tell you. I'm happy you could stop by and see it." Kate had come to a halt a few feet from the pair, feeling a sudden desire to maintain some distance from Sam and any suggestion of romantic interest between them.

"Jerry was about to tell me the origin of the store's name but I'd like to hear it from you, if you don't mind. I take it there really was a sea witch?" Sam focused his gaze on hers, his eyes a warm blue in the soft morning sunlight filling the store.

Jerry, an amused smile still on his lips, suggested, “Why not take Sam out to the patio and tell him the tale? He hasn’t seen the back of the store yet. I’ll just be a minute.”

Kate chewed her lower lip, laughing to herself. Smiling resignedly, she said, “Yes, actually there was a sea witch.” Then, gesturing for Sam to follow, she led the way toward the back of the store and out through a set of sliding glass doors to a small patio containing a round black wrought iron table and two chairs under a brightly colored umbrella. “This is our backyard, so to speak,” she offered. Sam looked around him and nodded admiringly at the thick green bushes, Cape Cod roses, and clusters of yellow day lilies crowding the little cement patio. A large hydrangea bush added a splash of blue to the overall scene. “Very nice.”

As they settled themselves at the table Kate, hoping to forestall any personal conversation, quickly launched into the tale. “Well, let’s see. It all begins about 1716 when a sea captain named Sam Bellamy arrived in the town of Eastham on the Outer Cape, just south of Wellfleet. Presumably, his ship had run aground in a storm, stranding him on the Cape. While Captain Bellamy was waiting for an opportunity to sail out again he stayed at Crosby Tavern, where he met a young girl of about fifteen or sixteen named Maria Hallett, the daughter of a prominent Cape Cod family.”

“Hallett? As in that old fashioned drugstore and ice-cream counter down the street Jerry was just telling me about?” Sam frowned slightly as if trying to remember. He leaned back in his chair, long legs crossed at the knee, fingers lightly tapping the table. Kate had a fleeting thought that Sam looked relaxed and quite at home on the Sea Witch’s little patio.

“Yes, as a matter of fact,” Kate replied qiuckly. “There have been Halletts on the Cape for centuries, along with Nickersons and Crockers...” She paused for a moment, her eyes catching Sam’s. He was looking at her with such warm interest that she quickly averted her gaze and hastily continued with her story. “Well, anyway, young Maria was quite taken with the captain and his tales of adventure and she soon fell in love. However, whether Sam Bellamy also loved her has been a matter of speculation ever since. Some say that he would have married her but for the fact that her parents wouldn't have him as a husband for their daughter. Regardless, after a few months he sailed away for the Caribbean, presumably promising to return with enough money to marry her. Unfortunately for Maria, however, her romance with the sea captain had resulted in her becoming pregnant and, some months later, she gave birth to a baby boy. Tragically, he died that same night. The birth caused such a scandal among the good people of Eastham that the poor girl was thrown in jail. In the end, this series of catastrophes, the loss of Sam, the pregnancy, birth and death of her child, and being imprisoned, caused her to lose her mind. She was eventually released from prison but by then it was too late. Maria became an outcast, disowned by her family. She is said to have lived alone in a hut on the beach and wandered the Atlantic dunes, staring out to sea, searching the horizon for her lost lover. As time passed, the townspeople began to believe she had sold her soul to the devil and called her a witch, telling stories about her increasingly bizarre behavior, such as how she would stand on the dunes under the full moon or during storms, screaming curses at the sea long into the night."

Kate paused again, and Sam, who had been attentively following the tale, interjected, "So this poor kid was the sea witch?"

Kate nodded. "Yes, that's right. Maria, or ''Goody,'' Hallett, the Sea Witch of Billingsgate, as the town was then known."

"Goody?" Sam queried, amused .

Kate nodded again, smiling. "A common appellation for a woman at the time, short for goodwife, I believe."

"So whatever became of Bellamy? Does anyone know?"

Kate laughed. "Well, yes. While he was in the Caribbean, Sam Bellamy turned pirate, commandeered a slave ship called the *Whydah* that was returning to Europe filled with treasure and sailed it up the coast to the Cape." Kate shrugged expressively, spreading her hands wide. "Some say he was returning for Maria, bringing enough gold and treasure to buy off her parents. Whether that was true or not no one will ever know. A storm came up off the coast and the ship was wrecked and sank in Cape Cod Bay. Black Sam Bellamy, as he was known then, did not survive. Some say too that Maria stood on the dunes that night and cursed the ship, using her witchy powers to run it aground."

Sam pondered this for a moment. "This sounds familiar somehow. Where did I read something like this?"

Kate smiled knowingly. "You can visit the Whydah Museum and see what's been salvaged of the shipwreck. The wreck was actually found quite recently, the only sunken pirate ship ever recovered, as I understand it."

"Ah, that must be it, then. Perhaps the next time I come to the Cape, you can go there with me. You'd make a great tour guide." Sam's smile warmed up a notch.

"Well, I'm not so sure about my skill as a tour guide," Kate laughed a little, shaking her head, and at the same time feeling a swirl of excitement surge through her at the thought of seeing Sam again. As she searched for something to add, Jerry appeared in the doorway. "Coffee, anyone?" With an apologetic glance toward Sam, he added, "Our coffeemaker doesn't produce the best coffee on the Cape, but it's drinkable."

Sam rose, holding up his hand and smiling. "Another time. I've taken up too much of your time and I need to get on the road, anyway." He turned toward Kate who had also risen to her feet. "I intended to go back earlier, but I really did want to see your store. It was nice to see you again as well."

Sam took a step toward her and lightly touched her elbow. "I really enjoyed the story. I hope when you come to Long Island you will stop by to visit and let me show you around my store."

Behind her, Kate heard Jerry chime in with "Actually, Kate will be out that way in the near future. Maybe as soon as next week, right, Kate?"

Kate turned quickly and gave Jerry an angry look, causing him to raise his eyebrows and step back toward the door.

"Possibly, yes." Kate turned back to Sam, smiling sweetly. "I have some personal business to conduct, but if I have the time, I'd enjoy seeing your store. I'll have my granddaughter with me, though."

"No problem, bring her along."

"Well, it was nice seeing you again, Sam." Kate extended her hand and Sam took it lightly in his, holding it for a few seconds. "Good-bye." Kate pulled her hand back, sliding both into the embroidered pockets on her dress.

"Hopefully we will meet again soon," Sam smiled and, turning to Jerry, added "Thanks so much." With a final wave, he was out the door.

Kate watched him go, then, shaking a finger in Jerry''s direction, said, "Don't put me in that position again!" and headed for the office, leaving Jerry looking after her with a bemused expression and Captain Ahab chiming in, "Don't do that, don't do that."

CHAPTER 28

Kate stood in the center of her living room, arms folded over her loose-fitting sundress, looking out her bay window at the sleek dark car pulling to a stop on the grassy verge beyond the low split rail fence. She had almost convinced herself David wouldn't really show up, would call and back out of this hastily arranged visit to see Glory with some tale of emergency family or business issues. No such luck, though, Kate thought, as she watched him unfold his long body from the car, carefully shutting and locking the doors. In theory, Kate wanted him involved in his granddaughter's life; in practice, if past experience counted for anything, she told herself, it was going to be hell. Satisfied that the car was secure, David turned and walked up the flagstone pathway to the front door apparently unaware of Kate's continued scrutiny. She noted with relief that he was dressed appropriately for the beach in swim trunks and sandals, his broad torso covered with a plain white tee shirt, his body looking tanned and fit. Kate shifted her weight, curling her toes in her worn leather sandals and tugging unconsciously at her swimsuit, concealed beneath the dress.

When David had called the other night, wanting an opportunity to spend some time with Glory, Kate had been reluctant to accede to his original request that he be allowed to take the child to his own home in Plymouth, where she could meet his wife Jill and whichever one of his two sons was home at the moment. Glory was shy and nervous with men, Kate had come to realize, and she didn't feel she could just turn her over to a grandfather she didn't know and a stepgrandmother whose feelings toward Glory Kate had not had the opportunity to assess. Or so she told herself. In any case, after some heated exchange, David had agreed to come to Yarmouth and spend an afternoon on the beach in the company of both Kate and Glory, a highly preferred activity for Glory that hopefully would create an initial positive experience with Grandpa. At least, that was what Kate thought was best and she was gratified when a phone call to Dr. Lawler confirmed this as the right course to take. Not that David would care what the psychologist thought, she told herself caustically.

The doorbell sang out its musical notes and Kate turned to smile at Glory, curled up on the sofa in her swimsuit and terrycloth beach robe, sandaled feet tucked beneath her. Kate felt a twinge of worry at the apprehensive look on the little girl's face.

"Hey, we're going to have fun! Your Grandpa's here to play with you on the beach. The three of us are going to have a blast together!"

Let's hope so anyway, Kate told herself, taking a deep breath and pulling open the door.

"Hello, Kate."

Kate smiled at David, standing quietly on the steps, hands by his sides, willing herself to relax.

"Hi, David, how are you?" Kate bit her lip wondering if she sounded a touch too cheery to be natural.

If she did, David gave no reocgnition of it. "I'm fine, Kate," he said in polite tones. "And you?"

"I'm good. A beautiful day, don't you think?" That was just stupid, Kate castigated herself, casting about something more intelligent to say.

"Beautiful. Are you going to invite me in?" David gestured toward the living room as Kate moved aside.

"Of course, David. I'm sorry, come on in. I'm just a little nervous about this."

"I understand completely. I confess I'm a bit nervous myself."

David stepped in, his gaze taking in the room and lighting on Glory, still curled up on the sofa.

"Hey." David's voice softened, his eyes on Glory, a gentle smile curving his lips.

Glory looked up at him, the familiar troubled expression in her eyes. Kate turned toward her. "See, Glory, I told you Grandpa was here." When Glory didn't move from her position on the sofa, Kate lifted her into her arms. The little girl quickly molded her small body to her grandmother's, her head on Kate's shoulder, her one visible eye gazing with some trepidation at her grandfather.

David tilted his head slightly, still smiling. "I hear you like the beach, Glory. Well, so do I. What do you say we head on down there? Are you ready? I know I am."

Glory's face cleared and a tiny smile appeared, pulling the one visible corner of her mouth upward. Head still on Kate's shoulder, she gave an almost imperceptible nod.

Kate and David's eyes met for a moment. David spread his hands out, hunching his shoulders. "What are we waiting for? Let's go."

The beach was crowded, the hot white sand studded with brightly colored beach blankets, chairs, and umbrellas alongside clumps of dried brown seaweed. Kate and David, loaded down with beach chairs and bags of their own, had silently trailed behind a more animated Glory through the narrow streets to the beach and now struggled through the fine dry sand, looking for a comfortable spot to set up camp, exchanging no more that a few cursory observations about prospective sites. Much of Kate's attention was directed at Glory anyway, already at the water's edge, letting the cool little waves lap at her ankles as she danced back and forth in the foam. Finally, David dropped his load of beach equipment with a grunted "Here, this is fine."

It took only a moment or two to spread out the blankets and open up the chairs and affix their individual shades and umbrellas. Once that was done, Kate and David looked at each other uncomfortably across the expanse of their private beach domain. Finally, Kate said as quietly as possible under the circumstances, "Look, David, we're going to have to get used to this if we're going to co-grandparent successfully. More successfully than we did with parenting Ally, anyway. It's been long enough, God knows. Surely we can do this."

David held up his hand to stop her. "Enough. We may not ever be the best of friends, but I think we can learn to be civil." He turned to look at Glory, who had plopped down on the wet sand, letting the waves break around her, her giggles audible over the sound the surf made as seawater dragged the sand under her legs and hands back to the ocean.

"She loves the ocean," Kate offered.

David nodded slightly, his eyes still on his granddaughter. "She certainly takes after her mother, doesn't she" he said more to himself than to Kate.

Kate looked at him, examining his features as he stood gazing at the small figure in the pink and green swimsuit, now up on her feet, playing tag with the waves, sunlight glinting off her wet skin. His expression was closed and guarded and, with a little sigh, Kate looked away again, removing her sandals and pulling her sundress over her head as she headed down the beach toward Glory, calling a "come on" over her shoulder and hoping he'd follow.

Kate reached Glory first, giving her a quick squeeze. "Hey, can I play?" When Glory smiled assent, Kate lifted her in her arms, carrying the child to where the waves were breaking in a spray of silver and creamy white. As Glory shrieked in delight, Kate lowered her into the retreating swirl of ocean, then lifted her up and over the foam as the next wave broke under her.

David came up behind her and now stood off to one side, smiling at Glory and calling encouragement. "Whoa, that was a big one!" and "That's the way to do it!" as Glory pulled her knees up to her chest to avoid the spray. After a few minutes, he moved in closer with a "Here, let me help" and soon he and Kate were on either side of the little girl, lifting her high in the air, hands firmly under her armpits.

They tired long before Glory, and Kate was able to retreat to the shade of the umbrellas and watch while David dutifully filled castle molds with sand, then turned them out in rows of neat little pillars, Glory observing cautiously, casting occasional glances in her grandmother's direction. However, once she began jumping gleefully onto the rows of castle walls, turning them into piles of wet sand, David retreated as well much to Kate's amusement, grimacing and muttering, "Here, you can do it yourself this time." He sat down heavily in the umbrella chair next to Kate. "Why do they all do that?" he asked irritably, as much to himself as to Kate.

Kate smiled benignly. "Who knows? Ally used to do it all the time. Remember that time you built her a big castle with walls and a moat? You and she must have spent an hour working on it and as soon as it was finished, she leaped right in the middle of it, smashing it to bits. You were so mad at her that day!"

"Yeah, I remember." David chewed his lip, staring pensively at Glory, who was running through the sandy ruins. He sighed audibly, leaning back in his chair and closing his eyes. "I've been remembering a lot of things lately, Kate. Ever since you called to tell me Ally was dead, I haven't been able to get her off my mind. I even dream about her. It's driving me nuts."

"Really?" Kate paused. "I dream about her a lot too. And not necessarily good dreams." When David didn't respond, Kate went on, hesitantly at first, to relate the dream of Ally climbing out onto the jetty and disappearing into the foam, and how she had whispered "Glory" after years of vanishing silently.

When she had finished, David sat unmoving for a few moments, eyes still closed, until Kate began to wonder if he might have fallen asleep. "Well, none of my dreams are as dramatic as that but it does feel like she's trying to tell me something, saying something I can't quite catch. She always looks so sad, so *worried*, and exhausted, like she hasn't slept in weeks."

Kate nodded, looking at David's expressionless face, his eyelashes black against his copper-colored cheeks. "Everyone keeps telling me to stop trying to find out what happened to Ally, where she was, what she was doing and why. Who Glory's father is. But I just feel, deep down inside, that it's vitally important that I know. And a big part of that is seeing Ally's face in my dreams, and sometimes even when I'm awake, trying to tell me something—something really, well, *necessary* to Glory's well-being. Do you understand that, David?"

David opened his eyes, taking in Kate's earnest expression. "I understand it."

Kate hesitated, debating whether to continue. "Look, I may not know what happened to them, David, but it probably wasn't good." Kate described the drawing, the play themes, the fire at the ranch where The Way had been staying in New Mexico.

When she was finished, David looked away from her, back down the beach where Glory stood in the surf with her back to them, still as a statue, gazing out toward the horizon. "Maybe knowing is the best thing and maybe it isn't. But it seems to me this is the only way to tell." He looked back at Kate, his expression still unreadable. "I'm concerned about it, nonetheless. Concerned in terms of Glory's well-being. So let me in on what you find out, okay?"

Kate nodded, her own expression guarded, until she caught sight of a slender figure in a dark blue one piece swimsuit, a few wisps of silver hair escaping a white swim cap, off to her right. Fran's blue eyes, vivid in her creased, suntanned face, were filled with curiosity as she took in the scene. Kate groaned inwardly before smiling brightly as she said, "Hi, Fran. Beautiful day, isn't it?"

"Yes, it is, isn't it? The ocean is just delightful, so refreshing. Swimming is such wonderful exercise, especially on a day like this." Fran seemed to be directing these comments to David, who returned her gaze with a politely puzzled expression.

"Fran, perhaps you remember my ex-husband, David? Ally's father?" Kate tried to recall whether Fran and David had ever actually been introduced. She and David had never lived here together, but surely, years ago, David might have met her on a visit.

Fran's look of curiosity turned to one of studied interest. "I'm not sure, dear. Maybe so."

Resignedly, Kate offered introductions and David murmured a "Yes, of course. Nice to meet you."

Fran hesitated, seeming unwilling to move on, her eyes taking in Kate and David and glancing out toward Glory playing at the edge of the ocean.

"So, how are you, Fran? Everything going okay?" Kate queried somewhat desperately.

"Fine, just fine." Fran's expression brightened suddenly. "It looks like I've got a renter for the cottage the week of Labor Day. A nice man, middle-aged, looking for a quiet place by the sea to take a late summer vacation."

Kate smiled, thinking Fran sounded as if she were quoting from the real estate agent who handled her rentals. "That's great, Fran. I knew you would get that week rented eventually."

"Yes. Well, I'll be sure to send him by the Sea Witch."

Kate smiled again. "Thanks. That will be great."

Fran took one last look around her and, with a small wave of farewell, reluctantly continued on down the beach. As she moved off out of earshot David and Kate caught each other's eye and both laughed out loud. David shook his head and leaned back against his chair, closing his eyes again. "Well, if nothing else, Kate, you're going to give your neighbors plenty to talk about."

"Oh, Fran's a sweetheart, really." Kate hesitated for a moment. "David, do you go to Mass?"

David opened his eyes and looked at her curiously. "Sometimes. Not every Sunday and Holy Day of Obligation like we did when we were kids, I have to admit. Christmas and Easter mostly. Besides, I'm divorced and remarried, remember? As far as the Catholic Church is concerned, I'm not exactly a member in good standing. Why are you asking me this?"

"Because I've been thinking a lot about religion, belief in God, spirituality, whatever, since I found out about Ally and this group she joined. I'm trying to make some sense of it." She shifted in her chair, the better to keep one eye on Glory and still meet David's gaze. The little girl had abandoned the sandy heap of her former castle and was squatting at the water's edge, examining seashells.

"Well, if you do, I'd like to be the first to know because it makes no sense to me." David shook his head in exasperation, then turned back to Kate. "How about you? Do you go to Mass, Kate?"

"No. I haven't been in years. I wouldn't feel welcome there either although, I don't know, from what I hear divorce isn't necessarily treated the same way it was years ago. It just stopped having any real meaning for me. I guess I still believe in a God, but I couldn't explain just what that means."

"I couldn't explain God to you either. I do know that I left that image of the old guy with the long beard sitting on some cloud up in the sky back in grade school."

Kate laughed. "I know what you mean. I'm not sure how much I believe in the rest of the Christian story, though. Enough, I guess, that I still have a Nativity scene as part of my Christmas decorations. I don't think there's any one way to understand God."

David had turned back to the ocean where sunlit waves showed patches of foam turned to scattered nuggets of gold. "You know, Kate, the end of our marriage was brutal, but it wasn't always like that. We had some great moments too. Ally's birth was one of them. She was a beautiful baby, much like her mother. I remember you holding her right after she was born, exhausted but alight with happiness at the same time."

Kate caught her breath, too astonished to reply.

"Didn't expect that, did you. Like I said, I've been remembering a lot of things. The way it ended..." David looked up at the turquoise-blue sky.

Anywhere but at me, Kate told herself, watching him and marveling at this turn of events.

David suddenly met her gaze as if reading her thoughts. "We should have done better, Kate. Our marriage didn't deserve that. Ally didn't deserve that." And then, without missing a beat, he added, "Why haven't you married again, Kate?"

Kate regarded him coolly, pausing a moment to collect her thoughts before replying. "I don't know exactly. I do know I like my independence. I like not having to worry about pleasing someone else, not having to compromise. I just have myself to deal with. Anyway, I guess I just haven't met anyone I'd want to marry badly enough that I'd be willing to give that up." Suddenly, Sam Ritter's face floated into her thoughts but she pushed the image away resolutely.

Glory ran up to Kate, having tired of exploring the water's edge. She was shivering as Kate wrapped a beach towel around her, pulling her onto her lap and holding her close.

"It's too bad. You would probably do well with someone who isn't me." David smiled at a speechless Kate as he reached out and stroked Glory's wet hair, brushing it away from where it had plastered itself to her cheek. "We should head back. It looks as though Glory has had enough of the beach for one day."

CHAPTER 29

Behind a one-way mirror in Dr. Lawler's office, Kate was attentively observing the therapy session between the psychologist and Glory. The little girl sat cross-legged on the floor, watching intently as Dr. Lawler conducted a conversation among the group of animal puppets. One of the puppets, the rabbit called Bunny with the big floppy ears, still didn't want to talk and the others, Pig and the duck called Mrs. Mallard, were trying to get him to do so, eventually concluding that the puppet would talk when ready. Glory smiled and even giggled a little at the puppets' antics as they tried to encourage their friend to talk but her expression became more serious as they tried to think of reasons why Bunny wouldn't speak. Maybe he was sad, maybe bad things had happened to him and now he was afraid to talk, maybe grown-ups had yelled at him for talking too much. Kate scanned Glory's face as the puppets suggested possibilities to each other, trying to decide if one was eliciting more of a reaction than the others. The suggestions took on a more humorous tone after a while, making Glory smile again, and Kate, sighing in frustration, decided that she could determine nothing conclusive from the little performance.

Dr. Lawler offered Glory the puppets and watched as she tried them on, showing her how to place her fingers so that she could make their mouths move. Kate looked on with some amusement as Glory made one of the puppets, Pig, talk animatedly to the quiet Bunny, moving her own lips as she did so but without making any sounds. As the monologue seemed to get more heated Dr. Lawler interrupted, asking Glory to label how Pig and Bunny might be feeling, using line drawings of faces with different expressions. Kate noted with interest that Glory chose angry for Pig and both sad and angry for Bunny.

With the puppet play over, Dr. Lawler suggested Glory draw for a while. Kate could see that, at first, Glory was just scribbling but after a few minutes a picture started to take shape, a much larger head of a person with big eyes and a big mouth standing on two stick legs in front of a group of much smaller people with round heads and faces that resembled the sad look in Dr. Lawler's line drawings. As soon as she was finished, she attempted to rip the drawing in two but, dissuaded by Dr. Lawler, she retreated to the door clearly wanting to leave. Kate, concerned, stood up, wavering between her desire to let the session play out and her need to comfort her granddaughter. Kate relaxed, however, as Dr. Lawler coaxed Glory back into the room to choose a face drawing to demonstrate her own feelings ("angry" and "scared") and receive a sticker for her efforts along with the opportunity to watch a DVD of her favorite cartoons. Once Glory was sitting in front of the TV screen following the characters' animated antics, Dr. Lawler called Kate in from the observation room.

"She's making a lot of progress, quite honestly," Dr. Lawler began, responding to Kate's troubled expression. "She's a bright little girl who can communicate quite well, even without speech. And she will speak eventually, when she's ready."

"Oh, I can see that. And I know this will take some time." Kate hesitated. "Dr. Lawler, I wanted to show you a picture Glory painted the other day."

Dr. Lawler looked at Kate with interest. "Certainly. Why don't you come over to my desk and have a seat, Mrs. LaRue." With a glance toward Glory, still watching the cartoon with rapt interest, Kate followed Dr. Lawler across the room. Removing Glory's painting from the large cloth bag she was carrying, she placed it on the desk in front of Dr. Lawler, the brightly colored halo of flames intensified by the soft light of the desk lamp.

"It looked to me like a painting of a building on fire," Kate offered "with a lot of people outside. See?" Kate pointed to the relevant parts of the drawing as she spoke.

"Yes, it certainly could be." Dr. Lawler nodded agreement as she studied the painting, leaning her head on her hand, elbow propped on the table.

"I think I told you that I have reason to believe my daughter was involved in some type of religious commune out in New Mexico." Kate paused and Dr. Lawler, looking up, nodded again. "Well, last night I went online and found a news story about a group called The Way who were burned out of the ranch they were living on in New Mexico not long before Ally seems to have arrived in San Francisco. So I'm wondering if maybe..." Kate gestured mutely toward the painting.

Dr. Lawler shrugged slightly. "Could be. It's a definite possibility. There are undeniable themes in Glory's play that suggest she may have lived with a group of people, rather than a more typical nuclear family." Seeing the question in Kate's eyes she added, "Her paintings and drawings often contain groups of people much like this. She seldom uses the smaller family units of toy people when she plays; instead, she sets up large groups with a variety of figures, and usually with the farm set, not the houses, which, incidentally, could seem like the more familiar setting to her. So I tend to think that Glory may have come from a somewhat unconventional background."

Kate sighed. "I'm still hoping to find out more about this 'unconventional background.' Sometime very soon, maybe as early as this weekend, Glory and I are going to take a trip to New York. While I'm there, I plan to visit this Yoga center that Ally was involved with. I'm hoping someone will be able to give me some information about this group, The Way, if that's who they were, and maybe identify Glory's father." Seeing the frown gathering on Dr. Lawler's face, Kate added, "Glory and I will be staying with my sister. I won't be bringing her to The Center for Yoga, Meditation, and Healing."

"Mrs. LaRue, I know you have Glory's best interests at heart, but I would warn you about what you might find out about this group, and possibly Glory's father. Whenever she engages in play with these themes, she enacts what seem to be violent and angry scenes. These groups often have a male figure who seems to be in charge and whose actions are often aggressive and upsetting to her. I don't know what you know about cults but it's possible that your daughter was involved with one. If so, you might create some serious conflict, particularly with her father, if you should find him. In any case, this wouldn't be an environment you would want for Glory." Dr. Lawler sat with her arms folded on her desk, her eyes locked into Kate's with the earnest intensity of a teacher lecturing a student.

Kate shook her head in amazement. "Look, I don't intend to turn Glory over to these people who may or may not be a cult. I realize that, whatever happened, the experience wasn't a good one for either Glory or Ally. I just need to know what *did* happen. It's important," Kate finished lamely, a heavy silence falling between them. Why did she need to know, anyway? What was it that made her continue to push this issue when everyone around her thought it was foolish, even dangerous? Everyone, that is, except David, she reminded herself with considerable annoyance.

Kate shook this thought off as Dr. Lawler, who had dropped her gaze back to the painting on her desk and its seeming halo of red-orange flames, looked up resignedly and said, "I don't agree with you that it's this important, not at this time. However, I assume you're going to do this, regardless. But in your desire to know what happened, I'd advise you not to take this any further than you absolutely have to, for Glory's sake."

CHAPTER 30

Five days later, relaxing in Maggie's comfortable family room, Kate watched as Glory cautiously observed Maggie's little two-year-old grandson Nathan push a train around a wooden track. Tucking her feet beneath her in the big floral patterned chair, Kate thought again about that conversation with David at the beach. It was curious to realize that he was feeling compelled like she was to know more about what had happened, as well as to know Glory and to be a part of her life. It was almost as if Ally were speaking to them somehow, trying to communicate something to both of them. From beyond the grave, Kate thought with some mild amusement, but she quickly dismissed this line of thought with an expression of annoyance and returned to her rumination on David's recent interest in their granddaughter, not to mention his comments on their marriage as well as herself. "It's a good thing," Kate told herself, "I want him to be more involved, right?" She sighed, squirming a little in her chair. "I'm just not sure if I want be involved with *him*. There's no way around it, though, if I want him involved with Glory. Besides, this may not be as difficult as I thought if that conversation on the beach is any indication."

Lost in her thoughts about David and Glory, Kate didn't hear Maggie as she came into the wide, carpeted family room, a tray of drinks and light snacks in hand. Kate jumped slightly as Maggie set it down on a polished side table, causing Maggie to laugh and comment jokingly, "Whoa, deep thoughts, there, sis. Either that, or I've become really scary with age." Kate smiled at that, taking in Maggie's attractively styled and colored hair, her carefully applied makeup, and her slender body dressed in dark blue Capri pants and a pale pink sleeveless blouse.

"Actually, I was thinking about David and his recent change of heart regarding Glory," she explained as she picked up a glass of cool white wine and contemplated the selection of cheeses Maggie had provided.

Maggie let out a snort of derision. "Right. He wants to see her. From what you said, I didn't get the impression he was offering to help in any practical way—like financially."

Kate smiled slightly, settling back in her chair with her Camembert and wineglass. "No. But I'm hoping if he gets to know and love her that will follow."

Ignoring the snacks, Maggie lifted her own wineglass to her lips, and, taking an appreciative sip, looked back at Kate with a sigh. "Maybe. Don't count on it, though."

"Maggie, listen to me. David was a good father to Ally. He stayed involved. He did his part financially."

"Wow. You're defending him. Things *have* changed."

"No, Maggie, they haven't. David could be difficult and I took issue with a lot of things he did like the motorcycle racing and the going to gun shows and rifle ranges. Not to mention keeping a gun in the house. He and I often didn't see eye to eye on how to deal with Ally but he was still her father. I never said he failed to live up to his responsibilities." Kate's voice was cool and firm and her gaze matched her tone.

Maggie threw up her hands in mock surrender. "Whew! Sorry!" She picked up her wineglass and took another sip of her wine, eyes locked on her grandson and grandniece, both now pushing individual trains around the track. "So what's next?"

"Well, as I've told you, what's next is that I need to go into the city tomorrow and visit the Yoga center where I think Ally met this John McCarty with whom she eventually went to New Mexico. I'm hoping someone might be there who knew them, or, better yet, knows where John McCarty is now. If you could watch Glory for me, it would be a big help."

Maggie waved her off with a shrug. "That's not a problem, you know that. Actually, I was thinking more about this Sam guy you were telling me about earlier. Do your plans for tomorrow include a drive out to Long Island?"

Kate smiled ruefully, trying to imagine what had possessed her to tell Maggie about Sam. "I don't know. Maybe." Kate had to admit to herself that she actually did want to see Sam again, and not just because she had a professional curiosity about his store. Nevertheless, she told herself, anything beyond business was out of the question. She sighed. "Look, Maggie, don't make too much of this. He's a nice man but I'm not really interested in a relationship right now."

Maggie cast a critical eye on Kate over the rim of her wineglass. "Kate, how many years has it been since you and David split up? Twenty-something? Don't you think it's time you got interested in someone else?"

"No, I don't, Maggie." Kate said wearily. "I think this is definitely *not* the time. I don't know when or *if* there will be a time. I'm sorry I even mentioned Sam to you at this point."

Maggie bit her lip, eyes focused on something above Kate's head. "Right. Sorry."

Kate kept her gaze focused on the two children, both of whom glanced over at Kate and Maggie, anxiety and confusion in their faces as the tense silence between the two lengthened. Nathan dropped the train engine he had been holding and ran over to Maggie, extending chubby arms and calling out, "Up, Grammy." Maggie lifted him onto her lap, murmuring soothingly. She looked over at her sister, watching as Kate reached out for Glory, pulling her close as the little girl instinctively reached for the locket, clutching it tightly to her chest. A determined expression crossed her features as Maggie took a deep breath and began to speak, words tumbling out in a torrent of quick emotion.

"You know, Kate, once there was a time when we could talk about anything; we were best friends as well as sisters. And we did talk about everything in our lives—parents, school, girlfriends, boyfriends, life, love, the meaning of the universe, whatever. I've really missed that. I've never had a friend I could confide in like I could with you because no one knows me like you do, no one shares the same history. But I guess you don't feel the same way, do you?"

Kate turned to stare in astonishment at Maggie, Glory's dark head under chin. "Maggie, I'm so sorry. I don't know what to say. I love you, and you will always be my one and only sister with a special place in my heart but..." Kate hesitated.

"But what?" Maggie's brightened gaze had turned to a frown.

"Well, whatever our history together may have been, you and I have very different lives now and I am not sure we understand each other all that well anymore. I like my life the way it is, and you... Well, whenever I've talked to you over the last twenty-something years, you were always trying to get me to change it." Kate tried to keep the irritation out of her voice but knew she had not, judging from Maggie's expression. Unable to restrain herself, Kate blurted out, "Besides, when did you *ever* want to hear what *I* had to say?"

Maggie shook her head sadly. "Maybe you're right; maybe I don't understand you all that well anymore. I'd like to, though. And I *do* want to hear what you have to say. Maybe you really are happy being alone and running that store. You're a good businesswoman, I realize that. Life's cut you a raw deal in lot of ways, and you've handled it all better that I ever could. I mean that," Maggie added, noting the look of shocked surprise on Kate's face. "To be honest, I can't imagine how you do it. I'd be so lonely if it were me. Don't you ever want to be with someone again? Even a friend...or a sister?"

Kate laughed. "Yes, sometimes. But as far as being with someone like Sam is concerned, I really *don't* know. As for you, I guess we'll just have to work on that."

Maggie smiled, releasing a wriggling Nathan, who trotted across the room and began rooting through a large brightly colored toy box. "You know, I've thought a lot about what you said to me that day on the Cape when your marriage was breaking up and I had come there thinking I would help you get your life back together. Remember? You told me you thought that after Dad died I was looking for someone to take care of me so I wouldn't have to be alone." Maggie paused, measuring Kate's expression. "Well, maybe you *were* right about that, at least a little. I like my life the way it is too, by the way. I wouldn't want to change it either. And I don't want to be alone. I didn't then and I don't now."

A mischievous grin tugged at the corners of Kate's mouth. "Well, just so long as you recognize that, I think you and I *do* have a chance."

CHAPTER 31

Kate stepped out of the shadows of the subway entrance and onto the streets of Manhattan, her arms wrapped tightly around her torso, her purse pressing into her side. The day was sticky with late summer heat and humidity, and Kate's thin white cotton blouse clung damply to her skin in patches. A crowd of kids dressed in the matching tee shirts of a summer camp pushed past her and onto the sun-drenched pavement, laughing and calling out to each other, oblivious to her presence. Above her the tall glass and steel buildings shimmered in the city heat haze. Although she did it often enough when buying for the Sea Witch, Kate was never really that fond of coming to New York, Manhattan especially. She always felt slightly claustrophobic from the crowds, the incessant traffic noises, the street smells, and the towering buildings. *I guess I prefer the peace and quiet of small town life*, Kate thought to herself, then stifled a giggle as images of the crowds and traffic on Route 28 in the summer passed through her mind.

With a resolute sigh, she pulled a small piece of paper from her purse and, after reassuring herself that she had remembered the address correctly, set off in the direction of The Center for Yoga, Meditation, and Healing. Kate moved along swiftly, weaving her way through the river of people without actually seeing them, her thoughts focused on what she planned to say when she arrived. She knew Kevin had called his friend Nick Maxwell, who, it seemed, recognized John McCarty's name but had been noncommittal about imparting any information about him. Knowing this, Kate had balked at discussing the situation over the phone with Nick, fearing he would just put her off. Instead, she had insisted on this face-to-face meeting, hoping she could persuade him to help her locate McCarty more easily.

Kate suddenly slowed her pace, nearly colliding with a harried-looking man perspiring heavily in a business suit, and found herself looking up at the broad windows and door that comprised the façade of the building her piece of paper said housed The Center for Yoga, Meditation, and Healing. Kate turned and quickly ascended the short flight of stone steps. As she climbed, she envisioned Ally, dressed in black clothes and her hair spiked in a rainbow of colors, doing the same some seven or so years ago, pulling open the door, consulting the directory...Kate shook herself, forcing thoughts of Ally out of her head. The Center, she noted as she scanned the directory, seemed to occupy most of the third floor. Kate spotted the bank of elevators down the brass and granite hallway and headed in their direction, wrapping her arms again around her rib cage, her fingers crossed beneath her elbows.

This is it, she told herself as the elevator glided upward. *If I can't get Nick Maxwell or someone here to listen to me, I'm out of options and I may as well give up.* Kate contemplated that for a moment before the elevator doors opened and she found herself standing in front of large frosted double doors on which the name of The Center for Yoga, Meditation, and Healing was inscribed in English and what thought might be Sanskrit, along with what she recognized as the symbol for the sacred sound *OM*. Pushing through the doors, found herself in a reception room with an attractive young woman of some Eurasian background, who smilingly told Kate to take a seat while she called Nick out to meet her.

Kate barely had time to peruse the magazine titles, all apparently on the subject of Yoga, before a middle-aged man whose lined face was the color of rich bronze set off by brilliant green eyes appeared and introduced himself as Nick Maxwell.

"It's a pleasure to meet you, Mrs. LaRue." Nick continued, adding as he spread his hands wide, "I'm not sure I can be of much help to you, but come on down to my office and we can talk for a bit and then, since you came all this way, I thought perhaps you might like a little tour. I could offer you some complimentary classes as well if you're going to be in town for a while."

They had reached the office by the time Nick had finished his little speech and he gestured toward a cushioned straight back chair which Kate sank into, grateful for the cool blast of air from the overhead vent. Nick seated himself behind the handsome oak desk and looked earnestly at Kate over his steepled fingers. "Now, from what I understand, Mrs. LaRue, you're looking for a man named John McCarty who you think may have been associated with the Center and who may be the father of your granddaughter."

Kate straightened up in her chair, interjecting quickly, "No, Mr. Maxwell, that's *not* correct. I don't think Mr. McCarty is Glory's father. I think he knew my daughter Allison, who was also associated with the Center several years ago. Ally is dead now but I have reason to believe that she and Mr. McCarty left here together to join a group called The Way. I also believe Mr. McCarty is here in New York now."

"Why look for him here? There are Internet directories—"

"Obviously, I've tried other resources without success." Kate held up her hand as Nick Maxwell began again to interrupt. "This is really important to me and to my granddaughter. I'm not blaming or accusing anyone of anything. I just want information about what happened to my daughter."

"Even if I knew anything about this Mr. McCarty, I think you realize, as I told you over the phone, that I would be unable to give you any information about him, especially any contact information." Nick sat back in his chair, his intense green eyes focused on Kate's.

"Yes, I know what you said." Kate pressed her lips together as she considered what to say next. "You know, Mr. Maxwell, I think it's very possible that Mr. McCarty would want to speak with me if he knew I was looking for him. I think he and Ally were close at one time; he probably cared a lot about her. And he probably doesn't know that she died. If you know where he is and how to get in touch with him, I think he would appreciate it if you gave him this information and told him how much I'd like to talk with him." Kate reached into her purse and pulled out a folded sheet of paper with one of her business cards stapled to the top left-hand corner and slid it across the desk to Nick, who picked it up with a small sigh. "I've explained the situation in this note, along with my contact information. If you want, you may read it yourself, if only just for reassurance that there's nothing untoward about this, then simply pass it along to Mr. McCarty when you see him."

Nick held the paper between his fingers, looking down at his desk and then over toward Kate, his eyes devoid of expression. "Really, Mrs. LaRue, what makes you think I'll ever see this man?"

"Please just give it to him if you do. There will be no harm in that. Mr. McCarty can do what he likes with the information."

Nick nodded and placed the paper off to one side of his desk. Watching him, Kate asked impulsively, "Did you know Allison LaRue? Or remember anything about a group called The Way?"

Nick pursed his lips slightly as an emotion flitted across his features, too quickly for Kate to identify it. "No, I'm sorry, but I don't remember your daughter. As you said, this was several years ago now and many people come through here, take a few classes, and move on. I don't meet all of them. As for The Way..." he paused, collecting his thoughts. "People who come to the Center are searching for something. Sometimes it's just a way to get some exercise but often people are seeking something more than that." paused again. "What do you know about Yoga, Mrs. LaRue?"

"Please, you can call me Kate. And can I call you Nick?" Nick nodded, his lips turned upward in a slight smile. "Well, Nick, I have taken some classes in Yoga and meditation. As a matter of fact, I attended a weekend retreat years ago, not long after Ally left home. I was having a hard time dealing with the fact that she had just up and left, with no word as to where she was or if she was okay. So I guess you could say I was searching for something."

Nick inclined his head in acknowledgment. "Yes, well, there you have it. Often people feel there is something missing from their lives, especially their spiritual lives, or they are trying to find a way to deal with whatever problems they are facing, so they come to us as a way to find solutions. Anyway, just to give you some background, even though you probably already know this, the word *Yoga* means 'union' in Sanskrit, a language of India where Yoga originated thousands of years ago. It refers to the union of mind, body, and spirit in communion with the ultimate reality, the eternal universal energy, if you will. The physical exercises are just a part of Yoga. The exercises that most people in this part of the world associate with the word *Yoga* are actually only one of several types of Yoga practice, which may be seen as branches or limbs. The others include meditation and self discipline—"

"Yes, I thought the name of this center was a little redundant." Kate commented quickly, unable to resist the opportunity to interject this observation.

Nick glanced at her appraisingly. "Yes, I suppose that's true; however, not everyone would understand that. As I said, the common belief is that Yoga is a form of exercise, not the complete philosophical discipline and lifestyle that it actually is. Most people in the Western world never even heard of it until the Beatles went to India to study with the Maharishi Mahesh Yogi in the 1960s."

Kate shrugged her acknowledgment of this as Nick continued. "Anyway, while many benefits may be obtained at all levels of Yoga practice, the full experience, anything even close to a true attainment of union or enlightenment, if you will, requires years of dedication, learning, and practice. We offer classes not only in all levels of *hatha* yoga, the physical exercises, but also in the other branches as well as opportunities to study the Vedas, the Upanishads, and, of course, the Bhagavad Gita, we consider to be the essential great spiritual texts of India. Some students have been with us for years and have become fairly advanced in their studies and their practice."

Nick paused, glancing at Kate to check whether she understood the references to the Indian religious texts, but seeing her nod in concurrence, he continued. "Well, sometimes people, while appreciating the process and the goals of Yoga, are impatient with the time and energy needed to achieve them and think that these can be obtained more easily through other methods. They leave and find other approaches or develop them on their own."

Nick hesitated again, organizing his thoughts. "I never met Joshua Emmanuel, as he called himself. However, I heard about him later. A very pleasant, charming, charismatic man, I was told, an excellent student of Yoga with an eclectic background of spiritual studies who brought some very interesting discussions to the groups and classes he was working with. He had some very creative and unique interpretations of religious texts, including those of India as well as others such as the Bible, some of the Christian Gnostic writings, Kabbalist writings such as the Zohar, the Tao Te Ching, and so on. Very intelligent, very well read, really quite dedicated to his studies. Anyway, I think he became more than a little impatient with the more traditional approach implemented here at the Center and soon started teaching classes of his own in his apartment. He was able to attract a number of the Center's students by, among other things, using a variety of techniques to achieve deep meditative states and sometimes advocating the use of certain drugs to aid in this, not something advocated here, of course."

Nick caught Kate's glance and, when she nodded understandingly, he continued with his narrative. "In any case, the Center became concerned about his activities and asked him to disassociate himself from us. He did, and soon after he left New York with a group of people, some of them former students and teachers here, to form a practice or communal group out west that they called The Way. Beyond that, I know very little. I don't know if The Way still exists, and I don't know what became of Joshua Emmanuel either. This sort of thing is distressing for those of us at the Center, by the way, because we hate to see the teachings and practice of Yoga distorted and the wrong impression given about who we are and what we do and this was a prime example of that." Nick stopped, needing to catch his breath a little after reeling off his last statement a bit too quickly.

Kate cleared her throat. "Nick, may I show you a couple of photographs? Just to see if you recognize the persons in them?"

Nick smiled resignedly. "Fine. I assume these photos are of your daughter, who I am sure I didn't know, but I'll take a look."

Kate slid the photograph of Ally standing on the street in New York City across Nick's desk and watched as he picked it up and studied it, his face blank. "This is my daughter Ally, Nick."

Nick looked up at her, sympathy in his eyes. "Mrs. LaRue, Kate, there are many young women who look like her in New York and some of them even come here, but I don't recognize her specifically." He held the photograph out to Kate but she shook her head in refusal. "Please put that with the note for Mr. McCarty. I have several copies at home."

"Fine," he sighed, attaching the photo to the folded note with a paper clip. He looked back to see a photo of another young woman on his desk. He stared at it for a few seconds, then shook his head. "No, definitely not. Who is she?"

"I don't know. I found it among my daughter's effects."

Nick handed the photograph back to Kate, who slipped it into her purse. "I wish I could help you, Kate."

"Please, just give the note and the photo to Mr. McCarty."

An unidentifiable emotion flickered across Nick's face and was instantly gone. "Yes, right," he replied, a touch of exasperation in his voice.

"I think I would like that tour you mentioned, if that's still possible," Kate said, seeing the look of dismissal in his eyes.

Nick smiled slightly. "Sure, why not." He rose from his desk, leaning over to speak into an intercom to the receptionist, and then gestured to Kate. "Come with me. I should tell you, though, the Center is quite large, so I will just show you a sampling of what we have to offer."

Kate followed Nick down the hall, their footsteps audible on the polished wooden floors, sunlight streaming through the wide windows to their right. They stopped at a door composed of a smooth blond wood that looked well varnished and contained a small window. Nick gestured to Kate to look inside. The room was large, well lit and essentially empty of furniture. A half dozen or so women of varying ages as well as a few young men dressed in loose running suits or sweats stood on brightly colored yoga mats, their bodies folded in half with their faces touching their knees and their hands wrapped around their ankles. An older woman, her long silver hair tied back in a thick braid, stood to one side in the same position, a short stack of small, slender books and notepaper beside her. Kate assumed she must be the instructor. She looked back at Nick with a small shrug.

"Yes, one of our beginner classes in *hatha* yoga," Nick replied, correctly interpreting her shrug. "The physical exercises are necessary to progress in the other branches of Yoga; of course, many people do not wish to go further and are satisfied with the benefits these bring."

Nick turned away picking up his pace slightly as Kate continued to follow him down the hall until they reached a pair of large mahogany double doors. "This is our library. I am not sure who may be here studying, so please be quiet." He eased open one of the doors and gestured for Kate to walk in ahead of him. The room was a wide rectangle, lined with books on two sides, a bank of computers in study carrels on the third. Over by the far wall was a small statue of a Hindu god that Kate thought might be Krishna, although she couldn't be certain of that. It sat on an ornate wooden table that also appeared to be mahogany, flowers and incense in small silver bowls placed before it along with flickering candles in carved silver candlesticks.

One male student of indiscriminate age sat at the long table in the center of the room, surrounded by books and deeply engaged in whatever he was reading. As Kate took in the scene, she noticed a middle-aged man with black hair lightly threaded with gray, his face narrow and lined with a small goatee on his chin, look up from a broad mahogany desk near the entrance. His eyes ran over Kate briefly and rested on Nick, his lips curving upward in a polite smile. "Good day, Mr. Maxwell," he greeted him in a low tone suitable for a library. "Giving a tour of the Center?" He glanced back at Kate offering the same polite smile he had given Nick.

Nick's voice tone matched his as he responded with "Yes, this is Mrs. Kate LaRue. Our librarian, William Rawlins." He pressed his fingers together at his lips, as if giving thought to his next statement.

"Mr. Rawlins has been with us for a number of years, twelve or so anyway," he said to Kate. Turning back to his librarian he added, before Kate could respond to this information, "Mrs. LaRue is here seeking information about her daughter Allison, who was a student here several years ago. She presumably left with Joshua Emmanuel's group, The Way." Kate saw William Rawlins's face darken, the slight smile he had maintained vanishing. "She has since died, leaving Mrs. LaRue with her daughter's child. Did you know an Allison LaRue, or remember anything about her?"

The librarian frowned, chewing his lower lip while Kate rummaged in her purse for an additional copy of Ally's photograph. She produced it just as he was shaking his head slowly, saying, "The name doesn't ring a bell." Kate slid the photo in front of him on the desk. Mr. Rawlins picked it up and studied it for a moment. He shrugged. "Possibly, but I can't be certain. Of course, all of our students and instructors are in the library at some time reading the texts and studying. She doesn't look familiar enough that I could identify her." Rawlins smiled sadly and shook his head. "I wish I could remember. So many young women who look like her come here; some stay and some do not. However, if she left with Joshua Emmanuel, then she wasn't really a serious student of Yoga."

He handed the photo back to Kate, who placed it in her purse with a polite "Thank you anyway." Nick gestured toward the door as the librarian offered, warm compassion etched in his face, "Good luck in your endeavor, Mrs. LaRue."

Back in the hall, Kate followed Nick around a corner to another polished wooden door with a small glass window. "One of our classrooms," he said, nodding toward the door. Kate looked in at a simply furnished room with a round oak table and chairs, tapestries covering three of the walls, another small shrine to a Hindu god, or maybe a goddess, Kate wasn't sure, set up in a corner. A group of a half dozen or so people sat at the table with books and paper, engaged in an animated discussion. A pair of computers was set against the one bare wall. Correctly interpreting Kate's thoughts as she studied the group, Nick added, "Our students and teachers are generally not Indian, but we have occasional guest speakers, instructors, and consultants. The Center is really designed to serve Western students of Yoga."

Kate nodded and they moved on to an open room at the end of the hall that contained a modern kitchen and beyond it, a dining room. "Among the subjects studied here, if you will, is healthful and appropriate eating, with the three nutritional *gunas*, known as *sattva*, *rajas*, and *tamas*, as a guide. We use Ayurveda, an ancient Indian healing system to achieve health and balance among the elements of life. This is one aspect of that." Nick glanced back at Kate who nodded again in acknowledgment.

He smiled politely. "Can I offer you something to drink? Water or herbal tea, perhaps?"

"No, thank you. I should be going anyway. I appreciate the tour and your time. If you would please—"

"Yes, I know." Nick paused. "I really wish we could have been of more help to you. I don't think you realize how many young women like your daughter are out there on the streets, especially here in New York. They are all looking for something, whether it is success or fame or just some meaning to life. If they come here, it's often very briefly and then they're gone and we never see them again. Most are not able or willing to put in the time or effort needed to truly achieve what they are seeking from Yoga. And many, like your daughter, are susceptible to those who promise an easier path. In any case, it's very hard to remember all of them."

Nick looked at Kate again, standing with arms folded, her face troubled. "Although our focus here is Yoga, we do offer some comparative thought and philosophies as well. You would be amazed at the similarities among them if you know where and how to look."

"Yes, I'm sure that's true" Kate responded keeping her expression decidedly neutral. She smiled politely, a tight little smile that did not reach her eyes. "It's all very interesting but I think I've taken up enough of your time."

Nick shrugged slightly. "Come with me and I'll show you the way out."

CHAPTER 32

A few minutes later, Kate was back out on the hot New York pavement outside the tall building that housed The Center for Yoga, Meditation, and Healing, the stifling heat already causing her blouse to stick once more to her skin. The image of Ally rose up once before her, a teenager in goth clothing standing on these very steps and debating her next move after her first visit here. What would it have been? Where would she have gone?

Kate looked around her at this crowded Manhattan street with its steel and concrete buildings on every side, the cars and buses fighting for space on the street, the flow of foot traffic pushing by her on the sidewalk and longed for somewhere private and quiet where she could try to sort through what she had learned. She turned in the direction of the subway stop for the ride back toward New Jersey and Maggie, following the crowds and feeling slightly numb when her eye caught the graceful lines of a brick and mortar church hemmed in by skyscapers. A small framed sign on a tiny patch of grass proclaimed it to be the Mary Queen of Heaven Catholic Church with a Mass schedule noted beneath it. Private and quiet, thought Kate, and hopefully peaceful and cool.

At the arched double doors she took hold of the brass handle praying it wasn't locked. The door pulled easily open and Kate found herself in the small darkened vestibule. As her eyes adjusted to the light her ears began picking up distant singing, notes borne to her on some seemingly soft sweet breeze. Kate slid into the church trying to be as unobtrusive as possible. Standing under a choir loft, she looked down the rows of empty pews to a beautiful stained glass window depiction of a blue robed Mary standing on an earthen orb, a snake beneath her feet while a ring of stars encircled her. Stained glass in delicate blue and green patterns wove around the otherwordly picture, completing the panorama. Above Kate's head a choir was singing an unfamilar hymn, voices blending harmoniously. Thinking she must have come in on a choir practice, Kate slipped into a back pew. She sank down on the wooden bench and closed her eyes for a moment, feeling the heat and the stress of the day draining from her body. The choir had begun a new, more familar hymn and Kate found herself humming it softly under her breath as their voices, accompanied by the rich tones of an old pipe organ, seemed to soar upward toward the high, arched ceiling and from there fill the entire church.

Kate opened her eyes and let her gaze slide over the familar face of the church of her childhood. The altar to the right of the stained glass rendering of the Blessed Virgin was covered with an elegantly embroidered white cloth and surrounded by potted plants, some with abundant late summer flowers, others with simple green or variegated leaves. To one side stood the lecturn from which the scripture readings and homily would be given, to the other carved chairs of dark wood and plush cream-colored cushions provided seating for the priest and, Kate presumed, the altar servers. A low wooden altar rail, polished to a high shine, still separated the priest from the congregation but Kate knew that those receiving communion would do so while standing before the priest or an eucharistic minister. She grimaced as she took in the tall crucifix directly behind the altar, portraying Jesus' bloodied body hanging from the cross bar, his thorn-crowned head falling to the side in death. Kate remembered how frightened she had been by a similar crucifix in the church she had attended as a child and how, much later as a young adult, she had questioned the need for such a gruesome display. The response from her parish priest had been that the Church wished to be direct and honest about what had happened on that long ago Good Friday and not downplay it with the simple crosses other churches used. Well, maybe, but she had not agreed with that argument then, and, Kate thought, she still didn't now.

Still listening to the sweet hymns flowing from the unseen choir above her, Kate took in the stained glass windows featuring scenes from the Bible's Christian Testament that lined either side of the church while on the walls between each window were carved depictions of the biblical scenes that comprised Stations of the Cross. Kate thought back to the Lenten Fridays when, as a child, she would follow her mother and sister around their parish church, stopping at each station to say the appropriate prayers and contemplate the meaning of the scene before them. When had she last done the Stations of the Cross? Kate thought about this briefly and concluded it had to have been before she graudated high school. Well, it had been a long time since the faith she had been raised in truly meant something to her but she could remember when it did. There never had been a sharp dividing line between believing and not believing, just a gradual drifting away that had begun when she was a teenager, and became more pronounced when she began attending college and was exposed to new ideas that did not always fit with the Catholic religious education she had received. *I was like Ally in many ways*, she reminded herself, *only I never felt any need to look for something embodied in a man preaching some kind of instant nirvana.* Kate shrugged inwardly. *Maybe I would have, though, had the right person shown up at the right time and with the right message.*

Kate realized suddenly that the voices and the organ music had faded away into silence, a hush that was followed by the rustling of paper, whispered voices, and muffled laughter. She listened as feet thumped and clattered down the steps from the choir loft behind her, expecting to be caught out and evicted from her peaceful sanctuary at any minute. Sunlight streamed in behind her as the doors opened and people exchanged good-byes and reminders of their next practice, along with Masses they were expected to attend. In the silence that followed, Kate heard muffled footsteps and looked around to see a slightly built older woman with curling gray hair and warm brown eyes approaching. Taking in her navy blue pleated skirt, sensible shoes, and white blouse, she would have surmised she was a nun, even without the small silver crucifix she wore around her neck.

Kate decided to jump right in before her companion could say say anything. "That was the loveliest singing I've heard in ages," she said beaming a smile, "and the acoustics in this church are just wonderful. Are you the choir director?"

"Yes, and the organist. I'm glad you enjoyed listening to us just now. I must say that has to be one of the most glowing compliments we've received. I'll be sure to tell the choir next time we meet." The nun smiled down at her and extended a hand. "I'm Sister Andrea, by the way. Are you a parishioner here?"

Kate took her hand in hers and pressed it lightly. "No, I'm afraid not. I'm visiting New York and needed a spot to sit and relax and be at peace, really. I was lucky enough to come upon your church when it was open and your choir was practicing. I suppose I will have to leave now," she added reluctantly.

Sister Andrea studied Kate thoughtfully. "No, not just yet. I have a few things to clean up before I go." She paused briefly and added, "Is there something I can help you with...?" Sister Andrea let the question hang for a moment.

"I'm sorry, I didn't introduce myself. I'm Kate LaRue," Kate filled in hastily. "Thank you for offering, but I don't know what help you can give me." She quickly reconsidered this. "Well, maybe there is something. Sister Andrea, I was raised as a Catholic by two very devout parents, but, despite that strong religious background, I don't feel connected to the Church any more. I haven't for a long time. It isn't as if I've found something else; I just haven't wanted to be a part of any church." Kate smiled apologetically. "I'm sure you've heard all this before."

Sister Andrea had sat down in the pew next to Kate. "Oh yes. As I'm sure you know, many people have this struggle with belief."

"Do you?" Kate asked curiously while at the same time feeling guilty asking the sister such a question.

"Yes, sometimes. So far, though, I have always managed to find my way back."

Kate nodded. "I guess I haven't reached that point yet. I don't know if I ever will. I am really more concerned about my daughter who apparently joined a religious cult a few years back. I tried to bring Ally up as a Catholic, but she never seemed to identify with the Church at all. I've wondered if maybe she sensed when she was a child that I was not really committed myself and that negatively affected her ability to believe." Kate looked at Sister Andrea, her frustration showing on her face. "I'm really not explaining this well."

"No, I understand." Sister Andrea's voice took on a more serious tone. "As I'm sure you know, people often look for answers to life's meaning in many different places; places that may not be where they began. They often return there when it comes time to pass on a set of beliefs to their children because it's familiar, but if they have not fully returned themselves, it can create the type of problems you spoke of." Sister Andrea kept her eyes on Kate's, kindness and sympathy in her gaze. "I hope for your daughter's sake she finds what she needs in a safe and stable place, even if it's not within the Church."

Kate struggled for a few seconds with telling this sister the whole story of Ally and Glory and decided she was too tired to go through it another time that day, and in any case, wasn't entirely sure how it would be received.

Sister Andrea looked at Kate assessingly for a moment realizing she was not prepared to continue the conversaton. "Well, I will pray for your daughter and for you. I'm afraid it's the best I can offer."

"Thank you," Kate replied, unable to think of anything better to say.

"It will take me a few minutes to get everything I need together. You're welcome to stay in our church until then." Sister Andrea gestured expressively across the church.

"No, I think I'm ready to go now. Thank you again, though."

"Well, Kate, you will always be welcome here should you decide to return. In the meantime, may God go with you."

Kate rose from her seat and took one last look at the mosaic of Mary Queen of Heaven above the altar before shaking a smiling Sister Andrea's hand and walking down the aisle and back out into the heat of the New York street.

CHAPTER 33

Kate sat back on the cushioned seat of Maggie's front porch glider, sipping a tall glass of sparkling water as she slid back and forth, looking out at the lights of suburban New Jersey below her, the skyline of New York City in the distance. Maggie's elegant home sat high on a hill, offering a sense of majesty and dominion over the pleasant, upper middle class community she lived in. It had been a long day, Kate thought to herself as she watched the sun, which moments ago had richly colored the landscape in gold highlights, begin to set, lighting the western sky with a pink and orange hue as it did so. Glory was already asleep, having had a busy day playing with her newfound cousin, a fact for which Kate was infinitely grateful. Maggie appeared and joined Kate on the glider, leaning back into a corner and eyeing Kate critically.

"You really look like you had tough day, little sister. Are you sure you want to head back tomorrow? A day relaxing and maybe puttering around town would be good for you. It's going to be another scorcher, you know."

Kate smiled wearily. "Really, Maggie, I would if I could. I've got too much going on back home. Besides, scorcher or no, I want to make sure I get back to the Cape before that hurricane, or what's left of it, gets here." She thought back to the news broadcast she and Maggie had watched while preparing dinner a couple of hours earlier, an overly cheery meteorologist pointing out swirling circles of white heading for the Carolina coast but with a projected trajectory straight up the coast with direct hits over the tip of Long Island and across the arm of the Cape.

"Mmm. I've also heard there's a good chance it will go out to sea."

Kate laughed. "I'm not waiting around to find out. I'll come back, I promise, maybe in the fall, once the tourist season is over. We can get together for Thanksgiving, certainly."

"Okay, fine." Maggie feigned a hurt expression. "But no backing out of Thanksgiving. And you have to keep me updated on Glory. Promise?"

Kate looked out over the darkening landscape, lights shining brightly from the houses farther down the hill, the New York skyline outlined in light in the distance. Somewhere out there was John McCarty, the one person she knew of who could provide her with the answers she needed, she was sure of it. Please please please, Nick Maxwell, Kate beseeched the gathering night, just give him my message, and I know he'll call me.

"Kate?"

Kate turned to her sister, her features obscured in the twilight. "Yes, Maggie, I'll keep you posted. I promise."

They sat together in companionable silence for a few moments allowing the glider to slide back and forth beneath them. "Did I tell you about the church I went to today?" Kate asked her voice soft and low in the darkness.

"No. What church?"

"It was in the city near the Yoga center. The Mary Queen of Heaven Catholic Church, a beautiful little church. It was cool and peaceful inside and a lovely choir was having a rehearsal. The choir director came down, and we talked for a bit."

"That sounds nice," Maggie said cautiously. "What did you talk about?"

Kate hesitated. "Maggie, is the Catholic Church still important to you? I mean, do you still go to church every Sunday and holy day, follow all the rules, or most of them anyway?"

"Um, I don't think you talked about what I believe, Kate. Anyway, I do still go to church most Sundays and holy days. I go to confession, fast on Fridays during Lent. We have a good pastor at our church; that really helps."

Kate moved closer to her sister and looked at her earnestly. "Do you believe in what the Catholic Church teaches, though? You know, Jesus as Savior who died for our sins and rose again, who was born of a virgin. That the Pope is infallible in his teachings?"

Maggie returned Kate's gaze with a more cautious one of her own. "Hmm. I do believe in the basic tenets of Christianity. I may not always agree with the Church on everything, though. Is this about Ally or you, Kate?"

"Both, I guess. I've been wondering if my lack of committed belief in Catholicism or even, as you said, the basic tenets of Christianity, turned Ally away from the Church and toward something she thought was better."

"That's a tough one to answer, Kate. Maybe. Ally could have chosen any number of ways toward God, or none at all. That she chose this one is not your fault." Maggie paused. "So I suppose what you're saying is that you've lost any faith in Christianity at all?"

"I don't know. There's a lot I find hard to believe in a literal sense, you know, the virgin birth, Jesus as divine and human."

In the interior of the house, a phone started ringing and just as quickly stopped. Maggie cocked her head as a masculine voice called out, "For you, Maggie. It's Beth. Want to take it out there?"

Maggie slid off the glider. "No, I'll come in." She looked down at Kate. "We can talk about this some more later. Don't stay out here in the dark by yourself too long."

Kate smiled in the darkness. "I like it out here. Calm, peaceful... much like that church I visited today."

Maggie shrugged and disappeared back inside the house. Kate, with a small sigh, contemplated the nighttime vista for a moment, then she pulled the case that held her computer over to her from where she had placed it next to the glider. Balancing the computer on her lap, she booted up, the screen providing a bright glow on the dark porch. Kate paused, considering the possibilities she might research and typed in Joshua Emmanuel. To her surprise and relief, a number of hits appeared, a few of which seemed useful. These she quickly opened, scanning the contents. One that seemed especially promising was a Web page proclaiming the ministry of the Prophet and Avatar Joshua Emmanuel, who would guide you on The Way to Union with the Divine Source of Being. Kate studied the text, seeing in it the threads of Yoga and Eastern religion she had been seeking, along with an undercurrent of Christian teachings and New Age philosophy as well. After all, how many Joshua Emmanuels could there be out there?

Joshua, who seemed to prefer a first name address, began with a flowery welcome to "all seekers of truth" and offered sympathy and understanding to those who had explored the paths of traditional organized religions and had not found in them the answers they sought. He, Joshua, could offer a new and better way, one that would teach you to connect with the deity within you as he himself was able to do as an incarnation of divinity, come to the world to provide this guidance to others. "Like you, I have passed through many births, lived many lives, dying many deaths, only to be reborn. However, unlike you, I remember these and have learned from them. I can help you to learn to do so as well, to gain true knowledge of yourself. I can free you from the turmoil of time and the material world," Joshua proclaimed, seemingly paraphrasing yogic beliefs. Then he went on to talk about "Christ consciousness," a level of being and awareness that united one with Jesus as another incarnate child of God.

Kate scanned sections on meditation and yogic practices, much like those at the Center, as well as brief biographies and stories from practioners of similar religious and spiritual traditions combined with more current testimonials from his followers. Another page included sections on those Joshua considered previous "avatars" such as Jesus, Buddha, Rama, Zoroaster and Krishna.

Kate perused these further, reading passages, apparently from the Bhagavad Gita, in which Krishna tells Arjuna how he manifests himself in the material world, taking part in human affairs whenever chaos and a falling away from religious practice threaten continued existence. Kate contemplated this, considering the meaning of these passages. Was Joshua actually equating himself with Lord

Krishna, seen in that classic work of Indian religion and philosophy, as an avatar of...Vishnu, was it? Kate searched her mind for what she remembered of the Bhagavad Gita which she had read in college, and then again at that long-ago retreat. Continuing on, she read another passage suggesting that the disciplined and loving worship of Krishna would provide the insight and understanding the seeker desired. Apparently, Kate realized with a grimace, Joshua was applying this concept to himself. She still could not imagine Ally "worshiping" anyone, whatever he might have had to offer. She shook her head, murmuring to herself, "This is obviously not the Ally I thought I knew, as a matter of fact, it would seem as though I didn't know her at all."

Kate's thoughts returned to Nick Maxwell and The Center for Yoga, Meditation and Healing. Nick, along with that librarian, was right, of course. Ally had always been impatient, more so as a teenager. She would have wanted results quickly, and years of study and practice to achieve "union" or "enlightenment" wouldn't have appealed to her. If someone came along who offered a shortcut she would have taken it, especially if the person offering it seemed to know what he or she was talking about. That much Kate understood about her daughter. It was just so hard to believe she would have wanted *this*.

CHAPTER 34

The day was already hot when Kate and Glory pulled out of Maggie's driveway and headed down the hill, Kate waving in the rearview mirror to Maggie standing on the sidewalk as she watched them leave, her slender body clad in a sleeveless cotton blouse and shorts and her face a mask of concern. Kate drummed her fingers on the steering wheel, feeling the first tendrils of cool air blow her hair away from her face as the air conditioner finally kicked in. She thought about how much she needed to get home and how long it would take her to get there as she tried to convince herself that a quick jaunt to Long Island to see Sam Ritter would be anything but quick. The morning weather forecast had not been encouraging, and even Maggie had to concede that they were likely to get hit with heavy rain and high wind by sometime tomorrow. If a hurricane was coming, there was a lot of work to be done to get ready for it, storing the Sea Witch's stock, shuttering the windows...Kate pushed away these thoughts with a decisive shake of her head, then pulled over onto a side street and took out her cell phone, punching in Sam's number from the address book. *Maybe he won't be there,* she told herself, *and then it won't matter anyway. I'll just go home*. Glory began to stir restlessly in her car seat, and, just as Kate turned away from the phone to tell her they would be back on the road in a few minutes, a familiar masculine voice could be heard.

"Hello, can this really be Kate?"

"Hi, Sam. Yes, it's me. How are you?"

"I'm okay, how about yourself?"

"I'm fine. Look, Sam, I'm in New Jersey and about to head back to the Cape but I have a little time and I was wondering—"

"By all means, come on by. I'd love to show you around the store."

"I do have Glory with me."

"Not a problem. Hey, I'll treat you both to lunch, how's that?"

Kate smiled into the phone. "Sounds great. We'll be looking forward to it."

After a few minutes' discussion of the best routes to take and a second phone call to an irritatingly amused Jerry, Kate was back on her way, now with the south coast of Long Island in her sights.

Kate and Sam sat at a small round table under an enormous umbrella, the remains of a lunch of fresh shrimp and clams still sitting on the bright mosaic of decorative tiles that lined the tabletop. The little seaside pub that Sam had taken them to fronted directly on the beach, and Glory, after wolfing down french fries and a hot dog, was happily running up and down the beach playing her favorite game of keep away from the rolling waves. Sam glanced over at Kate, a warm smile lighting his face. "I'm so glad you decided to stop by. It's been a pleasure to see you again."

Kate returned his smile, thinking back to their arrival, later than expected after getting lost navigating the streets of the picturesque little town, with Glory tired and grumpy with the heat and the longer-than-expected drive. Sam had been very gracious and understanding and immediately brought Kate and Glory over to a section of his store that sold a variety of children's gifts, including pretty little cloth dolls, doll clothes, sailboats, airplanes, puzzles, and coloring books. Over Kate's protests, he offered Glory a choice of complimentary gifts, insisting that this was a special occasion and that he would be hurt if Kate refused. Finally, Kate gave in and Glory's mood was considerably brighter as she trailed along after Sam and Kate on their tour of the Sandpiper, two new coloring books and one of the little dolls clutched to her chest. Kate, for her part, walked through the store admiring Sam's stock but also feeling somewhat smug in her assessment that her own stock was generally of higher quality. The Sandpiper was more gift store, admittedly charming and unique, but with much less of the high-end artwork that the Sea Witch featured.

Once the tour was over, Sam had left the store in the hands of an assistant and the trio set off down the street, enjoying a freshening breeze that had picked up off the ocean, until they reached this little restaurant. Kate, feeling sated with the lunch, stretched her sandaled feet out under the table. "I'm glad we were able to do this too, Sam. It's been a rough couple of days. This was just what I needed."

Sam nodded, having been given the full story of Kate's visit to the Center, although Kate had kept much of her conversations with Maggie to herself. "It's an interesting story, you know. About your daughter," he added to Kate's inquisitive look. "Common, of course, in some ways, but, I was wondering, have you ever had any experience with cults and the like?"

"No, why, have you?"

"Mmmm...well, yes and no. My parents were very devout Christians. They belonged to a small congregation of, I guess you might call it, Latter Day Puritans for want of a better description." Smiling at Kate's startled look, he added, "Well, not exactly. It was an independent, conservative denomination, however. I spent a lot of time in church when I was a youngster. Long Sunday services, Sunday school, midweek services. There were a lot of things other kids got to do that we didn't, Halloween parties and trick-or-treating for example. In the summer, I never went to the kind of camps other children in town did, always to the Vacation Bible School the church sponsored. I did go the local public school, but I was only allowed to play with other kids from the church we belonged to. As far as I know there were no Christian schools around, no home schooling at the time, or my folks would surely have sent us there or taught us themselves. The pastor was a very inspiring and charismatic preacher, at least my parents and the other congregants thought so. I can't say I was that impressed. Nevertheless, their whole life was bound up in that church."

Sam caught Kate's curious gaze out of the corner of his eye and smiled. “It was like a cult in some ways. A charismatic leader, a group that isolates itself from outside influences, a whole lifestyle within the rules and boundaries of the group which makes it difficult to leave because you have nothing outside it. My parents were fine with that, you understand, but I wasn’t.”

“So what happened?” Kate prodded when he paused, looking out to sea.

Sam looked over at her, the same smile dancing in his eyes. “I went to college, not the one my parents wanted for me, where I met people who were not part of all that. It was very liberating for me, but very scary for my family. I pretty much had to work my way through college, with the assistance of loans and the like, because there was no way they were going to contribute to what they saw as my downfall. And as fate, or luck, if you prefer, would have it, my senior year I had a girlfriend, my first serious relationship, who became enamored of the Reverend Moon.” Sam laughed softly, lost in the memory. “I can still remember how excited she was about it after she went to spend a weekend or something at a farm they had, a weekend when I was visiting my family and didn’t feel I could bring her along.” He shrugged expressively. “They, the ‘Moonies,’ as people called them, were very persistent, and nothing I could say or do could discourage her from listening to them. She may still be with them as far as I know. Anyway, the end result is that I think I have some knowledge of what the whole ‘cult’ thing is like.”

He said nothing more, still looking out over the ocean. Finally, Kate broke the silence. “So, do you belong to any church or, I don’t know, religious organization now?”

Sam looked back at her. “No. I don’t think I could do that again, you know, belong to any church. Too restrictive. How about you?”

“I was raised as a Catholic; so was Ally. It’s been a while since I’ve been to church, though, not counting the one I just spent some time in of course.” Kate considered for a moment, then asked “How do you get along with your parents these days?”

“I don’t. My father is dead and my mother lives with one of my brothers. He’s a deacon in the church. I’m an apostate who is beyond saving at this point; anyway, I'd just as soon they didn't try. We do send the occasional card to each other."

"I'm sorry." Kate reached out and gently touched Sam's arm.

"Don't be. The point is, I've seen firsthand how compelling all of this can be—religion, cults, whatever. Even people you think would never have anything to do with them can get pulled in if the message and the timing are right. So, don't be surprised about your daughter being one of them."

Sam and Kate sat in companionable silence for a while, Kate gazing out over ocean, a mix of grayish blue and green in the dappled sunshine, the whitecaps sending up their delicate sprays of foam. In the distance she could see clouds building on the horizon, feel the wind picking up as it began to blow in from the south. She turned to Sam. "I'm going to need to leave soon, in order to get home ahead of that storm." Kate gestured in the direction of the horizon. Sam inclined his head in his acknowledgment. "Yes, you're right; you'd best head out now. I don't like what I'm hearing about this. Sounds as if we're in for a tough ride."

Sam beckoned their waiter over, gesturing for the check. Kate made a show of reaching for her purse but Sam predictably waved her away. "My treat, remember?" Kate, smiling her thanks, rose and walked toward the beach, calling to Glory, who was crouched on the wet sand looking intently at some shell or small stone just at the edge of the water, its foamy fingers curling around her small feet before retreating into the sea. She glanced up at the sound of her grandmother's voice and, reading the meaning of her waving hands correctly, trotted toward her reluctantly.

Gathering up their belongings, the little group moved back out toward the street, Sam lightly touching Kate's elbow as they threaded their way through the inside of the restaurant. Kate drew in her breath, feeling that light touch like an electric charge running along her arm, but she didn't pull away and in a minute they were on the street. Once there, Sam let go of her elbow but he was close enough to her as they walked along that she could feel the warmth of his body, a prickling cascading down her arm and the length of her body to her toes. Kate clung to Glory's warm little palm like a lifeline, grounding her, barely aware of what Sam was saying and hoping she didn't seem like a total idiot, smiling and nodding. The walk was over soon enough as Kate spotted her little car up ahead.

Once inside with Glory secured in the back in her car seat, Kate looked up at Sam with a mixture of relief and regret. Sam leaned forward, placing his hand gently over hers as it rested on the steering wheel. "Safe trip home," he said, a smile playing on his lips but with a serious cast to his eyes. "You should get back well in advance of the storm but I wouldn't take any chances. My advice is to go straight back to the Cape from here." His smile broadened. "Until next time, Kate."

Kate returned his smile. "Until next time, Sam."

She started the engine, putting the car in gear as Sam stepped back. A quick wave, and she was headed down the street, watching Sam standing on the curb watching her until finally he was lost from view.

CHAPTER 35

Kate breathed a deep sigh of relief as she locked her front door behind her and looked back out across the familiar shadows that filled the darkening landscape outside the large bay window in her living room. Evening light was rushing in early accompanied as it was by the heavily clouded skies, the wind already whipping the tops of the pine trees. Kate had spent an hour or so at the Sea Witch helping Jerry and the remaining seasonal staff with the last of the storm preparations, listening to increasingly dire storm predictions on the store office radio and mentally chastising herself all the while for not getting back sooner. She might not have gotten back at all, she reminded herself, if she had stayed any longer on Long Island. All the way home, driving over the Tappan Zee Bridge and along Route 95 in Connecticut, she had listened to the weather reports on the car radio, the calls for evacuation and the proclamations of states of emergency in New York, Connecticut, Rhode Island, and Massachusetts. The warnings of road and bridge closures left Kate fearful that the Bourne and Sagamore bridges would be closed before she could get there, stranding her on the mainland until God knew when.

Glory had disappeared into her bedroom, seemingly oblivious to Kate's tension and anxiety. *Probably a good thing*, she told herself as she rummaged through desk drawers looking for candles, matches, and flashlight batteries. Putting her collection of these on the kitchen table, Kate then plugged in her laptop and set it on the table as well. She stared at it for a moment, ruminating over her Internet search of the night before and Joshua Emmanuel's odd Web page with its patchwork theologies and self-proclamation as an avatar, an embodiment of some type of divine being. She sighed, shaking her head. No time for that now she told herself.

Kate walked back into the living room, switching on the TV and hunting through the listings for the Weather Channel as she passed through. Listening to the nonchalant voice with one ear, she made a quick tour of the house, checking that the windows were secure and closing the shutters on her side porch. As she canvassed the house, she soon found Glory lying in the pool of golden light cast on the floor of her bedroom by the big Winnie-the-Pooh lamp, furiously coloring pictures in one of her new coloring books. Kate watched her unnoticed for a moment, thinking to herself that maybe Glory was not oblivious to the adult atmosphere of fear and anxiety after all. Just then, Glory glanced up at Kate, her big dark eyes unreadable, and Kate felt a twinge of concern that her granddaughter might be far more frightened that she had thought.

"Oh, sweetie, don't worry it's going to be okay. It's just that a big storm is coming, so we need to be ready. We'll be fine, you'll see." Kate stepped into the circle of light cast by the lamp and crouched down next to Glory. She cast a quick glance at the page Glory had been coloring, noting the overriding colors of red, orange, and black impressed upon the page with such considerable force, and irrespective of the picture lines that numerous small tears had been rendered in the paper.

"Are you hungry?" Kate quickly assessed what might be available for a quick dinner, realizing with a spurt of anxiety that she had not been able to stock up on basics in advance of the storm. Seeing the flicker of interest in Glory's eyes, she added, "How about some macaroni and cheese? I think we still have some of that ice cream for dessert too. Come on in the kitchen and let's see what we have."

With some reluctance, Glory permitted Kate to pull her to her feet and followed along into the kitchen, one small hand enclosed in her grandmother's, the other clutching the locket around her neck. Once there, she climbed onto a chair and watched, motionless, as Kate moved around the kitchen pulling out a package of macaroni and cheese and setting a pot of water on the stove, all the while keeping up a cheery running commentary on her progress in putting together a quick dinner. At the same time, Kate was making mental notes of her food resources and silently chastising herself for not getting home sooner so as to be better prepared. *What was I thinking? Was seeing Sam really that necessary? Of course not*, she told herself irritably. *I can't imagine what possessed me to do something so foolish.* But no sooner did these thoughts pass through her head than the memory of his touch sent a shiver through her body all over again. Kate shrugged helplessly, then, turning to Glory, still watching from her perch at the end of the table, said brightly, "I think I'll make a little salad to go with this. And we can definitely finish up that ice cream I bought last week!"

By the time night fell, the storm was upon them in earnest, the wind pushing against the house with enough force to make it shudder and emitting a high-pitched wailing that reminded Kate of the banshees in her Irish grandmother's stories. The electricity failed early, throwing them into utter darkness in the middle of a DVD of lighthearted children's cartoons. Kate had cursed softly to herself, feeling Glory stiffen in her arms; she had hoped they would be spared this until the little girl was safely asleep in her bed. Glory seemed even more anxious once Kate started lighting candles and seemed to relax only slightly when Kate exchanged them for a pair of glassed hurricane lamps and a flashlight, using the latter to read Glory Little Golden Book stories while wrapped in a blanket in the big rocking chair.

As the night wore on, Kate did her best to maintain a sense of calm and control, a forced attention to the frolicking animals, princesses, and bright-eyed children in the stories, but she could not help but hear the creaks and groans of the windblown trees followed by the sound of branches snapping, all of it overlaid by rain dancing a frantic beat on the roof and windows and know that Glory was listening as well. Finally, after what seemed an eternity of story reading, Kate felt Glory relax into sleep, fingers still curled around the locket that hung from her neck, no doubt lulled by the endless repetition that had threatened to cause Kate to doze off along with her. Kate shut off the flashlight, fearing the batteries were about to give out anyway and sat in the flickering light of the hurricane lamps, staring as shadows danced across the walls, seemingly in time to the continued wails of wind and rain beyond them. *A few minutes,* Kate thought drowsily, *I'll give her a few minutes to fall well and truly asleep, and then I'll carry her in and put her to bed, maybe in my room so that if she wakes up and is scared...*

Kate thought she was still watching the shadows but the dark dancers were only in her dreams as head dropped back against the rocking chair's cushioned headrest, her breathing slowing and becoming more rhythmic. The shadows changed shape and became tall, dark pine trees waving peacefully on a windy starlit night. Kate found herself walking along the street that led to the beach dressed for a day in the sun and surf, except for the fact that it was night. Next to her, clinging to her hand as she strolled along, enjoying the warm breeze, was Glory, clutching her pail and shovel and moving along in excited little skips. She looked up at Kate, eyes wide and filled with delight. "Can we build a castle? Will you help me, *please?*" Kate looked down, a thrill of joy passing through her. "Glory! You're talking!" As soon as the words were spoken, Kate realized her mistake. "Ally!"

"Come on, Mommy, please say yes."

Kate hesitated. "Yes, of course, darling. But you have to promise to stay on the sand this time."

Ally looked up at her, her face obscured as they moved into a dark canyon between houses. "Yes, Mommy, I know you want me to stay on the sand."

Suddenly, the beach lay ahead of them, the sand silver in the light of the stars, which were now joined by an enormous full moon, hanging low in the western sky. Beyond the sand the ocean, heavy and black, heaved its big white breakers onto the glistening beach. Farther away, Kate could see the great body of water throwing itself against the rocks of the jetty, the spray leaping into the air, sparkling in the light of the moon and stars. She paused, fear trickling down her spine, but Ally tugged hard on her hand. "Come on!" Ally continued to pull impatiently at the end of her fingers, a shadow dancing in the dark.

Finally, Kate was persuaded to move forward, her legs leaden, the happy pleasure of the beach visit gone. She struggled along in the sand next to her exuberant daughter until they reached the wet sand at the ocean's edge. Kate felt a sob rise in her throat as Ally broke away as she had so many times before, running, running toward the jetty, Kate pursuing, helplessly trying to call her back.

Ally reached the rocks, climbing up them, nothing more than a dark outline in the distance. Kate waded into the churning ocean, realizing that the stars and moon were gone and, as always, the storm was upon them, fiercely lashing them both with water from above as well as below. Kate caught sight of Ally leaping nimbly across the rocks as lightning lit up the sky but by the time she herself was up on the jetty, fighting to maintain her balance, it was pitch-black. Kate strained to listen but the roar of the wind and ocean obliterated everything else. Suddenly, the lightning zigzagged across the sky a second time, illuminating the scene before her. As it did, Kate let out a scream for she was perched at the very edge of the last rock in the jetty and a grown-up Ally stood in front of her, drenched in rain, eyes wide and feverishly bright. Ally reached for Kate in seeming desperation but she was swept off the rock by the gale before she could touch her, disappearing into the waves, her voice echoing back, "Glory! Glory!"

Kate jerked awake with a gasp, her eyes at first unable to make sense of her surroundings. As her heartbeat slowed, she realized she was staring into the inky blackness of her living room with the hurricane lamps at its center, still casting a pale glow around them, their wicks burned low. Kate glanced down as Glory stirred restlessly on her lap, whimpering softly in her sleep, caught in dreams of her own. Kate listened for a few seconds, hearing the steady beat of rainfall and the restless wind, then carefully lifted her granddaughter, flashlight in one hand, and carried her into the bedroom and laid her gently on the trundle bed. Kate watched until Glory had settled herself back into a quieter sleep, chest falling and rising in the dim glow of the flashlight before slipping back into the living room.

She stood there uncertainly in the darkened room for a moment, listening again to the storm, thinking that, despite the relentless rain and wind, the worst was over now. She picked her way through the shadowy outlines of furniture to the bay window, wondering how close it was to daybreak and whether she could legitimately avoid going back to sleep and the possibility of another repetition of the dream.

Pulling back the curtains, she saw with a sinking heart that the world beyond was still in total darkness and that, as her eyes strained toward the eastern horizon, she could see no hint of coming dawn. She was ready to turn away when lightning flashed, illuminating a street and yard drenched in running water and littered with leaves and tree branches, at least one of the scrub pines from Fran's front yard lying across the road. At the same time, Kate was startled to see a solitary, unfamiliar car parked along the grassy verge just beyond Fran's house and directly across from her own. In the brief seconds of light, before the lightning flash was extinguished and the boom of thunder sounded, Kate could have sworn someone was sitting in the car...watching her. She jumped back from the window with a smothered scream, letting the curtain fall and dropping the flashlight, extinguishing its light. Kate groped for it fruitlessly in the dim light of the lamps and then stood, heart pounding, against the edge of the window, looking around the curtain and into the blackness, seeing only the rain as it pelted the glass. She waited, forcing herself to breathe slowly, counting the seconds until the flash came again, farther away this time but still throwing the scene into a relief of electric blues and black. Once again, the car's distinctive outline was illuminated but if there was someone inside this time, she couldn't see him—or her.

Kate closed her eyes, leaning back against the wall. *It's late,* she told herself, *and you're exhausted.* The car surely belonged to Fran's new renter and the idea that anyone would be sitting in a car at this time of night in this weather was obviously a trick of her sleep-deprived imagination. Nevertheless, the thought of climbing back into bed and going to sleep did not appeal to her as the plot of every horror movie she had ever seen or heard of quickly played out in her head, never mind the fear of dreaming of Ally, the storm, the jetty...

With a sigh, Kate moved over to the hurricane lamps and turned up their wicks, heightening the glow of light in the room and revealing its familiar and unthreatening forms. Kate picked up one and walked through the house, checking the doors and windows as she had done before the storm broke and satisfying herself that all was still secure. Back in the living room, listening again to the drumming rain, she picked up the light, amusing romantic novel Maggie had given her in New York, curled up on the sofa next to one of the lamps, and began to read.

CHAPTER 36

When Kate opened her eyes again the room was full of sunlight. She lay still for a few minutes looking up at her bedroom ceiling and recalling the events of the previous night, half convinced she must have dreamed all of it. She barely remembered waking up from her doze on the sofa and stumbling into the bedroom with one of the lamps, having left the other one in the living room once she had extinguished the flame. Thinking perhaps she had better check she remembered that accurately, Kate threw off the covers and looked down in surprise at her rumpled clothing. The fuzzy memory of deciding at the last minute that she was too tired to even change flickered across her consciousness and she smiled ruefully. Looking over at the other side of the room, she noted that Glory was still asleep in the trundle bed. The sight of her little granddaughter curled up on the bed, half buried under the covers, brought back a sudden memory of their first morning together—how many weeks ago now? Kate smiled again at this thought and then, returning to the present, rose reluctantly, thinking that she should really get a quick read on the damage the hurricane had caused. It was going to be a long day regardless.

Once in the living room, it soon became apparent that they were still without power. *No big surprise there*, she told herself. *I just hope this won't last more than a day or so*. Considering what she had in refrigerator, Kate decided that maybe there was an advantage to getting back too late to stock up. Less to lose, she told herself grimly. Opening the curtains across the bay window, Kate felt a mild shock as she surveyed the destruction outside. The road, the sidewalks, the yard were covered in leaves and branches. While the pine trees in her own yard seem to have survived, minus some branches, of course, she could see two more trees down across the street. One of these lay across her split rail fence, splintering the top rail; a third further down the road seemed to have taken down some wires with it, one of which waved gracefully in the light morning breeze. Also, across the street the car that had so spooked her the night before sat benignly on the grass, covered in leaves and twigs but seemingly undamaged. *Probably a rental*, thought Kate, casting a critical gaze over it. *I can't imagine what this person was thinking, leaving it out on the road like that in a hurricane. Lucky for them a tree didn't fall on it.*

The sound of soft footfalls behind her caused Kate to turn and smile at her granddaughter standing in the living room behind her, her tousled hair half covering her face, one wide dark eye looking up at her, sleepy confusion still evident in her gaze. "Good morning, sweetheart." Kate leaned over and gathered the little girl into her arms. "I'm glad you're up," she murmured into Glory's tangled hair. "It's going to be long day."

An hour later, after a breakfast of bread and jam served with glasses of orange juice, the only serviceable breakfast foods Kate could find given her mistrust of most of what was in refrigerator at this point, she discovered, much to her dismay, that the phone lines were down. She breathed a sigh of relief and sent a brief prayer of gratitude to the powers that be when a quick check of her cell phone revealed that, miraculously, the local cell phone towers must have survived the storm.

Kate scanned her voice mails, noting calls from Maggie and Sam Ritter. She lingered over the latter for a moment, then decisively punched in the numbers for Jerry Stafford's cell phone. Much to her surprise, he answered on the first ring. Their exchange was brief; Jerry was already on his way to the store and it was clear from his quick update that the storm damage to the Cape as a whole was pretty extensive. Greatly concerned, Kate got herself and Glory ready to head out, wondering if perhaps she could arrange some childcare with Jen or Chris later should the Sea Witch have sustained a lot of damage.

The outside air was clean and refreshing, the sky blue and dotted with little powder-puff clouds as Kate and Glory cautiously picked their way through the rubble in the yard and driveway. Kate secured a still subdued Glory in her car seat, her new toys from Sam's store in Long Island next to her. With Glory safe in the car, Kate worked quickly to get some of the bigger branches out of her driveway, along with moving aside a couple of unfamiliar stray trash barrels. She had nearly finished when Fran emerged from her house across the street, eyes filled with concern, clearly ready to remonstrate with her over her apparent intent to drive in the wake of the storm damage.

"Good morning, Fran," Kate called out, hoping to head off the inevitable lecture. "How are you?"

"Kate LaRue, you aren't planning to take that child and try to drive anywhere this morning are you? Haven't you heard the news reports? I have a battery operated radio and I know for a fact that most of the streets just aren't passable. Trees and power lines are down everywhere and some areas are flooded too. Why, a couple of houses down the street here and some of those right at the beach have been flooded. The Sound came right up to their doorsteps last night."

Kate interrupted with a quick wave of her hand. "Fran, I appreciate your concern. I intend to be very careful and if I can't get through, I can't, but I need to try to get to the store and assess the damage there. Glory and I will be fine."

Fran stared at her in obvious disbelief, shaking her head a little at Kate's obstinacy. Looking to change the subject, Kate gestured to the car still parked out front. "Does that belong to your new tenant?"

Fran followed Kate's gaze, shrugged and nodded. "Yes, he arrived last night just before the storm broke. He was very lucky to get in at all."

"I bet. You'll have to introduce us some time."

As Fran's gaze shifted to the rental cottage next door, Kate's followed. In the shadows of the screened-in porch, both women detected a silhouette separate itself from the rest of the shadows and move toward the door.

"Well," said Fran softly, "now is as good a time as any." Then, more loudly "Hey, there, Mr. Christoforos! Come here! I want you to meet someone."

After a few seconds, the screen door opened and a tall, lanky man with thick dark hair emerged and slowly crossed the yard toward them, walking carefully to avoid the worst of the debris. As he reached the edge of the property, Kate, somewhat resignedly, crossed the street to meet him, conscious of Glory still waiting in the car.

"Kate, this is Michael Christoforos, from Helena, Montana. Mr. Christoforos, this is Kate LaRue, my neighbor, who is determined to try to drive across the Cape in the aftermath of a hurricane to check on that store of hers I was telling you about."

"A pleasure to meet you. Please, call me Michael." Michael Christoforos's dark brown eyes took in both women as he spoke, his voice warm and resonant.

Fighting down an urge to respond to Fran's last comments, Kate looked at him with mild interest, trying to place his age. She wasn't at all convinced he was "middle-aged" as Fran had suggested; however, his skin was creased and weathered, as if he spent a lot of time in the sun. His eyes, warm and friendly and yet at the same time somehow impersonal, nonetheless, implied someone younger.

"Nice to meet you too, Michael. I hope you can enjoy your visit here. I'm afraid this may have not been the best time to come to Cape Cod." Kate offered a pleasant smile, remembering that Fran was fond of sending her tenants to the Sea Witch's door.

Michael smiled in return. "Oh, I'm not concerned. I'm sure I'll enjoy my stay here."

Fran interjected, "Mr. Christoforos has never seen the ocean before although he has always wanted to. I was thinking we might take a little stroll down to the end of the street later. Perhaps you and Glory would like to join us?" Fran beamed at Kate, adding as an aside to her guest, "Glory is Kate's granddaughter."

"Perhaps." Kate smiled once more in Michael's direction and then waved briefly to Fran. "I really must go. Bye."

Before anything more could be said, Kate turned and walked swiftly to her car, aware of the gaze of both Fran and Michael boring into her back as she went.

CHAPTER 37

The Sea Witch sat on its sandy lot just as it always had, despite its now-deserted look, shuttered and closed against the storm. As was true everywhere, the parking lot was covered with litter and debris, including one large tree that, while appearing to have missed the roof by mere inches, had, nonetheless, succeeded in wrenching one of the shutters loose, leaving it hanging at an awkward angle and exposing a crack in one of the windowpanes.

Kate's relief was palpable as she squeezed her car into a relatively debris-free spot next to Jerry's pickup truck. The ride over had been tortuous, skirting fallen trees, overturned trash barrels, the occasional lawn chair, and the ominous downed power lines. As Fran had suggested, many streets were closed off, flooded with pools of water that covered sparking power lines. There were a number of homes and businesses that had taken direct hits from trees and other falling objects; next to one house lay the remains of its brick chimney, another was partially burned from lightning or downed power lines, Kate wasn't certain which.

Jerry, seeing them drive up, appeared at the door and beckoned them inside. He held the door as Kate and Glory stepped over the threshold, tears welling up in Kate's eyes at the sight of the familiar interior undamaged and safe. She whistled in greeting to Captain Ahab who promptly whistled back no doubt relieved to be home after a long night spent with Jerry, Kevin and Duncan.

"There's no power, of course," Jerry acknowledged once they were inside, "but the only structural problem I can see is that broken shutter and cracked window. They'll need to be replaced but that's really nothing. It could have been so much worse." He shrugged expressively. "How did you make out at home?"

Kate nodded, moving toward the back of the store and the office. "Everything seems to be okay except for the lack of power and the general mess." She waved in the direction of the parking lot. "We were certainly lucky. How about you and Kevin?"

Jerry looked a little grim. "Well, we suffered some damage to the roof along with a couple of broken windows. Quite a bit of rain got in, so there's some water damage as well, but, hey, like I said before, it could have been a lot worse from what I've seen. A number of houses too close to the water were destroyed, swept out to sea. A lot of erosion too, it looks like, as well as another breach out in Pleasant Bay."

Kate pondered this for a moment. The shoreline of the Cape was always changing, the sea reclaiming the peninsula bit by bit, and big storms like this hastened the process in dramatic and frightening ways. Kate knew that it was certainly possible that someday in the far future Cape Cod would no longer exist. She nodded resignedly. "Well, I guess that's to be expected."

Once in the office, Kate and Jerry sat down together and considered what needed to be done to get the Sea Witch open again, then spent some time clearing the rubble from the parking lot and examining the downed tree and the damaged window. In the early afternoon, assured by a quick phone call to Fran that the power was still out at home, Kate decided to call Chris Angelino and see if she would be willing to take Glory for a few hours. Much to her surprise, Kate found that Chris actually had power, the brunt of the storm having missed that portion of the Cape closest to the mainland. In any case, Chris was happy to have Glory, suggesting a sleepover rather than a short visit and Kate, recognizing that she was unlikely to get power restored at home any time soon, decided she would consider it.

In the end, with as much of the work done at the store as could be accomplished and arrangements made for the removal of the tree and the repair of the window and shutter, Jerry headed back to Wellfleet to tend to repairs at home. Kate secured Glory in the car for the trip to Bourne, interrupted only by a quick stop at a McDonald's that apparently had a generator or other power supply as Kate was too famished to care where they ate. While Glory munched her chicken nuggets between sips of soda and the occasional french fry, Kate punched in the numbers on her cell phone for first Maggie, then Sam. Maggie either wasn't home or not answering so Kate left a brief voice mail, reassuring her sister that she had made it back safely and that her home and business had not suffered much damage from the storm, as well as promising to call again soon.

Sam, on the other hand, picked up on the second ring and Kate felt the now familiar rush of pleasure at the sound of his voice and at the same time was irritated by it. They did not talk long as Sam was dealing with some fairly serious damage to the roof of his store. Nevertheless, he sounded happy to hear from her and genuinely relieved to hear that she had come through the storm without any major problems. When they broke the connection, Kate sat for a moment, staring past the crowds of weary-looking people jostling for seats and wondering just where this was going, if anywhere. She wanted to see him again, no question about that. She lingered with that thought for a minute, imagining walking along the beach with him in the moonlight, Sam leaning over to kiss her...and glanced down at Glory, who was staring up at her, eyes round as saucers. *Damn*, Kate told herself silently, angrily stuffing her cell phone back in her purse, *I don't have time for this.*

Reaching for the little girl, she lifted her off her seat and into her arms. "Come on honey, it's time to go."

A cup of tea warming her hands, Kate looked across Chris's kitchen table, watching as Glory, her new doll seated on a plastic doll-sized chair, busily arranged toy plates and teacups on a matching table, oblivious to Chris's two children racing around her in a pair of kid-sized race cars. Chris already had enough toys and equipment in her house to furnish that preschool she wanted to run someday,

Kate mused. The kitchen alone had a fort, a house, painting easels, and a small plastic slide, as well as the two cars.

"I hope you and Glory will consider staying for dinner. I've got plenty." Chris backed out of her refrigerator carrying two bags of premixed salad greens, swerving nimbly to avoid a collision with her son Mark as he rounded a corner of the table. "Go ride those in the living room!" Chris pulled Gina to a stop and gestured angrily toward Mark who immediately headed into the other room, his sister in his wake. Chris looked over at Glory who, with sidelong glances in Chris's direction, was now feeding her doll a bottle. "I don't think my two ever play quietly like that. I'm not sure they know how." Kate smiled over the rim of her teacup, watching as Chris first set the bags of salad greens down on the table next to a couple of tomatoes and a few green peppers sitting on a cutting board, then looked expectantly at Kate, hands on hips.

"It's a nice offer, Chris. I think I'll take you up on that since I'm not sure what the situation will be at home tonight."

Chris nodded in satisfaction, then pushed the cutting board in Kate's direction. "Great. If you don't mind..."

Kate laughed. "Not at all."

Chris returned to stirring a large pot of spaghetti sauce on the stove while Kate set down her teacup and began slicing the peppers into thin strips. Her eyes intent on the sauce, Chris asked, "So, you think John McCarty will contact you?"

Kate glanced up at her. "I don't know, I hope so. I think he will if Nick Maxwell gives him my message."

Chris looked in Kate's direction. "And you think this Nick Maxwell knows where he is?"

Kate nodded grimly. "Yes, I do. He was suspicious of something. Nick, I mean. As if he was protecting McCarty. But from what, I don't know. A paternity suit?" Kate shook her head in exasperation.

"Maybe from this guy you were telling me about, this Joshua Emmanuel," Chris suggested. "He sounds a little creepy to me."

"Yeah, to me too." Kate looked over at Chris again. "Does it make sense to you that Ally would have become involved with this group?"

Chris shrugged. "I don't know. She probably didn't read that Web site you described." Kate laughed. "Seriously, though, if the guy talked a really good game, I could see where she might have been pulled in and then, who knows, it might have been difficult to get out once she was out there in New Mexico with him. Like I told you, she was really into that stuff the last time I talked to her, meditation, Yoga, New Age philosophy. I just don't know."

"I suppose you're right." Kate thought back to Nick Maxwell's description of Joshua Emmanuel as a charming and charismatic man with an ability to attract many of The Center's students to his ideas. What if once you were a member of The Way, you were expected to stay? Kate mulled over the possibility that it was Emmanuel that Ally was afraid of, that she had escaped from the group, not just left of her own accord. Kate recalled stories she had read about cults like this, images of hundreds of dead bodies in a South American jungle coming to mind, the legacy of Jim Jones and the People's Temple, followed by images of shroud-covered bodies in bunk beds. What was that group called? Heaven's Gate? Then there was the fiery end of David Koresh's Branch Davidians...

Kate glanced down at her watch. "I need to go back to Yarmouth for a few hours, Chris. I've got someone coming out to look at the store and give me a quick estimate on the damage." Kate waved off Chris's look of surprise. "I know, I know, but this man is a good friend, and I should stop by the house first."

"Go ahead, don't worry about Glory." Chris wrapped up the freshly made salad and placed it in the refrigerator. "The spaghetti sauce won't be ready for a while yet anyway."

Kate got up, went around the table and gave Glory a quick hug. "Grandma will be back soon," she murmured soothingly to Glory's troubled gaze. "Have a good time with Mark and Gina."

As she turned toward the door Chris called out, "If you still don't have power you might want to think about spending the night. I can fix up the sofa bed, it's no trouble."

Kate glanced back in surprise. "Thanks, Chris. You're very kind. I will consider that."

CHAPTER 38

The house looked dark in the soft afternoon light, the litter of trees and debris undisturbed around it since Kate had last seen the house that morning. She pulled carefully into the driveway, skirting the stray branch and piece of trash lying in the road as she did so.

I was really lucky this time, Kate thought as she circled her home on foot, noting that the house appeared undamaged by the storm and recalling the havoc the hurricane had created over much of the Cape. Even the Sea Witch was relatively unscathed and the cost of repairs would be minor, especially when compared to what many on the peninsula would be paying. Kate thought back to her earlier appointment with her agent and the estimate she had been given. She and Jerry had conferred by cell phone and agreed they could easily get the window patched up to reopen for Labor Day weekend, the last hurrah of the summer season.

As Kate climbed her front steps she caught sight of Fran and her new tenant walking along the road leading down the beach. Fran waved enthusiastically and the two crossed the street, heading in her direction.

Kate smiled resignedly. "Hi, Fran" she called out, searching for her guest's name for a second and then adding, "and Michael. Been down to the beach? Is there a lot of damage?"

Fran had reached the fence with the politely smiling Mr. Christoforos in tow. "Could be worse, could be worse. There's certainly some beach erosion and damage to the houses along the beach like I said before. Flooding, you know. The waves are huge but the tide is out right now." Fran craned her neck to look around Kate. "Where's the little one?"

"Staying with some friends. We may be gone overnight if the power isn't back."

"That's probably wise," Michael commented his voice still containing the warm timbre Kate had noted earlier, but the expression in his eyes looked distant, as if he were thinking of something else. "I was hoping to visit your store while I'm here. Fran has been telling me so much about it. Was it badly damaged?"

Kate smiled. *Oh, Fran*, she thought, mentally shaking her head in amusement. To Michael she said, "No, thankfully, it's not. Just a broken window, actually. We should be able to reopen in a day or two, assuming we get the power back, of course. I'll let you know."

Kate smiled again and with a little nod and wave, opened her door and went inside. The interior felt warm and humid in the late summer afternoon so Kate opened a few windows, hoping to air it out as a pleasant sea breeze was blowing in from the direction of the Sound. After checking the contents of her refrigerator, most of which, she decided reluctantly, would need to be tossed, Kate moved to the bedrooms, got down a suitcase and put together a quick one-day supply of clothes for herself and Glory, wanting to be optimistic about when the power would be back on and not feeling particularly eager to sleep on Chris's couch. Tomorrow, she decided, they would come back home regardless. As she moved the suitcase into the living room, Kate heard the muffled sound of her cell phone's ringtones. Grabbing her purse, she rummaged through it in some frustration before pulling it out hastily and calling out an aggravated hello.

After a brief pause, an unfamiliar male voice said somewhat tentatively, "Hello, is this Kate LaRue?"

"Yes," Kate replied, mentally chastising herself for not checking the caller ID before answering. "This is Kate LaRue. To whom am I speaking?"

"My name is John McCarty, Mrs. LaRue. I understand you've been looking for me."

Kate felt a wave of shock and excitement run through her body as she dropped quickly into the nearest chair. "Mr. McCarty! Oh, thank you so much for calling me."

"You're welcome but I'm not sure what I can do for you, Mrs. LaRue, except express my condolences about Ally. Nick Maxwell told me she died recently, I'm terribly sorry to hear that."

"Yes, thank you. I don't know what Mr. Maxwell told you, Mr. McCarty, but I've been trying to find out more about where Ally was and what she was doing the last several years. As I understand it, you and she joined this group called The Way and went to New Mexico with them?"

"Yes, that's true, but that was five or six years ago now. I didn't stay long and I had no contact with Ally or anyone else associated with The Way after I left."

"Well, perhaps you can tell me more about The Way, why you and she joined, why you left, why she didn't," Kate said, a feeling of desperation overwhelming her, hearing the familiar note of dismissal in John McCarty's voice. "Ally had a daughter, a little girl named Glory. She's with me now, and I just want to know, to understand, what might have happened—"

"Did you say she had a child named Glory?" John McCarty interrupted, a concerned and somewhat confused tone to his voice.

"Yes, that's right," Kate replied, and then paused, anticipating some further comment but McCarty was silent. Finally she said, "Mr. McCarty, are you still there?"

"Yes, I'm still here." He paused before continuing. "Maybe there is something I can tell you. I actually happen to be staying on the Vineyard with some friends at the moment but I'll be heading back to New York tomorrow. Would you be able to meet me for coffee tomorrow morning in Hyannis?"

"Umm, yes, I could do that," Kate answered, startled, anxiety creeping into her voice. "Is there something wrong? What does Glory have to do with anything?"

"A lot, potentially. I think it will be easier to explain in person and, anyway, there's something you should see."

After they had arranged a time and place to meet, Kate broke off the connection and stared at the darkened cell phone, bewildered. *Well, at least this is progress*, she told herself. *He's willing to meet me, and he's even here on the Cape, amazingly enough*, she thought, reflecting on the fact that she had steeled herself for another trip back to New York should John McCarty ever call her. After a moment, she tossed the cell phone back in her purse, grabbed the suitcase, and headed out to the car.

Kate paced around Chris's narrow living room, stepping around the toys scattered across the worn carpeting, her cell phone glued to her ear.

"No, David, thank you, but I don't need you there. I can take care of this myself. I just wanted to let you know where things were, that's all." In the brief silence that followed, Kate could picture David, eyes closed, fingers rubbing his forehead, lips pressed together in frustration.

"Look, Kate, you have no idea who this man is. If Ally felt threatened by someone, don't you think it could well have been this John McCarty?"

"No, I don't. I think it was the leader of The Way, Joshua Emmanuel, to be honest. It seems pretty clear to me that Mr. McCarty knows something."

"Yeah, something he can't tell you over the phone; some mysterious thing he wants to show you. It sounds off to me, Kate, like the plot of a bad made-for-TV movie. But do whatever you want, Kate. As always."

Kate opened her mouth to retort but David had already broken the connection. Grimacing in frustration, she walked over to the open sofa bed and sat down on the edge of the narrow mattress. Glory was asleep, her breathing rhythmic, but occasionally her face twisted, small whimpers issuing from her lips. Kate reached over, lightly brushing Glory's soft hair away from her face. "Oh, sweetheart, I just want to help you. Why is that so hard for everyone to understand?"

CHAPTER 39

Early morning sunlight was filtering through the thick antique glass of the Sea Witch's windows as Kate made her way past tables and display stands back toward the front door, a small square of wood in her hand. Her mind was so preoccupied with her upcoming meeting with John McCarty that for once she barely noticed the softly gleaming glassware and crystal, didn't stop to admire, however briefly, the original artwork lining the walls, the Cape Cod seascapes illuminated in the pale summer light. She did stop to glance into Captain Ahab's cage to ensure he had enough food and water, and then moved on, ignoring both his restless shuffling from one claw to the other and his squawks and calls.

Kate felt a faint stab of guilt, remembering Glory's still sleepy eyes, confused and unhappy, when she handed her over to Jen in Falmouth with the sun barely up. She waved her free hand impatiently at the memory. What was she to do? Chris's kids had doctors' appointments later this morning. Kate wasn't about to bring Glory along on this morning meeting with John McCarty. What if he was someone she remembered, someone who had hurt her, or hurt her mother? Anyway, Kate told herself, she needed to fill the time until then in ways that would distract her and Glory didn't need that. Glory adored Jen and later this morning, if at all possible, she was going to take her over to the swings by the beach in Yarmouth. Glory would be thrilled and...Kate's stream of thought was broken as she approached the door, the outline of a man clearly visible beyond the glass panel, his face masked by the closed sign's clock face.

"Who on earth..." Kate reached the door and, after moving

the sign slightly with one hand, recognized the blurry outlines of Michael Christoforos's face on the other side of the thick glass. Kate swore softly to herself as she drew the bolts on the door. *He must be really bored* flitted through he mind as she pulled it open. "Mr. Christoforos...Michael...I'm sorry, but we're not going to be open today."

"Oh, I know, but I was hoping maybe you could show me your store anyway. I may not be staying on the Cape as long as I thought originally so..."

"Oh, well, I'm sorry to hear that, but this really is not a good time." Kate stood squarely in the partly open door frame, aware that Michael had taken a step forward as if anticipating her acquiescence and was now craning his neck to see around her. He looked down at her, smiling but with that distant look in his eyes that Kate suddenly found discomfiting. "Look, Michael, I'm delighted that you want to visit the Sea Witch to such an extent that you would come here even when you know we're not open for business but I have other work to do as well as an appointment to keep. We might be able to open as early as tomorrow if we can get the power back, so I would suggest you check back with me then or better yet, I'll give Fran a call when we're open. Thank you for coming by." Before Michael could argue further, Kate shut the door and drew the bolts, walking away in the direction of the office but at an angle that allowed her to keep the door in her peripheral vision. After a few seconds the outline in the glass faded from view and Kate paused, waiting for the sound of a car motor. When it didn't come after a few minutes, she circled around to one of the front windows, peering through the glass. She could see the wavy outline of Michael's rental car sitting motionless next to her own. Kate felt a pinch of fear in the pit of her stomach.

"What is with this guy?" she muttered to herself. She felt for her cell phone in the pocket of her jeans and, pulling it out, punched in the speed dial for Jerry's number, noting at the same time that she had a voice mail message from Sam Ritter. Well, that would have to wait.

"Hey, Kate, what's up?" Jerry's familiar voice sounded in her ear.

"Jerry, where are you?" Kate could hear the tension in her own voice.

"I'm on my way, be there in five or ten. What's wrong?"

"My neighbor's tenant is here, wanted to see the store. Didn't really want to take no for an answer and now he's just sitting out in the parking lot. I don't know about this guy. There's something a little off about him."

"Huh. Well, hang on. I'll be there shortly."

Kate folded her arms, hanging back as she stared out the window, the seconds ticking away in silence until Captain Ahab let out another squawk, making Kate jump. Suddenly, in her mind's eye she flashed back to the night of the hurricane when she had looked out her bay window and saw this same car sitting across the street and had been convinced someone was sitting in it, watching her. *Well, now he* is *watching me*, Kate thought grimly. *At least I think he is*, she added, realizing that she couldn't be certain he was actually in the car. The possibility that he could be circling around the store looking for a way to get in brought a rush of fear and Kate turned to look toward the rear door. Just then, the crunch of wheels on the shells in the parking area brought her head back around. However, as soon as Jerry's car pulled into the lot, an engine roared to life and Michael Christoforos's car backed out, quickly heading off down Route 6A. Kate moved over to the door, once again pulling the bolts and feeling a mixture of relief and annoyance.

Jerry walked in, a slightly bemused expression on his face. "I guess that was your neighbor's tenant? I must be scarier than I thought to chase him off like that."

"He's a little weird. At this point, I'll be glad when he goes back to Montana or wherever it is he came from. Come on, we've got work to do and then I've got to get down to Hyannis to meet this John McCarty," Kate stated brusquely as she reached for the square of plywood she had been holding earlier, the harsh tone an attempt to conceal her growing anxiety.

Jerry looked at her appraisingly. "The day hasn't started well for you, has it? Are you going to be okay, meeting this McCarty person on your own?"

"Don't you start, Jerry." Kate looked at him, reading the concern in his face, and bit her lower lip. "I'll be fine," she added, modulating her tone. "This little encounter with Mr. Christoforos threw me off, that's all."

"Right. Well, let's see what we can do here."

CHAPTER 40

After having seen the window securely patched and any remaining debris cleared away from the store, Kate was winding her way through the streets of Hyannis, the crystal clear air and pleasant temperatures bringing out a crowd of people to the narrow streets packed with stores and restaurants, some of which, Kate noticed with some chagrin, seemed to have their power back and were already open for business. The commercial hub of the Cape, she reminded herself with no small amount of irritation. She took a left fork in the road, heading down toward the ferry docks. The restaurant she and John McCarty had agreed on, with its shaded sidewalk café, was on her right, thankfully open and seemingly in good shape, despite neighboring stores with damaged roofs, cracked windows, and missing shutters. Kate slowed, picking her way carefully through the pools of water, searching the road for an available parking space. For once, luck was with her and she slid into a prime spot just as someone else slid out.

Kate glanced at her watch. She was a few minutes early but she could see the Martha's Vineyard ferry just pulling into its dock, hopefully with John McCarty on board. Kate climbed out of her car, inhaling the refreshing sea air and pausing a few moments to take in the sounds of the cawing seagulls above her head, the blast of the ferry's horn, the tinkling of laughter and voices. The effects of the hurricane could clearly be seen in the tangle of fishing boats and pleasure craft among the damaged piers, wooden planks and other debris floating in the blue water of the harbor, a number of people already busily at work restoring order.

The ferry was offloading now, Kate noted as she quickly turned, deposited her quarters in the meter, and headed for the restaurant. By the time she was seated under the brightly striped awning, a menu in her hand, the ferry had largely discharged its passengers, a new line of eager visitors and vacationers ready to take their place. A few were still exiting the ferry's boarding area and the swarm of people was starting to dissipate. Kate watched as a small contingent turned in her general direction and headed up the opposite side of the street. Soon the little knot of people began to break apart and her gaze rested on one man of thirty-something years, situated toward the back of the group and moving along at a moderate pace. He looked tanned and trim, dressed unremarkably in light-colored shorts and a blue T-shirt with a Martha's Vineyard logo, a darker blue windbreaker tucked under his arm, his face shaded by a battered dark-green cap. As she watched, he looked up, scanning the sidewalk tables, his face expressionless, and then, with a quick glance up the street for traffic, crossed on a trajectory that took him straight toward her.

"Kate LaRue? I'm John McCarty," he said as he offered his hand over the low railing. He smiled slightly, sensing her astonishment. "You look like Ally's mother. Anyway, Nick did a good job of describing you."

"A pleasure to finally meet you, Mr. McCarty." Kate watched with some amusement as he swung his legs over the railing, gesturing "I'm with her" to their surprised waiter.

"You should call me John, of course. And I can call you Kate?" Kate nodded agreeably. "What are we ordering?" John picked up the menu and scanned it quickly.

"I'm just having coffee, but you get whatever you want."

He looked up, a wide smile creasing his face. "In that case, I'm buying."

Kate laughed, feeling charmed by this man. What a shame, she thought, that Ally didn't choose to come back to New York with him. But then, maybe he really wasn't her type. No body piercings, no tattoos, much too nice. They made small talk for a few minutes comparing hurricane stories until their orders were placed, then

John turned to Kate, the smile fading from his face. "I truly am sorry to hear about Ally's death. Shocked, really. What happened to her?"

Kate gave him an abbreviated version of the phone call from San Francisco General and her subsequent trip there, the nature of Ally's illness and her dying words, Kate's shock at learning that she had a granddaughter, and her decision to raise the child as well as her determination to find out what had happened to Ally and Glory and who Glory's father might be. Kate's monologue was interrupted only by their waiter who, with studied cheerfulness, set John's breakfast down on the table in front of him and filled their coffee cups.

At this point Kate paused, looking at John who was listening silently while downing the eggs and bacon he'd ordered. "And what have you found out?" he asked, gesturing for her to continue.

"Not enough," Kate retorted. "I'd like you to tell me—"

"Please," John interrupted, "I'll tell you what I know, but first, it will help me if I knew what you have discovered."

Kate sighed in exasperation but continued, explaining what she had learned from David, Chris, Andi, and Tim as well as Glory's sessions with Dr. Lawler.

"Now, tell me what *you* know."

John looked at her for a moment, pushing away his plate and watching while the waiter cleared them from the table. After the coffee cups were refilled, he clasped his hands together as he gazed out over the water briefly before beginning. "As you already know, I met your daughter in New York City, several years ago now, when we were both taking a course in *hatha* Yoga at the Center. I was very taken with her. She was sweet and charming but with a definite edge to her. Tough but really very young to be out on her own. I think she was about twenty at the time." He waved off the inevitable protest he saw rise on Kate's lips, "but I was pretty young too. It was something we had in common, that and our interest in Yoga and meditation. We had some great times together, staying up all night just talking," he smiled at the look of disbelief on Kate's face. "Well, there were other things, too. But she was having a rough time at that point, and so was I, trying to survive in New York, not sure what she wanted to do, a bit lost and lonely. Part of her wanted to go home, but she was too proud to do that, didn't want the I-told-you-sos. The other part wanted to make it on her own, prove she could do it, make her own choices."

John looked away, not wanting to see the pain he knew was in Kate's eyes, and hurriedly continued. "You know, I'm impressed that Ally's friends thought of me as a possible mentor to her. I would never have thought that, but, I don't know, perhaps we mentored each other. Anyway, while we were studying at the Center, there was another student there, the man Nick told you about, Joshua Emmanuel. Very, very bright, very well versed in Eastern religion and philosophy but also Western religious thought. He could talk forever on religion and spirituality, but he never sounded like some religious fanatic, not then anyway; his ideas were very exciting and, well, sort of radical, I thought.

"After a while, he started inviting some of the other students, as well as some of the Center's staff, the ones who were most engaged by him, including Ally and me, over to his apartment in the evenings and on weekends. It was all very relaxed at first, food and drink and conversation, but later, it was more educational and more, well, experimental. And it wasn't just about spiritual ideas but about practice in everyday life. In general, what he had to offer that appealed to us was a way to deal with life and the broader world with all its stresses and demands, a goal that could be achieved more quickly and easily than what the Center could offer. Ally, in particular, was mesmerized by him, but then pretty much everyone who came there was." John stopped again, sipping his coffee and appearing to be collecting his thoughts before continuing.

"Eventually, the administration at the Center caught on to the fact that Joshua was promoting his own brand of philosophy and practice that they saw as counter to what they were trying to achieve. They clearly saw him as something of a charlatan and tried to dissuade those who were involved with him from continuing to participate. They succeeded with some. But, in the end, they asked him, and those of us who were still supporting him, to leave the Center."

He paused again, waiting while his coffee cup was refilled once more. He stirred some sugar into the cup, gazing intently into its dark depths until Kate finally prompted, "And so you all went to New Mexico?"

"No, not right away. But even before all this happened, the idea had been germinating about creating an experimental community, a bit like a monastery—don't laugh—" he admonished, seeing Kate's look of amused skepticism—"or maybe an ashram, or a kind of commune, one where we could support each other in our goals to achieve a kind of spiritual nirvana. I know it sounds incredible now, but at the time it did not. You have to understand, we were achieving some very intense and expansive meditative and consciousness-altering states."

"Were drugs involved?"

"Again, not at first. Actually, that was one of the reasons for going to New Mexico."

"Peyote?"

"Among others. We went there partly because Joshua had some connections in New Mexico. I think he had spent some time in the Southwest; most likely, he was from the area originally. Anyway, through his connections he was able to arrange to sublet the ranch, I guess you'd call it, out in the desert. It seemed like a great idea, worth a try. I had nothing to hold me in New York at that point and neither did Ally. So we went, probably about two or three years after we first met Joshua.

"In the beginning, it was a great experience, but before long, I started to get uneasy. I didn't like where this was going with Joshua."

"Well?" Kate asked, when John paused yet again, looking out over the harbor, watching another incoming ferry.

"In the beginning Joshua always asserted that the divine presence was in each of us, in everyone and everything; really, it was just a matter of accessing it, and with the tools he could give us, we could learn how to do that. Access the divine in ourselves, that is, and connect with the divine in each other. But after we were in New Mexico a while he seemed to be claiming that *he* was the only embodiment of the divine, that he was an avatar, an incarnation of God or a god. Because of all his years of preparation and study, he possessed, or so he said, a closer, better understanding of divinity and the human connection with 'God' and all that entailed. He also seemed to be saying that he could transmit to others, in different ways, this 'purer,' I guess you could call it, form of divinity that he possessed. At least one of those ways was through sex." John looked down at his coffee cup again, rubbing the empty cup between his palms. "When some of the women began having his children, he considered those children to be avatars too, because they were his and he had somehow transmitted this higher level of God-consciousness to them. He also gave them names that distinguished them as such, like Krishna and Jesus or, for the girls, Sophia or Shekinah, God's wisdom or presence on Earth or..."

"...Glory," whispered Kate.

"Exactly. Another metaphor for God's indwelling presence. Ally didn't have a child when I left, but...you said Glory is four, so she might have been pregnant. I don't really know what Ally was thinking at that time because our relationship had changed by then. Like I said, I left because I didn't like the way things were going but if Ally had a child with him, he would have made it difficult for her to get out unless she was willing to leave the kid behind. You see, in order to ensure that the biological mothers could not easily walk away with *his* children, he separated them at an early age and, to some extent, had them raised commune-style along with other women in the group he thought he could trust."

"So how do you think she got out? The fire?"

"Yeah, I heard about the fire. I don't know how she escaped, but that's as good a guess as any. In the confusion, she could have grabbed Glory and made a run for it."

Kate reflected on this for a moment, seeing Ally, desperate to save herself and her child, taking her from the burning buildings, and somehow finding her way out of the New Mexico desert. But how? Surely someone must have helped her. "John, when I met with Nick Maxwell I gave him some photographs that I wanted him to pass on to you. Did you get them?"

"No," he replied, shaking his head. "Nick told me about you over the phone, anyway. He just read me your note and gave me your number if I wanted to get in touch."

"Well, in that case, I'd like to show you some photographs, if you don't mind." John nodded agreeably as Kate reached into her purse and pulled out the photos she had shown so many times before. "I found these in Ally's apartment in San Francisco." First she laid down the two photos of Ally.

John laughed softly to himself as he picked up the one of Ally in New York. "Yes, indeed, that's her, all right. She really liked that look, so different from anyone I'd known at home."

"Where is your home, John?"

"I grew up in West Virginia. I still have family there."

"Do you mind telling me how you ended up in New York? I got the impression, I don't know, that maybe you..." Kate's voice trailed off.

John smiled and shook his head. "It's fine, I don't mind. Well, you have to understand that my dad, my uncles, my grandfather, they all worked in the mines. Working in the mines was what most men did where I came from; it was what everyone assumed you would do too. Then one of my uncles died when a mine collapsed. I was just a kid then, but I just knew this wasn't what I wanted to do. So after I graduated high school I packed up and moved to the big city. I have to admit that it wasn't a popular decision with my family and once I got there, it was a lot harder than I had thought it would be. The Center was a big help in dealing with all that I was going through. It still is; Joshua Emmanuel was just a blip on the screen."

John held Kate's eyes for a few seconds, looked back down at Ally's picture for a few more seconds then he put it down and studied the second picture. "This must be recent, not long before she died," he said, his voice matter-of-fact, detached, "and holding Glory, of course." Kate nodded, retrieving the pictures. She then placed the two photos of the empty landscape intersected by a road. John looked at these, seeming to be lost in thought—or memory. "The Way" he noted. Then, glancing at Kate, "This is the road going into the ranch. We called it The Way, the road to enlightenment, the same name as the group we were part of, and took photos that we used as meditative tools, a metaphor for what we were trying to achieve there."

Kate looked at the photos again in some surprise. "Huh. Well, I never would have thought of that explanation. Anyway, I wouldn't think she'd have wanted mementos of all that, especially given the circumstances under which she left."

"It wasn't all bad, you know. I still use many of the meditative techniques and guided visualizations he taught us. I can understand that Ally might have found some of these helpful as well especially given what you've told me about her situation. You have to remember there was a lot that was positive about The Way before Joshua got too caught up seeing himself as God or more godlike than the rest of us."

Kate shrugged as she put down the last of the photos, with its enigmatic image of a pretty, dark-haired woman with her mysterious half smile. John stared at it in obvious recognition. "Wow. Oh yes, I know her. This is Mary. I don't know her last name or even her real name any more than I know if Joshua Emmanuel is Joshua's real name although I'm pretty sure it's not. Mary was Navajo, I think. A really nice woman. She was, well, one of Joshua's main connections in the area, someone he'd known for years. Mary helped us get basic stuff we needed like food and clothes, furniture, and a generator. She also helped out as a midwife many times when the babies were due." John hesitated.

"What?" Kate tried to peer into his face, but he was shadowing it with his hand.

"It's interesting. After I left, after the fire, actually, I heard some stories. Well, I heard that Mary had gotten disillusioned with Joshua too, realized he was really taking things way too far, and that she had been trying to help people leave who wanted out." He shook his head decisively and looked at Kate. "I don't know what happened to her and I hope she's okay but if anyone helped Ally escape, it would have been Mary."

Kate looked again at the photograph, seeing the smile playing on Mary's lips. "You know, I have a birth certificate for Glory that says she was born in Los Angeles, father unknown."

John glanced back down at the photo. "Really? Well, I can't imagine that Glory was born in LA or even that she had a birth certificate. Joshua didn't allow that for the kids; didn't want government intervention or labeling I think he called it. I don't know but it would be my guess that Mary helped Ally get one. She was pretty resourceful and it would have been tough for Ally to get by without a birth certificate for Glory."

Kate sat back, slipping the last of the photos into her purse, her face a mask of emotions. John watched her for a moment before saying, "I have a photo to show you as well, Kate. One you really need to see." He began reaching into the pocket of his shorts, pulling out his wallet, and searching through the billfold. "I don't think you really want to find Joshua Emmanuel, Kate. But I'd be willing to bet he wants to find you, or, more precisely, Glory. You should know what he looks like because I'm guessing you don't." Kate nodded affirmatively and John unfolded a piece of newspaper and spread it out on the table between them. "I'm not sure why I kept this, to be honest. I stuck it in my wallet one day and never took it out. It's from an article in a small free press publication in New York that appeared not long before we left for New Mexico. Anyway, I did keep it and, well, I don't think there are too many photographs of him; he didn't like getting his picture taken so..."

Kate looked down at the grainy black-and-white photograph depicting a man standing in front of what looked to be the building that housed The Center for Yoga, Meditation, and Healing, his gaze focused somewhere along the street. Despite the quality of the photograph, there was no mistaking who it was. The recognition hit her like a sledgehammer. Kate could feel the blood drain from her face and see the table start to spin. She swallowed hard as the coffee she had drunk threatened to come back up into her throat. Weakly, she struggled to her feet. "Oh my God. John, Mr. McCarty, thank you so much, but I have to go."

John stood up, alarmed. "What's wrong? Are you okay? Do you know him?"

Kate looked at him, her face gray. "Yes...no...I mean, I know where he is. He's renting a cottage across the street from my house."

CHAPTER 41

Later, Kate could never remember how she got from the restaurant to her car, or who paid the bill for John's meal and the coffee they both drank. She had a vague memory of John's face, pale under its tan, offering to drive her home, or wherever else she wanted to go, and waving him off anxiously as she climbed into her car and pulled away. Desperately, she tried to recall exactly what Jen had proposed to do with Glory today. The playground, right? Before lunch or after lunch? Kate tried to visualize her conversation with Jen, seeing herself standing next to her on the porch of her parents' home as the morning sun was shining through pine trees, Glory between them, fussing in aggravated little sobs. Kate remembered giving Jen some money for a trip to McDonald's or Burger King. Would Jen have done that first and the playground afterward? Probably. But then, if Glory was really fussy and wanted the playground...

Rummaging in her purse with one hand as she attempted to steer her car around a corner with the other, Kate's fingers closed on her cell phone and she yanked it out of her purse. Hyannis was filled with cars and strolling tourists and Kate could do little more than crawl along, dodging people and the fenders and bumpers of surrounding vehicles. She glanced down and quickly punched Jen's number, listening to the distant ringing until her pleasant, familiar voice chimed in, sweetly asking her to leave a message. Kate blinked back tears of frustration. "Jen, call me as soon as you get this. Do *not* go to Yarmouth and if you are already there, *leave. Immediately*. Whatever else you do, *don't* go to my house. Call me!" Kate's voice broke in a sob.

Tossing the phone down, she rubbed at the tears that were flowing now from her eyes. Squinting to see through the blur, she bit down on her lower lip, struggling to get her emotions under control. "Oh, Glory, Glory, my poor baby. Grandma's coming," she murmured under her breath, blowing her horn angrily at a sleek and expensive-looking car that suddenly nudged its way in front of her from one of the side streets. Glancing down, Kate reached again for the cell phone, fingers pushing the necessary numbers, almost hoping this time for the canned request to leave a message. Almost immediately, David's terse voice sounded in her ear. "All right, Kate, tell me what happened."

Kate drew a deep breath, closing her eyes momentarily until she heard the horns blaring at her. "It's not him, David, it's not John McCarty." The words spilled out in a rush, agitation rising with each syllable. "He had a photograph with him, of this Joshua Emmanuel, the leader of The Way. He showed it to me. David, Joshua Emmanuel is Michael Christoforos, this man who is renting a cottage across the street from me. He's here to take Glory, he's her father, and he thinks she's some kind of divine incarnation, an avatar, Mr. McCarty says, like he thinks he is and—"

David cut her off, his voice cold and aggressive. "Jesus Christ, Kate. Where are you? Where's Glory? Is she with you?"

"No, no. I'm in my car, in Hyannis. Glory is with Jen but I can't get her on her phone. She may be in Yarmouth, maybe even at the house, I left her a message but..."

In the silence Kate could hear David's quick intake of breath, feel the vibration of anger and frustration, touched by fear, through the receiver. The traffic up ahead broke a little as they merged with Route 28 heading into Yarmouth. Then his voice suddenly cut back in, cold and hard. "I'll meet you there. Don't go in the house or get out of your car until I get there. I won't be long. And call me if that babysitter, whatever-her-name-is, calls you back."

Kate started to ask if he thought she should call the police but David had already broken the connection. What would she tell them, she thought to herself. This strange man who may—or may not—be my granddaughter's father may—or may not—be planning to kidnap her? He thinks she's some kind of divine incarnation and he wants her back?

No, she told herself. The first thing she needed to do was get Glory away from this man, this Joshua Emmanuel, or whatever his name really was, get her somewhere safe, and then she would have to figure out any legal complications. Legal complications. A sudden thought that some court or child protection agency would take Glory from her and give her to this man who thought he was an earthly manifestation of God sent tremors of fear down her spine and into her fingers and toes. The turn for her street loomed up ahead. Kate clutched the steering wheel, looking again at the cell phone on the seat beside her. *Jen, call me*, she pleaded silently. Visions of Joshua Emmanuel, or Michael Christoforos, or whoever he was, driving away down Route 6 toward the canal with a terrified Glory in his rented car, Jen hurt or maybe even killed trying to stop him, filled Kate with an overwhelming desperation.

As she turned into the street, skirting debris still scattered across it, she noted how deserted it looked. Certainly, no cars stood in her own driveway and Joshua Emmanuel's rental car was nowhere to be seen. Even the usual summer foot traffic was missing. Where was everyone? At the beach? Or off looking for buildings with electrical power? Kate noted somewhat grimly that the power lines were still down; obviously, this section of town wasn't high priority for power restoration. That could be a good thing, she reminded herself. Surely Jen would be elsewhere with Glory, somewhere safe. Kate pulled into the driveway and cut the engine, then sat staring at the silent house. The pine trees waved softly in the summer breeze casting patterns of shadow and light across its gray shingles, the windows veiled in darkness. As the minutes passed, Kate grew increasingly uneasy in the sunny quiet, a sense of foreboding rising along her spine. She could see Fran's house and its adjoining cottage behind her in the car mirrors, as silent and forbidding as her own, the gentle rustle of wind and an occasional bird all that could be heard.

Feeling she could stand it no longer, Kate got out of the car. She paused, hand on the car door frame. Glory and Jen were certainly not here now she told herself, but had they been? What if they had been in the house and encountered Joshua Emmanuel? What if he really had absconded with Glory and was right now heading up the coast with her? What if...? Kate hesitated, remembering David's admonition to not go in the house until he got there. Or leave the car, she reminded herself and she'd already done that. But who knew how long he would really be Kate argued with herself, and meanwhile... She turned and retrieved her cell phone from the front seat, gently shutting the car door. After crossing the lawn, she quickly pulled out her house key as she ascended the front steps, and, steeling herself for whatever she might find within, unlocked the door and stepped inside.

She paused, letting her eyes adjust to the dimness, breathing in the hot stuffy air, and feeling the stillness envelope her, a disconcerting change from the bright sunshine and soft breezes on the other side of the door. The house had simply been closed up too long in the late summer heat and humidity, she reminded herself. Kate took in a breath of the stale air and detected a faint odor of garbage. More food to be thrown away, she noted with mild annoyance. After a moment or two, she moved cautiously forward, past the triangle of light let in through the open door, a queasy nervousness taking hold. "Jen?" she called out, annoyed by the quaver in her voice. No one's here, she told herself firmly, the silence that followed seemingly agreeing with her. Kate looked around, walking through the kitchen, living room, and out onto the little side porch, confidence growing with each step. The house was empty, with no sign of anyone having been there. She reversed her steps and headed back into the living room and then down the hall toward the bedrooms. Checking each of them in turn, she noted again that nothing was disturbed, there was no Jen cowering in fear because Joshua Emmanuel had kidnapped Glory.

Kate felt the relief coursing through her veins and smiled to herself shakily, thinking that her worst fears were unfounded and overblown, and turned to head back down the hall—and then stopped, heart racing. Footsteps sounded softly in the outer rooms near the door...two, three, four. Then silence. Kate caught her breath, straining to listen. David? But wouldn't he just continue to walk in? Call out? He'd know she was here. Tears of panic sprang to her eyes as she glanced around fearfully. There was nowhere to go.

More soft footsteps. In the kitchen? Out toward the porch? Kate looked down at the cell phone still in her hand and quickly punched in David's number and listened again to the distant ringing.

David's voice in her ear, so abruptly she jumped, stifling a scream. "Did she call?"

"No," she whispered, aware the footsteps had stopped again. "I-I'm in the h-h-house. I think he's here."

The footsteps resumed, louder and more assured now, heading for the hall. Kate quickly backed into Glory's bedroom, not hearing David's response, her fingers around the phone slack with terror as it slid to the floor with a light clatter. She looked desperately around for a place to hide, a way out—but then he was there, his body seeming to fill the doorway. Kate looked up at him, feeling rooted to the floor, a sickening wave of nausea passing through her. He stared back at her for a second or two, then his eyes left hers and quickly scanned the room. He returned his gaze to hers and held it, studying her.

"Do you know who I am?" Joshua spoke softly but with an unmistakable undertone of anger and determination.

Kate tried to speak, hearing a tiny whispered "yes" that didn't sound as though it came from her throat.

"Then you know why I'm here. Where is she, Kate? Where's my daughter? What have you done with my Glory?" His voice had remained soft, but Kate could hear the anger rising in it, tightly reined in for now, but there nonetheless.

Kate swallowed, still struggling to find her voice.

He stayed where he was, blocking the door with his body, his eyes fastened on hers, cool, assessing, but wth a dangerous glint in them that made her shiver involuntarily. "Glory's mine. I'm her father and a child belongs with her father. I am sure you know that and I am also sure you took good care of her but now I'm here and I'm ready to take her home."

At this, Kate managed to find her voice as, lips trembling, she burst out, "You may be her father, but that doesn't mean you have a right to her. Ally left you and took Glory with her for a reason, and I know what that reason was."

"Do you? Are you sure? Glory is far more than simply my daughter, you know. Ally understood that, understood it very well, but in the end, she just couldn't accept it. Glory is very special, very unique; she's a gift to the world, not just an unwanted child, an orphan, to be raised by her grandmother like any other child." Joshua kept his eyes fixed on hers as if assessing how much she knew, then nodded slightly. "Actually, I think perhaps you do understand, at least some. I think you know that it is because of me that she is who she is." Joshua straightened himself, lifting his chin slightly. "However improbable as this may seem to you, I am an avatar, one embodied with God's presence, a state achieved through a higher level of consciousness than you are likely to ever experience in this life." He paused, weighing the impact of his words. "You've found this out, haven't you? You know now that she, like her father, has been blessed as an incarnation of heavenly Glory. And like other sacred children, she must be separated from the profane children so that she may receive the divine teachings she was born for. Try thinking of the Dalai Lama."

Kate's sense of utter disbelief must have shown in her face because, before she could speak, he continued, the anger and frustration underlying his voice unmistakable now. "You think that because your daughter gave birth to my child you have some right to her. Perhaps you think I am crazy, an unfit father." Joshua took a step toward Kate, a mocking tone in his voice. "Nevertheless, the truth is, your daughter was just the vessel, nothing more. Even knowing who the child was, your daughter thought she had the right to steal her from me, and now you've tried to do the same. Well, I'm here to get back my Glory, to restore her to her destiny. Glory needs to be with *me, not* with you, and you are going to tell me where she is." That same low voice, threatening now, clearly anticipating an answer, the answer he wanted and expected.

"I'm not sure exactly," Kate managed to whisper.

"You're not sure? Do you *really* expect me to believe that?" he replied in a voice heavy with contempt, his gaze still fixed on hers.

Kate gestured helplessly toward the window. "She's with her babysitter. I'm not sure where they went, maybe a playground, out to get ice cream, I just don't know. There's no power still. I don't have any idea when they'll be back."

Joshua Emmanuel looked down at the cell phone lying between them on the polished wood floor and swiftly picked it up, holding it lightly in his hand. "You're going to call the babysitter and tell her to bring Glory back here. What's the number? Is it in an address book?"

"I wouldn't sound...I couldn't sound normal. She...She'd know something was wrong." Kate voice quivered with fear and trepidation.

He eyed her appraisingly, then slipped the cell phone into his pocket. "Perhaps you're right. Well, then, I guess we'll just have to wait, won't we? Because no matter how long it takes, I'm not leaving without my daughter." Kate stood, rooted to the floor, watching the man between her and the door work to contain his anger as he considered his options. He looked back at her. "Do you have any idea who I really am or who she is? How much do you understand of what I just told you?"

"I know you think she's some incarnation of God and that you think you are as well." Kate tried to keep contempt out of her own voice but, by the look on Joshua Emmanuel's face, she knew she had not.

"Then I don't *think* you understand *anything* about it." Joshua Emmanuel took a few steps toward the window, not taking his eyes off Kate. He scanned the street and the yard quickly, and, not seeing what he wanted, turned back to face her. "This is not about something I *think*. My children, of whom Glory is only one, are the hope of the world, the divinity manifested in them in this time of greatest crisis, a time when faith and spirituality are waning. They will be the ones, along with me, to pull us all back from the edge of the abyss on which we are all standing. Do you *really* believe you have any right to interfere with this?"

"Glory is just a little girl. Ally was her mother. She's no more or less divine than you or I, and anything else is just...just...crazy." Kate struggled to keep her voice steady, breathing deeply to calm herself, casting about for some plan to get away, to get out of this, and find Glory and save her from this madman.

"You're wrong about that." Joshua Emmanuel's voice tightened with anger. With one swift motion, he reached for Kate, who had suddenly found her legs and run forward, trying to get around him, but she wasn't quick enough. Before Kate could react, he had her arms, pinning them to her sides, and had rammed her body hard against the wall. Kate felt pain explode in the back of her head as it met the wall's unyielding surface while Joshua Emmanuel's face, so close to hers, swirled into kaleidoscope patterns. Struggling to regain focus, Kate felt his grip on her loosen slightly. Somewhere in the distance, she thought she once again heard footsteps and knew he had heard them too. "Oh God, David," she mumbled under her breath. *Please let it be David and not*, nausea rising at the thought, *Jen and Glory.*

Joshua Emmanuel tugged at her, propelling her forward on unsteady feet, out of the bedroom and into the hall.

"Kate?" David's voice, cool, detached.

"David, the police, call—" a hand clamped itself over her mouth making it difficult to breathe. Kate scratched at it helplessly, feeling suddenly disoriented and confused. She felt her attacker stop, pull her in front of him, with his hand still across her face, waiting. Seconds later, David appeared at the end of the hall, still as stone, his eyes fixed on Joshua Emmanuel, metal glinting in his right hand, lit by the sun coming in the open front door. Kate's eyes widened over the hand held tightly across her face, disconnected thoughts swirling through her brain, memories of all the times she had argued with David over the dangers of keeping a gun in the house and now...Kate felt a scream rise in her throat as she struggled once more to free herself, black dots swimming into her vision, her lungs burning from the lack of oxygen.

"I just want my daughter. She belongs with me. I'm her father. I have a right to her. Give her to me and I'll let Kate go." Joshua Emmanuel's voice was still commanding but had nonetheless softened with appeal, and Kate thought that, through the buzzing that was filling her ears, she could hear a hint of underlying fear. He had seen the gun too she realized.

"I don't know who the hell you are, and I'm not giving you anything, let alone my granddaughter." David's voice cut through growing noise in her head. She felt movement behind her, followed by a muffled shout, but the blackness was rapidly descending as the floor rose up to meet her. Just before consciousness left her, she thought she heard a gunshot ring out, echoing through the darkness as it enveloped her.

The beach. Kate was on the beach running along the water's edge, bare feet slapping in the wet sand, eyes desperately searching crowds of laughing beachgoers who turned to stare at her as she passed. A group of teenagers playfully pushing each other into the surf parted as she approached and suddenly, Kate saw her far up ahead, weaving through the crowds, a flash of braids and tanned arms and legs. Kate tried to scream at her to stop but she was out of breath and only a whisper came out. The jetty was up ahead. Always the jetty. Tears flowed down Kate's cheeks as she struggled to breathe, struggled to call out. Now she was on the rocks and Kate could see that it was more than tears blinding her. It was rain. Thunder sounded and lightning danced and everyone was gone. Everyone except Kate and the small child skipping across the jetty. Exhausted, Kate pulled herself up on the rocks, stumbling along them, fighting for breath. The lightning flashed and Ally's face looked back at her, her eyes lit by a smile, and then she was gone. Gone and once again Kate was left clinging to the jetty, sobbing as the storm crashed around her.

"Relax, Mrs. LaRue, it's okay. You're going to be all right." Somewhere, someone was talking soothingly to her, a voice she didn't recognize. Someone at the beach? No, of course not. Where was she? As Kate struggled to open her eyes, it all came flooding back—Joshua Emmanuel. David. The house. The gunshot. Kate gasped as her eyes flew open, and she took in her surroundings. Dear God, a hospital. She looked to her left and saw the speaker, a middle-aged woman in a flowered smock, looking at something above her head.

"Glory...David...where...what..." Kate pleaded.

"I'm over here." David's voice. Kate struggled to sit up, staring at David, standing by the door of the room. The nurse patted Kate's arm—"I'll come back"—and moved around David and out the door.

"Are you all right? What happened? Where's Glory? Did Joshua Emmanuel—"

"You know, Kate, twenty years after a divorce, and I'm still trying to deal with your stubborn..." David caught himself, shaking his head, shoving his fists in his pockets, and focusing his gaze at the far wall. "I'm fine. Glory is fine. She's still with the babysitter, Jen, at the moment. Unfortunately, Mr. Emmanuel, whoever he really is or was...is dead."

Kate''s eyes widened. "Oh, God, David, no, you didn't..."

"I did. The man came straight at me, trying to use you as a shield. Then when you fainted...What else was I going to do? Let him take the gun? Kill us both? I'm just thankful I didn't hit you as well." He paused, letting out an explosive breath. "Don't you ever *listen*? What the hell did you go in that house for? Jesus Christ, Kate, I shot a man. Something I never believed I would ever do. As it is—"

"I'm sorry, David. I am truly sorry, but I'm glad you were there. You saved me and Glory too. Anyway, it was self-defense, David, you know that." Kate fell back against the pillows, feeling the tears welling up in her eyes.

David sighed wearily. "Yeah, I know. Please don't cry. I'm glad you and my granddaughter are okay. You just have a concussion, I think." His shoulders sagged. "Look, I've had enough for one day. I'm going home. I'm just...really...tired." Kate looked at him, seeing the utter exhaustion in his face. Catching her glance, David rearranged his face into more animated lines. "Your manager, business partner, whatever he is, is here. I'm sure he'll give you a ride home if they let you go. Although I imagine the police are going to want to talk to you. I've already had one discussion with them."

Kate nodded, biting her lip against the salty flavor of the tears that were trickling down her face.

David glanced down at her and added, his voice low and tired but not without concern, "Take care of yourself, Kate. Glory too. I'll be in touch." He reached out and gently squeezed her hand, then turned and headed out the door, striding swiftly down the hall.

Kate closed her eyes, thoughts whirling through her mind, replaying that last scene in the hall. Joshua Emmanuel's smothering hand across her face, cutting off her air, her head aching from contact with the wall. David appearing at the end of the hall, gun in hand. How many times had she seen David with a gun, any gun, in his hands, aiming at targets at the shooting range or hunting in New Hampshire and Vermont? And always a gun in the house, sometimes more than one. Kate mentally shook her head. What difference did it make? Surely there would be no question of self-defense. She had put them both in an impossible situation. What else could he have done?

Footsteps sounded in the hall and Kate jerked upright in alarm, then slumped back as relief filled her.

"Hi, Jerry."

"Hi, Kate." Jerry looked at her, a worried smile tugging at his lips. "How are you doing?"

"Okay, I guess. David said I had a concussion but I'm all right. I haven't seen anyone else."

"Yeah. Christ, what a story. Working with you never used to be this dramatic, Kate."

Kate laughed, then started to cry.

"Don't cry. It's all going to work out." Jerry patted her hand awkwardly, concern etched into his face. "Maybe I shouldn't tell you this but I talked with Sam Ritter a little while ago."

Kate looked up, startled. "What?"

"He'd been trying to get hold of you. I guess he was looking to get some updates on how we were doing with the hurricane clean-up. Anyway, when he couldn't get hold of you, he called me. I told him the whole story and, well, he's worried about you. He wants to see you."

"Jerry..."

"It's too late. He's on his way already." Jerry paused. "He likes you, Kate. Give the guy a break."

Kate laughed again, wiping her eyes. "I'll think about it, Jerry."

"Attagirl. By the way, Glory and Jen are here. I think you may be surprised by what they have to tell you."

Before Kate could respond, Jerry disappeared down the hall, leaving her to contemplate this statement. *I'll be surprised? By what? What kind of surprise?*

A minute later, they were at the door, Glory's little face a mask of confusion, her eyes wide and dark, her hand clinging tightly to Jen's. At the sight of Kate, she released her hold on Jen and ran toward her grandmother. Kate swung her legs over the side of the bed and pulled herself to her feet, gathering the little girl to her in an all-encompassing embrace. Kate buried her face in Glory's soft hair, fighting back a fresh assault of tears.

Jen, behind Glory, leaned down. "See? I told you she would be here." She looked at Kate, tears filling her own eyes. "She *asked* for you, Kate. She did. Really. When we came to the hospital, she said, 'Grandma, Grandma.' It's the truth. I don't know why, but I think maybe she was afraid..." Jen's voice trailed off.

Kate pulled back, taking Glory's face in her hands and looking into her wide dark eyes, too flooded with emotion to speak as Glory, lips trembling, whispered, "Grandma" in a voice soft and muted, but unmistakably hers, nonetheless.

CPSIA information can be obtained
at www.ICGtesting.com
Printed in the USA
LVHW09s1019240918
591165LV00002B/37/P

9 781478 792048